THE THORNSCARP PROPOSAL

KAMI KING LARSEN

❋ Created with Vellum

The Thornscarp Proposal is based on the short story "The Princess and the Promise" first published in *Bittersweet Breadcrumbs* under my pen name of Aster Rye. Readers may think they know the story, but I can assure you, this is so much more! While this novel is a cozy fantasy romance that is meant to be a light and fun experience, it does include profanity, mild descriptions of sex on page, violence, references to death of a parent, references to infidelity, references to abuse, and imposed servitude. Please be aware.

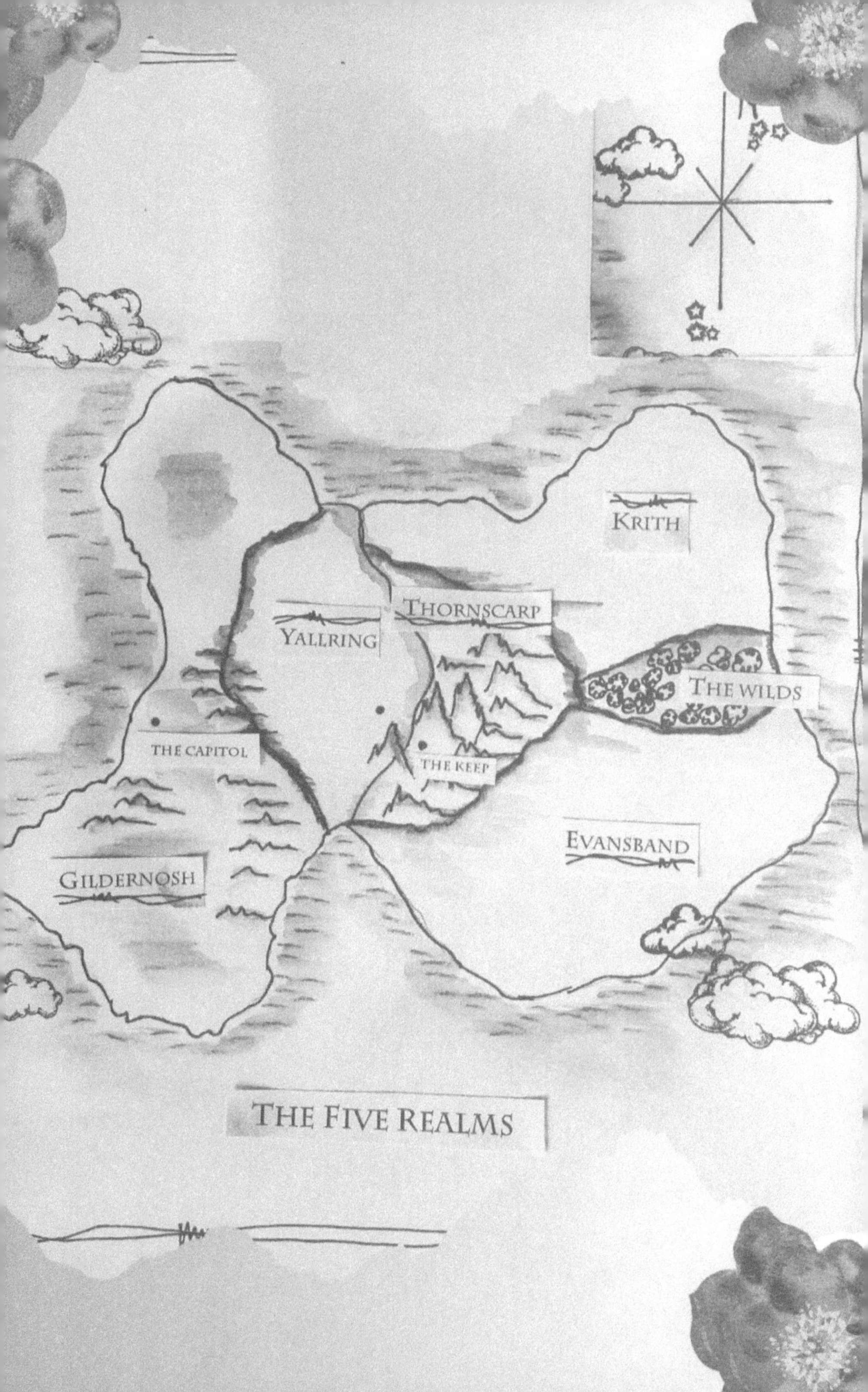

KRITH
THORNSCARP
YALLRING
THE WILDS
THE CAPITOL
THE KEEP
EVANSBAND
GILDERNOSH
THE FIVE REALMS

$\mathcal{U}$nwilling or Unable

MILA WASN'T SURE IF SHE HAD EVER BEEN SO MISERABLE IN HER life. Cold, wet, and rushing headlong into what she desperately hoped wasn't a fool's errand, she waited outside the keep gate and told herself this was a good idea. It would work. It *had* to work.

When she threw her hood back and called to the guards, she ignored the freezing pellets of rain as they stung her skin. Spring in the mountains was as similar to spring on the coast as piss was to dandelion wine—they might both be amber liquid, but they offered very different experiences on the tongue.

The grumpy sprite perched on the pommel of her saddle cursed loudly at the guards to be quick, but it still seemed to take ages for them to send a messenger up to the castle and even longer for the messenger to return.

"Oh, for the love of troll ta-tas," Glow grumbled. "Are we to believe they didn't have their spies following us all the way from the border? They know who you are as sure as I do."

"We don't know that for certain," Mila said.

The sprite craned her neck and scowled up at the woman behind her. "Yes, Mila, we do. And even if we didn't, how often do you think travelers just saunter into Thornscarp?" Glow twisted her lips to the side and waited all of two heartbeats before continuing. "I'll tell you. Never."

The road from Yallring had been quiet, almost eerily so. They'd passed the occasional wagon or rider on horseback, but as the area west of the keep was largely uninhabited, those had been few and far between. Each time, they kept their hoods up and their eyes down, and no one paid them any interest. How many of them were spies, Mila couldn't say. At the wall, the guards seemed fairly unsurprised when she announced herself and requested an audience with the sovereigns of Thornscarp. By all appearances, it would seem they had been expecting her as they were stoic and unwelcoming, but they weren't aggressive or threatening.

"We could always turn around and head for home." The chipper voice came from Mila's right and down a couple of feet, where Puddi sat atop the goat she'd taken for a steed.

"We aren't leaving," Mila said, looking down at the apple cheeks of the golden-haired gnome. "Not until I've had an audience with the king and queen."

Puddi smiled at Glowildeen and sat up straighter in her saddle as she threw a sopping wet, golden braid over her shoulder. Mila sighed as the sprite made a vulgar hand gesture at the gnome. The pair had been with her for years and were more than companions. And as much as they both hated to admit it, they loved each other as much as they loved her. The idea of traveling without them was absurd, but even if it hadn't been, the thought of leaving Puddi and Glow behind to deal with her father in her absence would have been beyond cruel.

Pulling her hood up to stave off at least some of the rain, Mila looked at the guard tower again. It had been a longer wait than she'd expected, and her bones were chilled, her back and rump sore from seven days on the road. But if they wanted her to wait, she would do just that.

Eventually the gate rose and a guard dressed in the Thornscarp colors—vermilion and golden ochre—gestured for them to follow him inside. She tried to ignore the clatter of the guard's hooves on the flagstone as they walked but failed miserably. Hooves. He had *hooves*. She shouldn't be surprised, but somehow she still was.

As soon as they passed within the massive stone wall, what had been a steady rain let up to more of a misting drizzle. Wiping the water from her eyes, Mila found herself momentarily stunned. The castle was . . . striking. And in a way she hadn't expected. Set into the side of a rocky outcrop, its walls were all smooth gleaming stone and breathtaking arches. Tall windows and intricate carvings looked down on the lush green spaces below. It was so at odds with the villainous idea of the Thornscarp she'd heard tales of. She had expected dark broken block and dusty dim shadows. Not this. Like the guard's hooves, it was nearly impossible for her to ignore the contradiction with the reputation of the place.

She was better at ignoring the sniggers and laughter as she was escorted from the gate to the castle's entrance where she dismounted and allowed a stable boy to take the reins of her horse as well as the rope Puddi had been using as a lead for her goat. Mila watched the boy, fascinated by the long scale-covered tail trailing from the back of his breeches. Slim and sleek with a small golden tuft at the end, it swished from side to side as he walked. It was only when Glow fluttered next to her face and nudged her in the right direction that she snapped to and followed the guard into the castle.

Not many who made the journey to Thornscarp ever

returned. Everyone knew that. She'd hoped her position might provide her some leniency, but now she wasn't so certain.

The laughter and mocking died the deeper into the castle they got.

Mila attempted to ignore the hostile looks and the turned backs as she made her way to the throne room. She attempted to ignore the myriad forms and features, the horns and fangs and wings. Most of all, she attempted to ignore the thundering of her heart as she knelt before the king and queen of Thornscarp and asked for a marriage alliance with their son, the mighty and brutal Prince Edonier.

"AND WHY, CHILD, IS IT YOU AND NOT YOUR NOBLE FATHER COME to us?" King Edon of Thornscarp asked, a laugh playing at the corners of his flinty mouth.

Balls and bastards. Mila had to fight not to roll her eyes. She could feel the mocking tone right down to her toes. *Child.* She was far beyond her childhood years and he knew it. Did he think this was fun for her? Did he find it amusing she was forced to kneel and to beg? Did he think, for even one moment, she wanted to defy her father and give her body and her title once again to some man she did not know?

The king was a large man with a waterfall of tawny hair and a beard to match. Small tusks jutted from his lower jaw and curled toward his nose. No crown adorned his head, but his posture screamed authority and power and dominance. She'd seen images of the king before, but in person, he was even more intimidating than she'd expected.

"He was unable, Your Majesty." Mila kept her eyes downcast and spoke with a calm she did not feel.

"Unable or unwilling?"

She had no good way to answer, tensions being what they were. She didn't want to give him another reason to turn her away or to dislike her people, but she refused to lie. "Both," she said simply.

Her father was unable as he was currently in negotiations with the Yallring parliament to avoid a full-blown invasion of his lands. Of *her* lands, she reminded herself. She hoped he still didn't know she where she was. In Thornscarp of all places. *Begging* for this alliance. When he did find out, he was bound to be less than pleased. Hence, the unwilling bit.

The king grunted, and she sensed him shift in his throne.

Mila still didn't look up, but upon entering the room she'd noted the pair of massive thrones on the dais. The queen's chair had been identical in every way to the king's. It was no secret they shared power equally. That at least appealed to Mila. Prince Edonier would be accustomed to a woman holding power, even if she wasn't a trained bloodthirsty soldier. At least she was to be the queen one day. *If* she did what needed to be done.

Guards stood to either side of the royal couple, and when Mila did venture to look from the stones under her knees, it was at them. On the left was a woman with scaled skin the color of moss and golden feathers flowing from her head in a long cascade down her back. A thin scar ran from one of her lavender eyes, across the bridge of her nose, and into the neck of her armor.

On the right stood the biggest man Mila had ever seen, towering above the king and queen. *Who makes his armor?* His face was both human and not unattractive. He too bore a beard. Unlike the king's, however, it was short enough to still make out his strong jaw. Soft chestnut waves covered his head and curled over his ears. From beneath the waves, large horns shaped like those of a bull grew from his temples, angled up and running parallel with one another as they pointed to the ceiling. Without those horns he still stood well over every other person in the room, and the slight curve of the pointed horns gave him at least another eight inches. If that alone wasn't enough, his lower legs were those of some mighty beast—complete with fur and claws—great cat paws rather than feet.

If the pair of guards noticed her gaze on them, they didn't show it. Both stared straight ahead, blank unfeeling expressions on their faces.

"And you take this responsibility on yourself?" Queen Augustina asked.

Mila cautioned a glance toward the woman but immediately regretted it. If the king was fearsome to look at, the queen was downright brutal. Long twisted horns sat over a face at once stunning and cruel. Her long auburn hair was braided to her waist, her leather breastplate scarred by countless slashes.

The queen was not someone to be tangled with.

"I do, Your Majesty." Mila could sense Glowildeen and Puddi, where they knelt behind her. She had wanted the pair to listen for once and wait outside, but in true form, they'd flat out refused. She hoped Glow would keep her composure intact and her feral mouth shut. The last thing Mila needed was to save her tiny friend from being eaten by one the guards.

"And why is it you think we should even consider this offer?"

The question was fair enough, but Mila still felt the disapproval from the warrior queen. She knew what the queen was thinking. How could a woman from Gildernosh ever be enough for a battle-hardened prince of Thornscarp? Despite being the monarch-in-waiting to the throne of Gildernosh, she was still just a woman. Not a soldier. Not a sorceress. Not a monster or a goddess.

And yet, there she was.

All the realms knew the royal family of Thornscarp had deemed it time for Prince Edonier to find a bride. Rumor was that they planned to finally create a solid alliance with one of the neighboring kingdoms, and while Mila's realm had wealth to spare, it had also been under constant siege from its neighbors to the east—one of which was the very same kingdom where her father was currently trying to negotiate. Or bribe, depending on one's perspective. In past years, it seemed there were constant whispers of an army at their doorstep planning to storm in and take by brute force what they couldn't get with political alliance. Gildernosh was ripe with fruitful gem mines and a vast coastline dotted with ports ideal for trading. They had fertile lands for crops and money to spare. What they didn't have was a populace trained for war.

Mila, knowing the risks, had suggested to her father an alliance with Thornscarp. Her face still stung from his slap and from the shame of being thrown out of his presence. The beautiful people of Gildernosh would never debase themselves by forming an alliance with the demon beasts of Thornscarp. No matter the cost to the kingdom or its people.

And while Mila would never agree to such a blanket dislike for an entire country or her father's disgusting use of the words "demon beasts," she had to admit, the sight of the fierce guards, and even the royal family, gave her some pause.

But Mila loved her people and she loved her home. She would sacrifice for them by sealing an alliance with a prince who could rally his troops to defend her homeland. In time, her people would come to accept the price that needed to be paid for their safety and their freedom. She only hoped her father would too.

It had taken her no more than a day to decide. Having accompanied her father on his visit to Yallring, Mila was closer to Thornscarp than she'd ever been in her life. In the dead of night, while the beautiful people of Gildernosh slept in their comfortable beds and her father played politics with the Yallring parliament, Mila saddled her horse, packed up her companions, and set out for the border with Thornscarp.

"Your Majesty," Mila began, "Gildernosh may not have armies as vast and as trained as yours, but we can offer wealth enough to supply your soldiers with any and all weaponry needed. Our people are hard-working"—the queen scoffed—"and our harvests are plentiful. We may supply your people with food enough to ensure not a soul goes hungry. Add in our harbors on the west with access to the seas at your disposal. In exchange, I seek only your assistance in sending a message to those who would seek to invade our lands and take these things—which I offer you freely—by force."

The queen tilted her chin down, not in a nod of agreement, but in contemplation. Mila's heart sank as the queen's eyes lit up and a smirk stretched her full lips.

"Interesting." Though the way the queen's lip curled, Mila got the impression the idea was anything but. "Here I was thinking you were still mourning the loss of you truest love. Clearly I was mistaken. Rumors whispered on the winds can be false, it seems. But you've deigned to travel here—to the land which other realms despise. I applaud the effort, but to imply your people are well intentioned victims seems . . . disingenuous."

Mila sensed more than saw Glow bristle behind her. The statement was not unexpected, but it did come earlier in the proceedings than Mila had anticipated. She'd known this introduction was going to be tough, but she'd hoped the real dung flinging would wait until she'd at least cleaned up from the journey.

"Your Majesty, my late husband has been gone over a year. My period of mourning is well and truly over. I've removed my bands." She held up a naked wrist for the woman to seen. "But if I've offended you in assuming my previous marriage would not be an issue, I offer my sincerest apologies. As far as being despised, I can only assure you, if you accept my offer, that will no longer be the case. At least so far as Gildernosh is concerned."

Her father might not like it, but as soon as she delivered a healthy heir, the kingdom would be hers and she would keep her word. The idea of a mutually beneficial alliance wasn't just a fairy story. It was the key to keeping her people safe.

The queen seemed unmoved by her words, but neither did she seem offended. Mila hadn't risen to the bait about her own people, and she counted it as a small victory.

"And I suppose you have a plan for how our nations will be united without a shared border? Perhaps the leaders of Evansband or Yallring will simply throw open their gates for passage?"

Mila gritted her teeth. Was it too much to ask for a cup of tea or a nap before this all began?

Like in her previous marriage, Mila had worried this might be a sticking point. She didn't in fact know how that bit would work. She'd been hoping the royal advisors would hatch some miracle after the wedding took place. Thornscarp was landlocked and without a port; all trade and transport relied on crossing into one of its neighboring nations. As far as she knew, it didn't happen often.

"It is my belief the coffers in Gildernosh should be stout enough to pay any tariffs or taxes needed to ensure a route between our people," Mila said. Her father would be furious if he found out she was already offering access to the treasury. But what choice did she have?

The queen tapped a finger against the arm of her throne, head tilted while she studied Mila. "You've shown bravery coming here, and for that I commend you. Stay with us the month, and we shall see if you are truly a worthy bride for my son."

Puddi let out a delighted chuff. The young woman had a taste for adventure and an obsession with romance. What could be more adventurous than staying in Thornscarp Castle or more romantic than a wedding?

Mila released the breath she'd been holding. A month in the

castle was easy enough and more than she had hoped for. If she truly meant to wed Prince Edonier, she would be spending more time than that in the company of the fearsome family. "You do me a great honor," she said.

"Thak," the queen commanded. "Take the princess to the blue room and find somewhere suitable for her companions. I trust you to see that she is comfortable during her stay."

The large horned guard stepped forward and dipped toward the queen in a bow. Mila's gut clenched, but she hadn't spent a lifetime in court without becoming practiced in indifference. She wouldn't show a drop of her unease at the choice of escort assigned her.

"Yes, Your Majesty." His voice was deep and rich.

Mila rose from her stooped position and glanced back at Puddi and Glow. The gnome had not a trace of reluctance where the guard was concerned. She wore a grin from ear to ear and batted her eyelashes at the imposing figure—she came up to his knee—as he passed her, while Glowildeen scowled at everyone and everything. It was a shame really, as the sprite's smile could turn tides and end battles even if it was filled with needle-sharp teeth. She simply never chose to employ it.

The guard took no notice of Puddi or her flirtations just as he took no notice of the ten-inch magenta-haired sprite hovering behind him and staring daggers into his back.

The massive man dipped his head to Mila and strode toward the doors. Mila took a step to follow but stopped short and turned back to the queen.

"I beg your pardon; might I at least meet the prince?"

The queen's face was unreadable. "Of course, child. At some point, I suppose. He is currently assigned to an important task. I'm sure you're aware of his position with the military?"

Mila nodded numbly. She wasn't even to *meet him*?

"Edonier comes and goes from the castle frequently. I'll be sure to have him make himself known to you at some point in the coming weeks. For now, you'll need to make due with us." Her lips tightened into a bitter smile. "And there is Gregor—my younger son. I'm confident he can provide an adequate distraction for the time being. I'll see you are introduced to him this evening."

2

S entient Pine

THE GUARD WALKED SEVERAL PACES AHEAD OF MILA AND PUDDI as they walked from the throne room to a grand stone staircase leading up into the castle. Glowildeen flitted back and forth between the guard and her companions, the fierce frown never leaving her face. Mila once again found herself attempting to ignore the frosty looks of those in the castle. She could see the wave of whispered insults fall quiet as soon as the servants, courtiers, and soldiers saw the large guard enter their periphery. Curious people occupied every room and passageway of the castle. Her escort took no notice of the others as he led her silently through the stone walkways. His legs were considerably longer than Mila's—and magnitudes longer than Puddi's—but he matched his pace to theirs.

Things hadn't gone as perfectly as she'd hoped with the monarchs, but at least they hadn't flayed her on sight.

It wasn't that she'd expected to have the prince accept her

and proclaim his undying devotion at their first introduction, but she had hoped to interact with him a bit. She was no stranger to blind unions, but some small part of her had hoped since she was taking this on herself, she could in some way direct the process. Once again, she was wrong. It was unfortunate, but she still intended to do what needed to be done.

When they reached a solid wooden door at the end of a long hallway several floors above the throne room, the guard stopped and dipped his head toward Mila.

"Thak, is it?" she asked. He nodded. "May I use your given name, or do you prefer something else?"

"Thak is fine, Your Highness." He stood next to the door, those oddly monstrous feline legs slightly parted and hands behind his back.

Puddi cleared her throat, and the guard looked down at her. Hands clasped beneath her chin, with a flick of her head, she tossed her long golden braid over one shoulder and smiled demurely. "You may call me Puddi if you like, Thak."

The guard tilted his head and raised a solitary eyebrow. Mila noted how lovely his large brown eyes were. "No title, my lady?"

"Oh yes. I come from a long and distinguished line of Pilmoulder Gnomes of Krith, but I don't like to brag. Puddi will do just fine."

"And you, my lady?" He tipped his head at Glow.

Her delicate damselfly wings beat hummingbird fast as she hovered near Mila's shoulder. She crossed her arms and looked down her nose at the hulking man. "If you value your miserable hide, you'll refrain from calling me anything at all."

The guard's eyes widened, and his brows reached toward the horns atop his curly-haired head. Mila thought for a brief moment that he was going to smile, but he merely dipped his head in the sprite's direction.

"Her name is Glowildeen Rosewink, and I apologize for her tremendous lack of manners." Mila frowned pointedly at the sprite. "The past days have been tiresome for us all, and I'm afraid Glow has let the travel get the better of her."

Puddi snorted, knowing full well the travel had little to do with it. Testy was Glow's default personality.

Mila smiled tightly. Tiresome was an understatement. A bath and some tea. Dreams were made of lesser things.

"No apology required, Your Highness."

She smiled. "Oh, we can't have me using a familiar name and you sticking with *Your Highness*. Please call me Mila."

"I'm afraid the queen would not approve," the guard said.

Of course she wouldn't. Mila sighed. "Very well. This is our room, then?"

"It's your room, Your Highness. One of the maids can arrange a room nearby for your companions. Unless you prefer the servants quarters."

Mila grimaced. "That won't be necessary. Puddi and Glow can stay with me."

"We don't take up much space," Puddi added merrily.

The large guard chuffed. "You're certain?"

"Quite. Thank you." Mila's tone was clipped. They weren't servants. Not to her anyway.

He nodded and tilted his horns toward the door. "Sentient pine," he said as if Mila should know precisely what that meant.

She pursed her lips and nodded, at a complete loss.

"We'll have a guard near at all times, but the door will respond only to a select few. You can open it from the inside, but only your touch will allow it to be opened from the hall."

Mila's lips formed a small "O" as she took in the meaning.

"And those few are?" Glow demanded.

"The three of you, the queen, her Master Covert, and the maid assigned to your chamber."

"The Master Covert?" Mila asked.

"The person in charge of keeping the realm safe. You needn't worry about him, however. He's a busy man."

"And what about you?"

He shook his head. "You'll need to allow the guard to enter should it be needed."

This seemed to satisfy the sprite.

"You'll need to run your palm down the length of it," he explained when Mila made a move to turn the handle.

Puddi giggled. "Run your hand down the hard wood? Let me try!"

Thak grunted a soft chuckle.

Mila closed her eyes and took a long suffering breath. "I think I've got it handled, Puddi." She lifted her palm to the center of the door and drew her fingers down the center. The wood sighed and shivered beneath her touch, and Mila prayed to the Maidens and all the other celestials that Puddi would refrain from commenting.

She bit back a yelp as a scratchy baritone pulsed from the heart of the wood. "Please enter, Princess."

Sentient wood indeed. It could actually speak. How had she never heard tales of that?

Thak nodded brusquely and pushed the door open. He dipped his head to avoid hitting his impressive horns on the jam as he stepped inside. Mila followed and took it all in. The room was clean and tidy, if sparsely furnished. A large stone fireplace occupied one wall, and a simple oak-framed bed sat against the other. A thick piled mattress and a sea of lush quilts and comforters nearly buried the bed frame. Matching velvet drapes covered the windows, and blue glass shades covered the lamps on both the table and those affixed to the walls.

"There's a washroom through there." Thak pointed to a door in the corner between the bed and the windows. "The castle is fed by hot springs deep under the mountain. The piping can be tricky at times, so one of the maids will instruct you on how to open the taps effectively. Despite the springs, it gets cold in the night. I'll light your hearth before you retire, and I'll have one of the maids bring up a set of cushions for your ladies."

Hot springs. A hot bath. The day got marginally better. Mila turned and took it all in. "I've left my horse in the stable along with my bag. If you'd be kind enough to show me the way, I'd like to tend to her and retrieve my things." The bath and tea would need to wait.

The guard's eyes widened once more. They were a deep rich brown, nearly the same shade as the hair covering his lower legs. And his lashes. She'd *kill* to have those lashes. It seemed almost a waste on his otherwise masculine face. He was terrifying, but if she could keep herself from looking below his knees or above his brows, she could pretend to herself he wasn't.

"Is that a problem?" she asked.

He spoke directly and with little inflection when he answered. "Not at all. However, I assumed you'd like a servant to fetch your belongings."

"I need to learn my way around if I'm to be a guest in the castle. There's no sense in having someone else tend what I can easily do myself."

He dipped his head. "Of course, Your Highness."

"I'm tagging along too," Puddi chirped, not bothering to hide the way she eyed the guard.

Mila in turn didn't bother hiding the smirk blossoming on her face. "If you insist. Glow, why don't you stay here and settle in? Puddi and I can clean up when we return."

Glow crossed her arms and flew up to hover eyelevel with Thak. "I'm trusting the princess will return unscathed. Should she have a single hair out of place, I'll be taking it out of your hide, big man."

Once again, Thak dipped his head, his left horn dancing dangerously close to Glow's fluttering wings. "Noted."

The guard escorted Mila and Puddi back down the stairs, but rather than exiting from the door they had come through earlier in the day, he took them around through the kitchen and out a side door to the stables.

They were met by a boy of perhaps twelve, smartly dressed in a clean set of breeches and a fitted white shirt. His leather boots were polished to a shine at the tops but were dusty with hay at the toes. As he turned to show them the way, Mila noted his slender pointed ears with small tufts of sable fur at each tip. If he had any other demon traits, Mila couldn't see them.

The princess and heir to the monarchy of Gildernosh was shown to her horse while the little gnome went off in search of her goat.

MILA SPENT NEARLY AN HOUR BRUSHING THE STALLION AND whispering in its ear as she fed it carrots from a bucket by the tack room. Every now and then she'd hear the joyful giggles of Puddi floating in from the yard. No doubt she was unabashedly flirting her way through every stablehand, soldier, and groundskeeper in the place. For all Mila knew, her small gnomish friend might be flirting with Prince Edonier himself. The queen hadn't mentioned when he'd be back. It could be an hour or a week or not at all.

As she ran her hands down the horse's neck, Mila silently thanked the cosmos for gifting her such wonderful friends in Glow and Puddi. Because of them, this whole endeavor might just be a tad less horrendous.

Thak stood silently by the entrance while she tended to the animal until she was satisfied. She retrieved her belongings as well as her companions' things. Another benefit to traveling with a sprite and a gnome—less luggage.

When she was ready to return to her room, the guard attempted to take her bags, but she refused. "There is no sense in having you labor when I can easily handle my own satchels."

The guard set his mouth in a tight line. "You've had a long day of travel, and I don't mind, Your Highness."

Mila hefted a leather bag onto her shoulder and grasped a smaller traveling case in the other hand. "The offer is appreciated but unnecessary." She gave him a tight smile.

"You may carry my things if you like." Puddi stood with her hands clasped at her waist and batted her eyes toward the leather case at her feet.

"I would be honored." Mila listened for the sarcasm she was sure to find in the guard's response but found none. Thak bent at the knees and lifted the luggage easily in one hand. Mila had to stifle the grin threatening to overtake her as she watched the large man handle the gnome's bag as if it were no more than a coin purse.

They reached the door to the blue room, and Mila ran her hand down its front as she'd been instructed. Thak pushed it open but did not step inside. "Water should have been drawn for your bath. Dinner is in an hour. I'll be out here when you're ready to go down."

"Thank you." Mila glowered at Puddi until the gnome took her luggage from the guard. Puddi tossed her braid once more and wiggled her hips as she entered the room. Mila followed, stepping past him to shut the door behind her.

It took all of Mila's strength not to break into tears as the door thudded shut. She knew the citizens of Thornscarp had the blood of demons running through their veins, and she'd heard tales of the differences among them. She'd even met a few in the past at functions back in Gildernosh or at summits in Yallring and Evansband, but the denizens of the mountain realm largely remained within their own secure borders. The few who did travel as ambassadors or emissaries had looked almost completely human. She recalled one envoy with orange irises and another with a lupine nose and tail to match but nothing as startling as what she'd seen in the past half day. She hadn't properly prepared herself for the scars and horns, scales and teeth.

The prince she'd just offered herself to went by many names. Brutal Prince Edonier. Prince Edonier the Mighty. The Demon Prince of Thornscarp. Despite his reputation, she'd never seen a likeness of the man. As far as she knew, no one had. Not in Gildernosh at least. He had gained almost mythic notoriety—many knowing of his deeds, but few having ever witnessed them for themselves. It was said that any who got close enough in battle simply did not walk away from the encounter. He was fierce and courageous. Beloved by his soldiers and feared by his enemies. She could repeat any number of stories relating to his deadly reputation, but she knew nothing of the man himself.

The royal family never sent him on delegations or to the occasional summits held between realms. They sent only a few emissaries on their behalf. No images of him were printed or shared. It was as if he were a ghost and all the more frightening for it. Perhaps that was by design.

What if he was covered in plates or fur? What if he had his mother's horns and the teeth of a viper? She wasn't concerned with loving him. She'd survived one loveless marriage already. But if she feared him? That simply would not do.

All the possibilities roiled around in her head and in her gut, but none of them were going to be answered now. Best to put on a brave face until she knew for certain what she'd just offered of herself. And who knew, perhaps the royal family or the prince himself would reject her offer by the end of the week.

Then she'd be right back where she'd started.

Mila walked through the chamber, pulling her braid loose. A melodic voice drifted from the bathing chamber, and Mila smiled. Though Glow hated performing for anyone but herself, she had an enchanting voice—robust and smoky, and not at all expected from such a tiny creature. On occasion, when the mood struck her, she'd share her talent with small groups of only her closest associates. But the tunes she'd sing were always bawdy and just shy of indecent. It was only in moments like this —when she didn't think anyone was around—that she'd sing the luscious tunes of her homeland in the center of Evansband.

As much as it pained her to end the sprite's song, Mila knew Glow would be in even worse form if she knew they were listening to her. So Mila dropped her travel case with more force than was needed. The loud thump it made as it hit the wood plank floor cut the lyrical spell as she knew it would.

Puddi sighed, shook her head, and motioned Mila over to the chair and plain desk in the corner. Mila turned the chair rear facing and sat while her friend climbed up to perch behind her. The gnome mumbled something about birds' nests and began to detangle the mess of her long ebony locks. Mila cringed, knowing a week's worth of travel grime was being sifted around her. It wasn't just twigs and leaves tangled in her hair. A fine layer of sweat and muck, dust and horse coated her skin. The rains couldn't wash all of it away. As much as she had wanted to lay eyes on Prince Edonier, perhaps it was for the best that he hadn't been in the throne room with the king and queen. She doubted he'd be too pleased to see a filthy woman in sodden riding leathers asking for a marriage bed.

As Puddi was finishing, Glow exited the bathing chamber along with a thin cloud of eucalyptus-scented steam. Her tiny cheeks—both on her face and her ass—flushed a faint rose under the river stone grey of her skin.

"I brought your things in with mine, Glow. Feel free to put on some clothes before we go down to dinner." Sarcasm dripped as Mila addressed her small nude friend.

"Let 'em all have an eyeful if they like." Glow swooped down and landed on the bed.

Eyeing where her friend had landed, Puddi giggled.

"What is it now?" Glow asked.

"Do you suppose the bed is constructed of sentient wood as well?"

"It better not be." Mila threw a wink at the gnome and smiled.

Puddi smiled back. "Too bad. If it was, perhaps it could tell us all sorts of naughty bedtime stories."

As close as she'd been to falling apart, at least Mila could count on her dearest friends to lighten the mood.

Thak was right. The maids had brought up extra cushions while she'd been in the stable and must have shown Glow how to work the water taps. As she entered the small bathing chamber and pulled her tunic off, she was relieved to see steam rising from the deep tub in the center of the space. She hadn't seen warm water in what felt like ages, and her muscles ached at the mere sight of it. Kicking off her boots and shedding the last of her clothing, she sighed and stepped into the blissful warmth.

An array of scented soaps took residence on smart wooden shelf to the side of the tub. Mila smelled each one before lathering up with a creamy almond-scented bar. She scrubbed away the last handful of days on the road, paying particular attention to her face and hair. If she was to meet a prince, even if he wasn't the one she had hoped, she needed to look as fresh faced as possible.

By the time the water had cooled, her fingers were wrinkled and her head was calmer. She didn't know why the thick, soft towel at the tub's side surprised her so much. Surely even the mightiest of royal families needed a good bath on occasion.

She dragged her fingers through her long midnight-hued hair and studied her face in the looking glass. Bottle green eyes stared back from bronzed skin that had seen its fair share of sunny days. The faint smattering of freckles that dotted her nose and the single dimple of her left cheek were as they'd been for years. She sighed knowing full well her assets lay in more than her appearance, but when interacting with royals from other realms, any imperfection might be a detriment. She sighed and pulled on her sheath and called for Puddi to take her turn in the bath.

Digging into her bag, Mila retrieved one of only three decent gowns she'd been able to fit in her pack. It was slightly crumpled but would have to do. The deep teal color sat nicely against her warm skin. She only hoped it would be enough to win at least a glance from Gregor.

Glow lounged on a pillow picking at her minuscule nails with a dainty dirk. She'd done as Mila had asked and had gotten herself clothed. To call the diaphanous scrap of fabric a dress was pushing it, but Mila had little energy to argue. If Glow didn't mind eyes roaming her tiny figure, than Mila was in no place to tell her otherwise.

As always, Puddi was beyond excited and took no time at all in getting herself cleaned up. She too wore a plain but elegant gown—a beautiful tangerine velvet number that cinched in tight at her chest and waist. She'd left her cap off and wore her flaxen braid in a crown around her head.

"You both look wonderful. Perhaps we'll make a decent impression after all," Mila mused.

"We don't need to make an impression of any sort, Mila. You do." Glow sheathed her dagger and launched from the bed. "And if this lot of ball lickers can't see how amazing you are, it's their loss. Not yours."

Puddi nodded. "Agreed."

"I love you both beyond words."

"We know," Puddi chirped and waggled her hips. "Now. Let's go mingle."

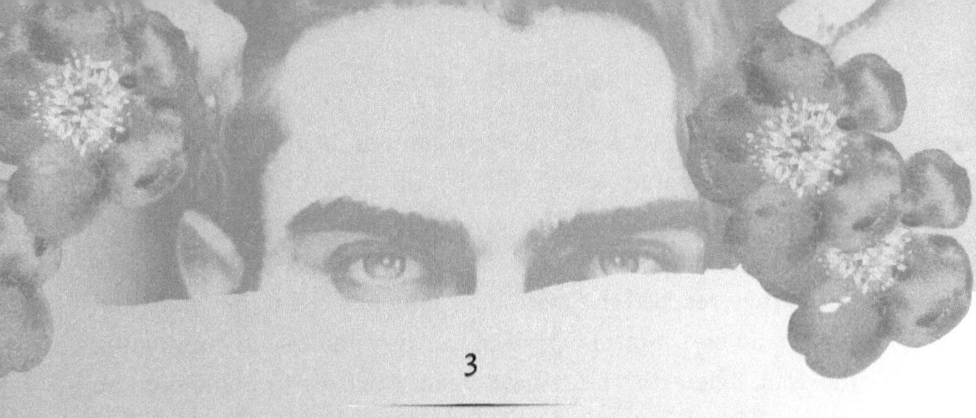

3

*H*ow Difficult It Must Be For Your Mother

THAK, TRUE TO HIS WORD, WAS WAITING PATIENTLY OUTSIDE THEIR door when Mila opened it. "Oh, I hope you aren't going to be stuck standing out here all week on my account."

There it was again, the slight widening of his soft brown eyes when she spoke. There but gone in a blink. He wore the same crimson tunic and charcoal leather breeches he'd had on earlier. Perhaps it wasn't an overly formal affair and no one would judge her wrinkled gown.

"Your Highness." He nodded. "This way please."

When he led the trio through the castle this time, they went back toward the throne room and the main halls. Mila took in her surroundings, paying more attention to the details than she had earlier in the day. The walls were built from the same sturdy grey stone she'd seen in her own chamber and the throne room. The flagstone floors were clean and the furniture tidy. Crystal globes hung from the ceiling, each filled with oil

23

burning lamps to keep the spaces well lit. She noted large ornately decorated vessels filled with an assortment of evergreen branches, mountain ferns, and the occasional stalk of bluebells or other hardy flowering plants.

As they reached the main hall, Mila glanced to her right and took in an enormous portrait of the king and queen dominating the wall. The artist must have been a master to paint such an image. King Edon stood tall and foreboding with his tusked mouth set in a hard line. His rich scarlet velvet tunic was adorned with gold epaulets that matched the shine of his thick mane of hair. In the depiction, rather than bearded, he sported a thick mustache. His tusks curled over it, and oddly, the combination was more interesting than she would have supposed. Despite the grim expression, the artist had managed to catch a twinkle in his eye that was wholly unexpected. His hand rested on the shoulder of the beautiful woman seated next to him. Queen Augustina had also been captured in all her glory. Her twisting horns shone brightly, and her mouth curved into a beautiful joy-filled smile.

Mila was so taken aback by the image she almost missed the subtle hint of something missing. The spaces to either side were bare, but she got the impression they'd once housed smaller frames—the wall was slightly brighter in rectangular areas, as if it had been protected from the elements by now-missing canvases.

She could have studied the beautiful work longer had her attention not been brought back by the sound of music drifting from up ahead. The air took on the wonderful aroma of roasted meat. Her stomach made a loud rumbling noise, and she grimaced. "Sorry," she directed at the guard when he glanced over his shoulder at her. "It's been a long day and we haven't eaten much."

"You should have said something." He turned his head forward, and Mila wondered how difficult it was to navigate the halls without hitting his impressive horns on the archways. "The queen will be displeased if her guests are not treated with hospitality."

"No. You've all been . . . lovely." Mila cleared her throat and continued behind him. Glow scoffed but thankfully didn't comment further.

The doors of the great hall were thrown wide—music and laughter flowed out as they approached. Thak stepped back to allow Mila, Puddi, and Glowildeen to enter ahead of him, and the noise dulled almost instantly. Heads turned their way, and they were greeted with a volley of sneers, smirks, and whispers.

The room was a decent size for a gathering hall, filled from corner to corner with a vast array of people and creatures. Many in attendance were clearly denizens of Thornscarp as they boasted an eclectic mix of horns and tails, claws and fur. She witnessed women in beautiful gowns to match their feathers and jewels to match their scales. Clearly the fashion in Thornscarp danced the edge of immodest yet still remained elegant and tasteful.

She saw men with snouts and soldiers with wings, the latter causing a stab of envy to surge through her body. Wings would be a dream.

Several people had entire heads with nary a trace of human features, and others were human in every observable way. In addition, there was a variety of brownies, pixies, trolls, and gnomes. A small cluster of sprites eyed Glow with barely concealed distaste, and a band of tree folk were playing lively music from a corner stage. A pack of dogs resided in the back, and a lilac stag was tethered to an iron ring in the front. The stag preened as a trio of women with scarlet hair stroked its flanks and antlers. Serving girls in loose flowing pants and adolescent boys burdened under massive trays hustled between tables, delivering steaming plates of food and refilling jugs of wine and mead.

Chatter in the hall picked up, but it wasn't nearly as loud as it had been before they'd entered. Mila motioned for her companions to remain with Thak, then lifted her chin and walked between the tables until she stood before the king and queen. They were seated at a table like everyone else in the hall, albeit a bit larger than the others. It wasn't an elevated dais or a long head table as Mila was accustomed to. Seated to the queen's right was an achingly beautiful man not much older than she was herself. He had hair the same lush auburn shade as the queen, cut short on the sides and swept back from his face. His features were chiseled as if crafted from marble by a master artisan.

Mila dipped into a curtsy and did not rise until the queen spoke.

"Ah, child. You've made it." Coldness ran through her voice but not in her eyes. They were the same eyes the artist had captured—full of light and life and completely at odds with what Mila could gather of the woman. Perhaps she simply enjoyed toying with her prey.

Doing her best to ignore the "child" once again, Mila dipped her chin in affirmation. The beautiful horned woman rose with a warrior's grace and beckoned to the gorgeous young man at her side. "May I present to you my son, Prince Gregor of Thornscarp."

The impact of the queen's words left Mila temporarily immobilized. It was only when Thak, having escorted Glow and Puddi to a table not far from the royals, stepped up and bowed that she realized how foolish she probably looked. She turned to the prince and dipped her head in his direction. "Your Highness."

Gregor studied her for a moment and, with an exceedingly bored look on his face, turned his attention to the soldier seated beside him.

Color flooded Mila's cheeks, but she held her head high and

smiled at the king and queen. They had their heads together whispering and she caught the king's eyes jump to her more than once, but the queen refused to look back at her. Feeling dismissed, she dipped again into a subtle curtsy and looked for her friends. Thak extended an arm, directing her to the neighboring table with two empty seats.

Puddi, looking uncertain and slightly confused, watched as she approached. Mila did her best to reassure the gnome with a cheerful quirk of her lips and gratefully sank into her chair. Mila was pleased when Thak took the other open seat, pointedly ignoring the sprite who scowled at him as if it were his doing that the prince was so rude. Despite how terrified she was of the guard in general, he seemed the least of all evils at the moment. Thankfully, they wouldn't be alone with the group of soldiers and courtiers who likely would rather see her starve than offer her cordial dinner conversation.

The surrounding chairs were occupied by three other men and a young woman who all appeared to be related. Two of the men and the woman had silvery white hair and upturned noses. They also had bright green eyes with elliptical pupils running vertically through the centers. The third man had the same catlike eyes but was without a single frosty hair on his head. His ears held a series of looping gold rings up either side. Mila noted how the others at the table had left ample room for the big guard and his impressive horns. He nodded to the group and dipped his chin toward Mila. "Princess Mila of Gildernosh and her companions, the ladies Glowildeen Rosewink and Puddi Pilmoulder. Your Highness, ladies, this is Ograt, Nox, Ram, and Petra." He pointed to each in turn.

The bald man, Ograt, smiled broadly, revealing a set of canines to rival the fiercest of wolves, and raised his cup toward her. "A pleasure, ladies."

As if his words were a signal, the other three also turned in their chairs and raised their cups.

Mila smiled in return. "Thank you for having us at your table."

One corner of Thak's mouth twitched. He quickly grabbed his goblet and took a long drink.

"Are you also guards?" Mila asked as she pulled her own goblet of wine up to her lips. She was happy to see the serving girl had provided smaller cups for Puddi and Glow.

"Not guards in the castle but part of the Corps," Ograt explained.

"The Corps?"

"The military, Your Highness."

"And you're all related?" It seemed obvious, but she knew too little of the people there to presume.

"Indeed we are. Siblings. Petra there's the baby of the family, but truth be told she's the toughest of us all."

The young woman laughed, showing off teeth every bit as intimidating as her brother's.

"How difficult it must be for your mother."

Thak snorted, and Mila immediately corrected. "I mean that you're all soldiers. Not that you're related. I only meant if something should happen in battle, it would be terrible for your mother to worry over losing all of you."

"No offense was taken, Your Highness." Ograt chuckled. "Mum probably hopes a few of us would take the sword most days."

"Their mother is a commander in the Corps," Thak said, as if this explained everything.

"So. You're after marrying the prince, are ya?" Ograt asked in a good-natured tone. He seemed to do the talking for the siblings.

Mila could sense Glow rising from where she'd been perched on the rim of an empty goblet but chose to ignore the movement. "That is why I'm here, yes."

"And you've never met the man?" Ograt pressed.

Mila shook her head.

"Seems like a big leap of faith to offer yourself as wife to a man you know nothing about."

As predicted, Glow flew over and dropped in front of the bald man. She didn't say anything, simply crossed her arms over her chest and raised an eyebrow in his direction.

"You'll need to excuse my friend. She has a tendency for overprotection at times. I assure you, her bark is worse than her bite."

"Not by much." Glow flashed a grimace and revealed the rows of tiny needlelike teeth hidden behind her delicate lips.

"Ah. So you're from Evansband, are ya, little one?" Ograt's smile widened. Mila could see all the way to his molars.

"It's the land of my birth, but these days my alliance lies with Mila and the throne of Gildernosh." She turned her back on him and strutted across the table. When she reached the end, she turned her head over her shoulder and ran her tongue to the tip of an incisor.

Ograt threw back his head and laughed. "Oh. I like you."

Mila sighed. Encouraging Glow would only lead to more antics. She turned her focus back to the soldier's question. "I know all I need to. I know he is fierce and brave. Loyal to his people and his soldiers."

"Aye. That's all true. But brave and loyal doesn't translate to respectful or kind. He could be cruel. He could be spiteful. He could have horrible breath. And you'd be none the wiser," Ograt said. "Then again, maybe it's the dark and dangerous you're after. Bad breath, though? I'd wager it might be a deal breaker. Not that I've gotten within kissing distance myself to judge whether it's good, bad, or somewhere in between."

Mila glanced at Thak, unsure how to react. The comment was surely no more than a jest, but she didn't know if the guard would be offended on the prince's behalf. Perhaps he didn't take kindly to soldiers insulting the crown he served.

To her relief, he smirked at the soldier. "I very much doubt he'd take to kissing a man as ugly as you, Ograt."

Ograt dipped his head in agreement, a grin playing around his mouth, and Thak raised his goblet in salute before draining it in one go.

Mila took note of the guard's hands as he placed the empty goblet on the table.. Strong hands, flecked with a dozen scars small and large. She often found herself judging men by their hands. It was an odd thing to be either attracted to or turned off by, but she couldn't help it. Some woman cared about shoulders and jaws. Others what was below the waist. She liked strong hands. Not that she should care about a guard's hands. Edonier's. Those were the hands she would need to judge.

Ograt didn't seen to notice the effect his comment had on Thak. Perhaps the guard was generally tense by nature. Or maybe they weren't friends at all. It didn't matter one way or the other. The bald man's attention had been snagged by something or someone behind her. When Mila turned her head, she noticed the feather-headed guard who'd been in the throne room with Thak earlier. The woman didn't even glance toward Ograt who was eyeing her hungrily.

Mila stifled a smile as she thought about Ograt's words. "All of those things could be true, I suppose. You're right. I'd have no way of knowing. It's why I'd hoped to meet him this evening, but the queen mentioned he was unavailable." She looked to where the other prince sat at the high table. He was currently ignoring the serving girl trying to fill his goblet and frowning as he stared directly at Mila. Her heart sank a bit.

"And still you'd marry him?" Ograt pushed.

"For the people of Gildernosh, I would."

Ograt nodded and called for one of the serving girls to refill his wine. The discussion was over. The next time Mila looked toward Thak, he seemed much more relaxed.

Over the next hour, Mila ate more than she'd care to admit.

The staff were constantly bringing heaping dishes to the table, and Mila sampled them all. Roast pheasant with cloudberry and walnut stuffing. Gooey cheese and apricot jam. Fresh green sprouts drizzled with honey and orange zest. Small cakes and warm breads. Each dish was better than the last. When she finally felt as if she would burst, she pushed the plate aside and reached for her goblet.

Puddi too seemed sated. She leaned back in her chair and sighed as she rested her hands over her stomach.

"Glad to see you've enjoyed the kitchen's hard work," Thak observed.

As the shimmering lamplight caught his face, Mila noted for the first time the smattering of freckles over his nose and cheeks. Then the light caught his horns, and she looked quickly away. "It may have been the best meal I've ever had," she replied with honesty.

"You can't mean the wealthy kingdom of Gildernosh has no decent cooks," Ograt said.

Mila nodded. "We do. Just maybe not as good as the mighty kingdom of Thornscarp."

Ograt laughed and thumped the table. The others joined in, and even Thak was close to smiling. Mila chuckled along. She was swirling the wine in her goblet when the laughter suddenly hushed. She looked up and saw thunderclouds in Thak's eyes. Turning in her seat to see who'd deserved such a severe response, she was startled to see the prince.

"If you all are done playing the fools over here," he sneered, "perhaps I might borrow the princess for a dance."

Thak started to stand but caught himself before he'd cleared the edge of the table. Lips set in a hard line, he focused on the empty plate in front of him.

Mila looked from the guard to the prince. His reaction didn't fit with his earlier response to Ograt's disparaging questions about Edonier, but perhaps the guard didn't feel as protective of

Gregor. She didn't have time to worry over it. She was there to meet the prince and secure a marriage alliance. If that meant getting on the good side of his brother, so be it. What one guard did or didn't think of him was of little consequence.

She righted herself and placed her goblet on the table. "Of course, Your Highness. I would be delighted."

As she stood and took the prince's outstretched hand, she couldn't ignore the others. Puddi looked hopeful. Glowildeen bored. The soldier siblings all looked as if they were preparing for battle, their once smiling faces now deadly calm. If Thak felt anything at all, she couldn't say. He simply stared down at his plate, refusing to meet her eyes.

The prince led her to a small open dance space in the center of the hall. The musicians struck up a standard waltz common in several kingdoms. The prince clutched one of Mila's hands in his, and she placed the other on his shoulder. As he wordlessly swept her onto the floor, she caught herself studying his face.

Up close he was just as striking as she'd first thought. His deep brown eyes were set in a face that could have been sculpted by the heavens themselves. Full lips and high cheekbones with a strong square jaw. Auburn hair immaculately trimmed and not a speck of dirt on his tunic. No horns or scales. No fur or feathers. He was perfect to look at. If the Maidens felt charitable, perhaps his brother shared some of his traits.

However, dancing with the man sent unease through Mila. She couldn't place it at first, and then it hit her. He was like the polished men of her father's inner circle, never saying the words but letting her know all the same that she was not quite up to snuff. She'd refused to cower to those men, and she'd refuse to cower to this one as well.

"How should I address you, Your Highness?" Mila asked. "Do you prefer Gregor or your title?" She didn't know why she'd assumed his given name would suffice. Perhaps because the guard, Thak, had preferred it. Clearly she was wrong.

"Your Highness will be sufficient." The disdain dripping from his words was wholly unexpected.

"I see. Well, you can call me—"

"I don't really think it's necessary to go further. Your Highness will do as well. For now."

Mila pursed her lips, clamping down on the biting words she wanted to use. They would have time to get to know one another over the coming weeks.

Several other couples joined in the dance. The prince took no notice of them. Mila, however, had trouble ignoring the ugly looks sent her way. One woman in particular looked murderous as she twirled by. She was a petite thing, with acid yellow eyes and short dark hair. She wore a flowing translucent skirt in a shade nearly identical to the vibrance of her eyes and a silver top with small capped sleeves and a hemline just below her breasts. The fashion left much of her skin exposed, but it was in line with what most of the other women in the hall were wearing. Aside from the queen—still dressed in her scarred leather garb—and a handful of soldiers and guards, everyone was wearing much less modest clothing. As Mila and the prince drew nearer the unusual beauty and her partner, Mila noted that her fingers ended in dagger-like claws. The open threat in her expression had Mila making a mental note to steer clear of the woman in the future.

"So," the prince drawled, "you've come to snag yourself a husband, have you?"

Mila forced herself to smile. "An advantageous marriage would seal an alliance between our kingdoms."

"Advantageous? Perhaps." He looked her over and ran his tongue across his lower lip. "In some ways at least."

Mila swallowed against the ire rising in her. "In many ways,

Your Highness. Gildernosh has many assets that the good people of Thornscarp might benefit from."

He smirked. "The good people indeed."

"And in exchange, the military might of Thornscarp could help protect the people of Gildernosh." Mila let him lead her in a simple turn. As she swept under his arm, she caught sight of the clawed beauty. If looks could kill she'd be a bleeding lump in the center of the dance floor, the denizens of the realm sullying their boots with her blood.

"Hmm. Perhaps. But only if the king and queen deem you worthy." Boredom dripped from his lips. "You do realize, however, Thornscarp has been seeing to its own for quite some time? Even without the hefty coffers of Gildernosh?"

Ignoring the question, she responded with one of her own. "Are the stories not true? Does Thornscarp not wish an alliance beyond its borders?"

"That is not for me to say. And you didn't answer my question."

Mila's brow furrowed. "And Edonier? Does he have a say, then?" She thought about getting the prince in her arms on her side. "Could you sway him, or do you answer only to the king and queen?"

"And you still evade my questions. But I'll answer yours. Apparently, unlike you, in matters such as this, I do as I'm told." The music was coming to an end, and Mila felt like her opportunity was slipping through her fingers. She snatched at it with an iron fist. If the prince did as instructed, she'd need to convince his parents. It wasn't ideal. She'd hoped for a union that would be at least marginally better than her last, but she was born to lead. And leadership often meant not just sacrifice but also determination.

"So what must I do to convince them?"

He barely looked at her as he released her hand, his deep brown eyes flicking to the woman with the claws instead. "My advice would be to act like a princess. Convince them you are *actually* worthy to marry their son."

Feeling both insulted and rejected, but no less determined, Mila stood alone on the small dance floor. The prince never looked back as he made his way to his table.

The revelry lasted several more hours, but Mila didn't speak with the prince again. Instead, she sat quietly at the table she shared with Thak and the cat-eyed siblings. She'd encouraged Glow and Puddi to dance and try to mingle, but both had refused, choosing instead to sit at her side and whisper stinging insults about all manner of things from the fashion and music to the prince himself. While neither wanted to discourage her, even Puddi seemed all too ready to slip the man a tincture of skullcap mushrooms and call it done after witnessing his vile treatment of her after their dance.

"Perhaps talk of regicide might wait until we're out of earshot of the very men and women who have sworn to protect him?"

"Oh, Mila." Puddi waved her hand and smiled sweetly. "He's not yet a king. It's merely murder at this point."

She didn't think anyone heard, but nonetheless, the air of joy the table had exuded earlier had evaporated and been replaced by a quiet calm. Not unpleasant, just subdued.

Eventually, Mila asked if she might retire for the night. Thak nodded and rose to escort her and her ladies back to their chamber.

"Really, it isn't necessary. We know our way. You should stay and enjoy the evening with your friends."

He looked at her steadily. "I insist. The queen has commanded me, and I won't neglect my duty."

"Of course. I'm sorry," Mila replied.

"Don't be."

They walked to her room in silence, and Mila thought it odd she felt comfortable with the intimidating guard after such a short acquaintance. Despite his size, the rather petrifying horns, and the beastly paws tipped with equally beastly claws, he carried himself with such grace and composure. She found herself comparing him to the handsome prince and the uncomfortable feeling she'd gotten when dancing with him. He was beautiful to behold, everything she liked in the male form, but. . .

But if Edonier was like his brother—haughty and aloof—her future might not be a happy one.

Silently, she scolded herself. It would do no good to think ill of the man she hoped to marry. It was her duty and one she would see through, if possible. She needed to win him over, and to do that, she'd do well to try to convince herself he wasn't as his reputation suggested. Along those lines, it was possible Gregor wasn't all bad either. It was possible, though not likely, it was an act to test her resolve. She certainly hadn't expected him to fall at her feet and pledge his undying devotion with just one look.

The problem was the time. She had only a month to convince the royal family she was a worthy bride but was still unsure how to accomplish the task. Her own courtship had been arranged. And before her marriage, only one other man had shown her interest and he was worse than her husband had been.

"Thak," she said as they approached her door.

"Yes, Your Highness?"

He stopped at the door and stepped aside. She was reaching up to stroke the wood, when Puddi pushed in front of her and rubbed vigorously below the handle.

"What?" she asked innocently when Mila raised an eyebrow at her. "We need to make sure it works for all of us. Just in case we're separated."

Mila blinked and shook her head, and the wood intoned, "Enter."

Thak pushed the door open and went into her chamber. Dipping his head to avoid snagging his horns, he barely avoided a midair collision with Glow who'd flitted in over him.

Mila rolled her shoulders as she came in behind them. "How do you suppose I might go about convincing the queen I'm a worthy bride for Prince Edonier?"

He turned away and knelt in front of the small fireplace, arranging the blocks of peat. Mila studied the way the muscles in his back stretched beneath his tunic as he worked. She'd never seen anyone built like Thak and found herself fascinated by his movements.

"Should you not be trying to convince the prince himself?"

"Yes. I should be. But as I have no idea when I might make his acquaintance, that task is easier said than done. And according to Prince Gregor, he has no say. It's the queen I should worry about."

He made a noncommittal noise in response.

"This isn't my strong suit. Charming princes and making royals love me." She sat on the bed, still watching Thak as he bent and stretched. He struck a match and placed it on the kindling. Her voice was quiet and far away when she said, "Not one. My father included."

Thak sat back quickly, bumping his horns on the mantel above the hearth.

"I can't imagine that's true, Princess." He turned at the waist and faced her. "You were married before, were you not?"

She smiled sadly. "I was. But surely you must know, a royal marriage is seldom born out of love. Mine was no different. As for my father, well, you have no idea." She wasn't sure why she was telling him this. Sitting up straighter, Mila plastered a smile on her face. It wouldn't do to share too many personal details with a man she knew next to nothing of. Despite his kind eyes and graceful demeanor, for all she knew, he'd be running off to sell her story to the first interested party he met. "Anyway. I'm here to do what I must and time is short. A month is barely enough to decide what to gift Puddi for her birth celebration or to convince a new gardener I won't execute him if he plants the wrong flowers. And here I am trying to convince an entire country to accept me. So, any tips would be helpful. I feel like this is some great test and I am failing miserably."

"You're likely doing a much better job than you suppose." Turning full toward her, he asked, "You'd take advice from a guard?"

"I'd take advice from you most certainly." *Why* was still a question she hadn't answered for herself. "Should it matter that you're a guard?"

A tap sounded at the door, and Thak stood, walked over, and pulled it open. A young woman with long dark hair coiled into a braid atop her head stood there, eyes downcast and hands clutching a tray holding a small white teapot and matching cups.

"Quince. Please come in," Thak said.

The girl startled when he said her name, but she hurried in, never once looking at the tall guard. Mila thought she might be afraid of him.

"Heya, Quince," Glow called from her spot across the room.

While the maid's garb wasn't nearly so scandalous as what some of the woman at the revelry wore, Mila was still surprised at how much it revealed. A light charcoal material wrapped around her torso and up the back of her neck, leaving her shoulder blades bare. Loose pants in material of the same color, though of slightly heavier weight, pleated over her waist and hips and flowed over her legs until it disappeared into her boots. It revealed the delicately patterned scales that covered her torso and neck, more like jewelry than skin. The entire ensemble looked not only ridiculously comfortable but also quite practical for the work the maid surely performed.

"Lady Glowildeen." The girl bobbed her head in the sprite's direction. It was then Mila noticed the long serpentine tail peeking out from the top of the girl's trousers.

"Not lady, remember. Just Glow will do." The girl poured the tea as Glow explained. "Quince was up earlier. Brought the cushions and explained how the plumbing worked."

"Oh, well then, a thank you is certainly in order," Mila said. "The bath was divine."

"You're welcome, Your Highness. Is there anything else I can get you this evening?" The girl's eyes shot to Thak once more before she focused again on a spot several feet in front of her on the floor.

"No. Thank you," Mila replied.

The girl scurried out, careful not to bump into Thak on her way.

The act made him look a touch uncomfortable as well. He wasn't far behind the maid and seemed just as happy to leave Mila and her companions.

Before he left, he turned his head. "It is. A test. Everything the queen does is a test. Remember that when next you speak with her. Try to get some sleep." With one foot out the door, he paused. "I expect you won't sleep well."

The way he emphasized the words felt odd. But then again, everything in the past day had felt odd.

The door clicked shut, and Puddi jumped up on the bed. "What did that mean? You don't suppose the castle is haunted, do you?"

Glow scoffed as she pulled off her dress and dropped in on her bag. "Not haunted, but I wouldn't put it past this lot to send one of those claw-tipped bitches in here during the night."

"An assassination? They wouldn't." Puddi squealed and sniffed at her tea.

"No one's sending in assassins, Glow. Puddi, I'm certain the tea is fine. And there aren't any ghosts either." Mila threw the words over her shoulder as she walked into the bathing chamber to scrub her face and put on her night dress.

By the time she finished, Puddi and Glow were asleep on their cushions near the hearth.

Mila turned down the lamps and crawled beneath the thick quilts covering her bed. The mattress was slightly lumpy, but only in one spot, and heaven compared to the rough nights she'd spent on the road over the previous week. She fell into the half slumber that comes before dreams take over, Thak's words, and his face, in her mind.

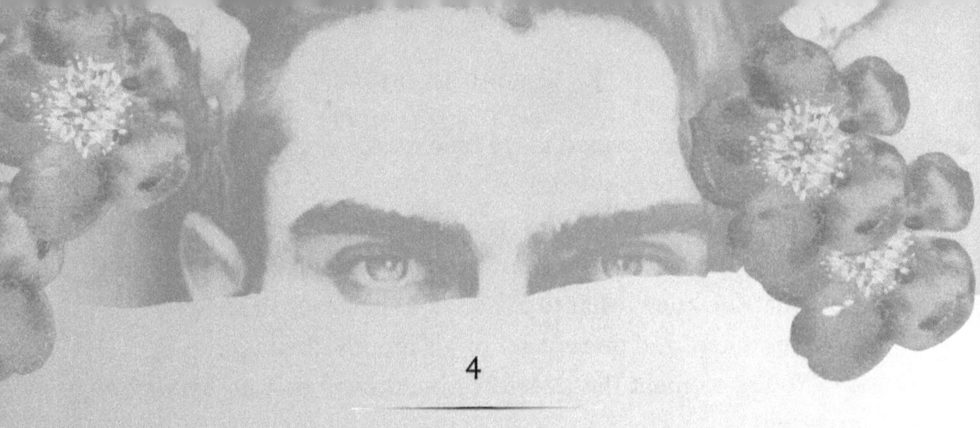

4

o You Ever Wear Boots

MILA WOKE THE FOLLOWING MORNING IN A WARM, COMFORTABLE bed, Thak's words from the night before still muddled in her mind. Why would he suggest she would not sleep well?

The mattress was piled high with thick sumptuous layers. The comforter was warm and snug. Even the fire—which had kept her cozy the night before—had burned down and prevented the space from being stifling.

Next to her, Puddi and Glow slumbered soundly. Evidently, they'd both migrated from their cushions to her bed at some point in the night. She slipped out of the sheets, careful not to wake them.

She pondered what the horned guard might have meant as she cleaned her teeth, brushed her hair, and put on her now-clean traveling clothes. She gently prodded her friends awake and instructed them to come down for breakfast when they were ready. Both seemed more than a little peeved that she'd let them sleep as late as she did.

As expected, Thak was waiting outside her door as she emerged, just as imposing but perhaps a smidge less terrifying now that she knew what to expect. Did he never sleep?

She smiled, and one corner of his mouth tilted up.

"You're to meet the queen for breakfast," he said by way of greeting.

Mila stepped out into the corridor. "I'm curious as to what I ought to expect."

Once again, he was mindful of his much longer legs and adjusted his stride accordingly. "I'd expect toast and eggs."

Was that a joke? Mila could barely contain her laugh.

Thak glanced at her and let out a long breath. "You should expect for the queen to treat you like the visiting princess you are. A guest in her home."

"And will the prince be there?" Mila asked.

"Which one?"

"Oh. I didn't know Edonier was here now. I meant Gregor."

Thak stiffened. "I expect he won't. It's a bit on the early side for him."

"It isn't that early," she replied.

He didn't acknowledge where Edonier was in the castle, so she assumed he was still out roaming the hills with the Corps, doing whatever military type things he was known to do.

When Thak didn't comment, she continued. "And what does he do with his days? Gregor I mean. Train with the soldiers?"

The big guard snorted but quickly recovered. "On a good day, he practices his swordsmanship. On many others, you're likely to find him otherwise occupied."

Mila thought on this as they made their way into the dining hall. Prince Edonier was known throughout all the kingdoms for his skill on the battlefield. She'd not heard the same about Gregor, but he was a prince of Thornscarp and they were warriors. All of them. Surely he must do some training with the men to maintain some level of ability and respect from the troops.

Once again, Thak pushed open the door to the banquet hall and stepped aside so Mila could enter before him. He'd swapped out the vermilion tunic he'd worn the day before for one in a deep mustard color. It was finely made and tucked into the fitted black trousers that were tailored at the bottom to seamlessly accommodate his unusual lower legs. Mila wondered if all the royal guards were outfitted so impeccably or if Thak's obvious rank had something to do with it.

"Do you ever wear boots?" The question was out before Mila could stop it.

He looked over his shoulder at her. "Your Highness?"

"Boots? Do you wear them? Or. . ." Her eyes drifted down to his paws. "I apologize. Do you find that offensive? I was just curious."

He chuckled. "Not offended, no. And at times, yes. In winter or in battle."

"The cobblers must be quite talented."

One corner of his mouth threatened a smile. "They are. Quite."

She nodded as they made their way inside.

Though the room was the same, it had a completely altered feel from the night before. Gone were the throngs of people and boisterous energy. No musicians greeted them. No warm candlelight danced from the walls. Rather, bright morning sunlight streamed through the windows and only a single table appeared to have been prepared.

Mila sat at the small round table laden with cold meat, some cheese, and crusty bread. Several large carafes of warm tea were placed along with the food. Mila watched as Thak grabbed one and poured himself a large steaming mug of the brew. She poured herself an equally large portion and added a heavy dose of honey to it.

Thak chatted with another guard, a woman with woolly hair and a thick brow. The guard muttered to him, her eyes never leaving Mila. After a few more hushed words, Thak informed Mila the queen was seeing to other affairs and suggested she eat.

She filled her plate, and the door opened to admit a slightly disheveled gnome and a rather surly sprite, both of whom grabbed small breakfasts before settling at an empty table in the corner of the room—close enough to act as her chaperones but far enough away that they weren't obtrusive.

Mila was nearly done with her breakfast when the queen was announced.

The princess stood and dabbed her mouth with a napkin before dipping into a curtsy as the queen sat opposite her. She looked regal despite being dressed in utilitarian clothing, or perhaps because of it. She'd forgone the scarred leather breastplate, but Mila had no doubt the woman could kill her efficiently should she choose to. Her dark horns were twisted and gleaming, her auburn hair braided away from her face and trailing down her back, and her simple dagger strapped to her side.

"I trust you slept well?" The queen drew the statement into a question.

Mila, unsure how to answer, flicked her eyes toward Thak. She was sure no one other than her saw the almost imperceptible movement of his head to the side. She had no reason to trust him. If the game he was playing was at her expense, things could go very badly for her, but. . .

"Uh, unfortunately no," Mila said. When the queen raised a single elegant eyebrow in question, she stammered. "I mean to say, I slept well enough I suppose. The room was quite comfortable, but I had difficulty calming my mind." The latter statement was true even if its implication was false. Mila still didn't understand the rules of the game she was playing.

"Interesting." The queen took a drink of her tea and studied Mila over the rim of her mug. "Dedication and duty to your people surely weigh heavily on you. Perhaps this evening you'll find better rest."

Mila assured Queen Augustina she would. Her Majesty then informed Princess Mila of Gildernosh there was to be another celebration after sundown.

The Queen bid her farewell after entrusting her safety for the day to Thak.

ONCE AGAIN MILA WAS MORE THAN A LITTLE AMAZED BY HOW graceful the large guard was. For a man of his size, he moved with a fluidity and calm that were near mesmerizing. He walked a step to the right and just a hair ahead of her, ready not just to lead in the proper direction but to open doors and fend off curious denizens of the keep. His hand on the butt of his short sword at all times gave the impression she might also be in a fraction of danger. It made sense to have part of his assignment be to prevent any unfortunate attack.

In the event of her untimely death, the surrounding realms would look down even further on Thornscarp and its love of brutality, but it wasn't as if it would lead to any all-out hostility. None of the four—save perhaps Evansband—could come close to matching the military of Thornscarp. Least of all Gildernosh.

What precisely, would her father do in such a situation? Likely marry quickly and hope for the speedy production of another heir. If such a thing were possible. The succession ran through her mother's line. She had to wonder if her death would bring about a clash for the throne, some distant cousin or other laying claim by blood rather than by marriage like her father. Mila hoped it would never come to that, but as her own actions recently showed, it was strange times indeed.

They were headed toward the stables when Thak spoke. "Thought you might like to see the grounds on horseback."

"I'd love to, but honestly, Thak, shouldn't you be resting?" The guard didn't seem tired, but surely he must be.

"I got some sleep last night."

She raised her eyebrows in surprise. The sentient door was reassuring, but Thak had made it sound as if someone would be stationed there just in case.

He added, "One of the other guards spelled me after you retired. I'm fine. Really."

Mila was still skeptical. "You're sure?"

"It's my duty to escort you, remember?"

"That hardly makes me feel better. But yes, I'd love to get out and have a look around."

Mila wanted to know everything about the realm that might one day be joined to her own. If, that was, her offer was accepted. She'd read about the kingdom's history and had spoken with advisors in Gildernosh, but there was a surprising paucity of information about the centrally located realm. It had secrets yet to be revealed, and there was no better way to start unraveling them than experiencing it herself.

As they neared the stables, a whirring at Mila's left snagged her attention.

If she hadn't been so accustomed to the pattern of Glow's wingbeats, she might have mistaken her friend for an overly large hummer beetle and attempted to bat her out of the air. As it was, she simply ticked her head to the side and glanced at the sprite, a question in her eyes.

"Don't think you'll be heading out without me," Glow grumbled. She'd traded in her gauzy shift for a more practical vest and trousers. Individual snake scales lined the leather over her shoulders and wound down the bodice to wrap around her ribs, the movement of her shimmering wings sending the armor into a rippling pattern. "If you'll recall, we were brought along for a reason."

"Of course I remember. But I hardly think I'm in mortal peril. Thak is being kind and showing me around. That's all."

"And if the big man has orders to make sure you don't return intact?" She eyed the guard with nothing short of death in her stare. Mila would have laughed at the notion, had her mind not been on a similar path not two moments earlier.

"Then I suppose I'll have a rather eventful and terribly unpleasant end to my little adventure."

Thak's low voice held no anger when he addressed both the sprite and Mila. "I can assure you I have no such orders."

"Forgive me if your assurances mean jack fuck all to me."

"Glowildeen. That's enough." Mila raised her eyebrows as she stared at her companion. It was both a command and a plea.

Crossing her hands over her chest, Glow hovered at eye level with Thak. "I'm watching you, guard."

He subtly dipped his head in acknowledgment.

Mila watched the exchange, unsure what to make of it all and was only distracted when she heard Puddi huffing in great lungfuls of breath as she finally caught up.

The gnome was dressed in a bright robin's egg blue dress with goldenrod leggings to match her perfectly placed lace cap. It was a new outfit to what she'd been wearing just that morning and one Mila was sure she hadn't seen before, much less packed for their impromptu voyage from Yallring to Thornscarp. It was a tad more revealing than her typical garb. The colors happened to set off her hair and complexion beautifully, and Mila couldn't help but wonder who the gnome had charmed already to ensure she had a perfect new wardrobe.

Puddi smirked when she noticed Mila taking in her new outfit. "Isn't it gorgeous? And you have to feel the material, Mila. It's the softest. Like silk almost. But they say it's made from some sort of mountain grass that only grows here in Thornscarp."

"Impressive." Mila ran her fingers over the material at the gnome's shoulder. "Oh, that is lovely."

"And light too. So much more freeing than our thick gowns."

"You'll be joining us as well then?" Mila smirked. While Glow's purpose left little room for doubt, Puddi's was just as obvious to Mila. While she was chaperoning her friend, it wasn't only Mila she was hoping to pay attention to.

"Of course. I just had to freshen up a bit." Puddi smiled demurely at Thak.

"For the love of all the gems in Gildernosh, girl. Put your tongue back in your head." Glow too could see what game Puddi was playing.

"I don't know what you mean." The gnome huffed and strode away.

Rubbing the spot between his eyes, Thak dropped his head. Mila was close to certain he was attempting—and failing—to hide a bemused grin. "Well, then." He cleared his throat as he lifted his eyes again. "If we're all here? Tryn"—he nodded toward the boy with the fur-tipped ears—"should have our mounts close to ready."

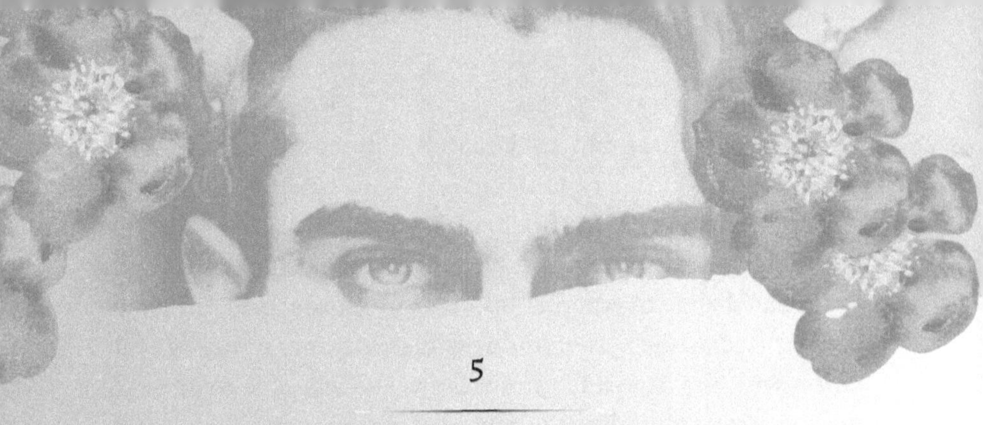

5

The Divine and the Cardinal
Or
A Land Full of Monsters

THEY SPENT THE BETTER PART OF THE DAY EXPLORING HIDDEN riverbanks and small-town streets, open meadows and tiny cramped mill houses. Thak was an excellent tour guide, and while they never stopped to talk to the citizens of Thornscarp, on several occasions Mila saw villagers pause what they were doing to watch as they rode by. As they were passing through the village beyond the keep grounds, Mila noticed an open field surrounded by wooden benches. To one side of the grounds, a large gold and crimson tent was being pitched.

"It's for the upcoming festival," Thak explained. "You showed up at just the right time for a little entertainment."

Mila was going to ask more, but Thak had changed subjects and was explaining the hot springs and how not only the castle relied on the waters for warmth, but the villagers too. Thak talked more in that chunk of morning than Mila had heard him

49

say in the previous day. He couldn't hide how much he cared about the land he had been raised in.

After leaving the town behind, they crested a low hill. Mila took in the devastating beauty around them. She hadn't fully appreciated the topography upon their approach the previous day, focused as she was on the possible outcomes of her conversation with the king and queen. Now, she was able to embrace the majesty surrounding the capital of Thornscarp.

To the east, the imposing figures of craggy snow-topped mountains crashed against the crisp azure sky. A large golden hawk rose on a thermal in lazy loose circles, undoubtedly looking for any creature fool enough to venture out from its hiding place. A carpet of tiny white flowers blanketed the roadside. Here and there more aggressive bunches of flame-colored blooms broke up the sea of white.

Puddi's goat took the small buds as invitation to graze, and despite her best efforts, she was unable to get him moving.

Thak looked over his shoulder and pulled up on his reins. "Lady Puddi has the right idea. This is a good spot for a rest." He dismounted and tethered his horse—an impressive beast which stood a good four hands taller than Mila's mount—to a low branch. The horse's saddle was a thing of beauty, all polished leather and sparkling chrome that somehow highlighted the horse's grey and white dappled coat beautifully. It even had specially designed stirrups to cushion and accommodate the guard's wide paws.

Mila followed suit, laughing as she watched Puddi lie back in the bed of flowers and their underlying loamy soil. As a gnome, she was connected to the land and all that blossomed from it. Judging by her look of bliss, and that she hadn't flirted with Thak at all since stopping, Mila assumed the land here was rich and comforting to her soul.

"It really is breathtaking." Mila stood, arms wrapped around her waist, staring at the mountains in the distance. Were there really so many different shades of white and purple, grey and green? "Is all of Thornscarp so stunning?"

"I've always thought so. Though, truth be told, I have little by way of comparison."

Mila shifted her hands to the small of her back and arched into a stretch all while never taking her eyes from the peaks. "You've never been to the other realms?"

Thak's voice came from a few feet behind her. "To Evansband a handful of times. And just over the borders of Krith and Yallring. Never to Gildernosh. I'm told it has its own merits."

"Well, I've been to all five of the realms, and each is lovely in its own way. But this"—she dipped her head toward the towering giants—"is something special."

"Gildernosh has the sea. They say it's a sight to behold. And mountains. You must, if you've got the mine output to keep the coffers heavy."

Mila nodded. "The sea is likely just as striking as you've heard. The power it holds is immense. As for the mountains, I'd call them little more than weathered hills when I compare them to these monsters."

She bent and plucked a handful of the velvety soft flowers and brought them to her nose. They had a peppery smell she found ridiculously pleasant. Finding a shallow depression through the field, she strolled farther away from the road. Ignoring the delicate flowers under his paws, Thak padded up alongside her, hands clasped behind his back.

"Have you not heard, Princess? Thornscarp is nothing if not a land full of monsters."

Mila twisted her lips into a wry smile. "Yes. That is how the stories go."

She didn't want to admit it, but she understood why. For all of Thak's gentle nature and Ograt's pleasant banter, something in both of them spoke of danger. It wasn't just their outward appearances either. Something deeper shimmered below the surface. A promise of violence should one find themselves on the wrong side of their favor. And that was nothing—*nothing*—compared to the cold welcome of the king and queen, the vicious stares from the claw-handed beauty, and even the actions of Prince Gregor. Were they monsters? She couldn't yet say. But something had her heart in her throat since the moment she'd passed through the castle's gate.

She couldn't express any of this to the guard at her side. For whatever reason, he'd been tasked with accompanying her and it wouldn't do to make him miserable in the task. Instead, she buried her nose in the peppery petals and inhaled deeply. Letting our her breath, she said, "I suppose the stories tend toward the unfair."

"Most things in life are unfair," he answered.

"True, but the stable boy, Tryn? He's no more a monster than I am."

"Wait 'til you see his horns and see if you think the same."

"His horns? Did he have horns and I missed them?" She'd stopped walking and glanced at him suspiciously.

"No. Not yet. But they'll come."

Her glance turned into a quizzical frown. "They'll come?"

"You didn't think I was born with these, did you?"

Mila turned her face upward and squinted against the sun. Ridiculous as it was, she'd nearly forgotten Thak had the vicious things sprouting from his temples.

"I. . ." She paused. "Weren't you?" She sounded like a complete fool even to herself.

Thak chuckled and shook his head. "My mother is one tough piece of work, but even she might find that a daunting task." His tone was serious, but there was mischief in his eyes.

Mila couldn't help but smile. "And is your mother also a soldier of the realm?" Thinking of Ograt and his siblings, it would make sense if their mothers were commanders together and their easy friendship born of that.

He shook his head. "Not anymore."

Something about his tone suggested it was a topic he didn't want to pursue further, so Mila changed the subject. "So how old were you when they grew?"

"Not much older than Tryn is now. Old enough to appreciate them but young enough to find them unwieldy on my gangly youth's frame. It took some time for my body to catch up."

Mila's eyes raked from the tips of the horns down his trunk to his long legs. His body had indeed caught up. She flushed when she realized he was watching her watching him. She swallowed.

Out of nowhere, Glow raced by, cackling as she flew. Her wings caught the light as she dumped an armful of white petals over Puddi's face.

"Does it run in the family?" Mila asked.

"Being a gawky teenager?" He looked genuinely confused. "I can't imagine my father ever being gawky or awkward."

She laughed. "The horns."

"Oh." His expression cleared, then he dipped his head and pinched the bridge of his nose.

"How do you know Tryn will get them?"

"I don't. Not for certain anyway. But if I were a wagering man, I'd say it's likely." He looked out in the distance. "Why do you ask?"

"I'm sorry. I'm just wondering how it all works. Ograt and his siblings look so similar, but the prince doesn't really look like either the king or queen." That wasn't precisely true. His face and the queen's were quite similar. It was just everything else that was different.

He nodded. "First off. You apologize entirely too much. You don't owe me remorse for not understanding. But to answer your question, some things do. Similar to eye color, hair, or skin. You can have families that take after one another and others with just flashes of traits. A blending of some and omission of others."

"And the horns? Do you and your parents all have them?"

He hesitated a moment. "Uh, no. We—"

"I'm sorry," she cut him off and winced as she apologized again. It was becoming clear he didn't feel comfortable talking about his family. Perhaps they were estranged or even dead. "It's none of my business. I just feel so bumbling, not knowing anything about how the demon—" She stopped herself again and cringed at her ill-mannered choice of words. Honestly, she was in line for the throne and had always been the picture of diplomacy, but in the past two days, she felt like a complete ninny.

Thak graciously didn't react. His voice was calm and inquisitive. "How demon traits work?"

She could feel her face flushing a deep crimson. "I'm sorry." Again! What was wrong with her? She took a deep breath. "Offending you is the last thing I want to do. I don't know exactly how to speak about the people here even though I desperately want to understand everything. And there are so many things I don't know."

For all of her tutoring and lessons, the intricacies of Thornscarp and its populace had been glanced over at best. Whether this was from lack of knowledge, distaste of the realm, fear, or something else entirely, she couldn't say.

Thak continued strolling along as if she'd simply asked how he liked his tea. "I don't suppose you would. The people here have largely been self-sufficient for centuries. We trade on occasion, but since the dawn of our history, we've not been eager to reach beyond our borders."

That would make sense as to why she'd only encountered the occasional ambassador from Thornscarp and why she'd never been invited to the realm for any official business. It just seemed so odd, for a kingdom surrounded on all sides by other realms, to keep so isolated. She wondered if it had to do with their physical appearance of if there was more to it.

"Why is that?"

"Do you know any of the old tales, Your Highness?'

"Plenty of them about Gildernosh. We share many of the same celestial deities with Yallring and few creation and goblin tales with Evansband. Puddi talks often of Krith as well, but I know only bits and pieces from Thornscarp."

She paused. "I was told once by a governess that the demons here were created by the union of a devil and an angel. She was a complete snob though, so I never took stock in anything she said."

"Well, for starters, most of us prefer the term chimera to demon." He grinned. "But as for the rest, she wasn't far off."

Mila's eyes widened. He must be teasing her.

"Why do you have that look on your face, Princess?"

She wasn't going to give him an inch. "What look would that be, Thak?"

"The look that says you refuse to believe a word of what I am about to say."

"Not a refusal of what you believe. I'm just surprised the woman knew what she was spouting. And. . ." She stretched out the word.

"And?"

"And an angel and a devil? Surely you know it sounds a little farfetched."

"I know no such thing." He tilted his head to where Glow continued to shower Puddi in all manner of vegetation and soil. "The gnomes and the sprites. The pixies and trolls. . . They all have a place in their respective homelands. Why shouldn't we have angels and devils?"

She stopped walking and crossed her hands over her breasts, cupping her elbows in her palms.

"Because they don't exist, Thak. But pixies and gnomes.

Sprites and trolls. They're all real. It's not the same thing. I'll not have you putting me on just for your amusement."

She wasn't angry really. But she was frustrated. She knew the queen in particular hadn't been keen on her proposal the day before, but she had hoped they would at least give her a chance to prove herself. Gildernosh needed this. She needed this. After her last rubbish fire of a marriage, she wanted something to finally go in her favor. Needed it to. How else would she gain a marriage of her own choosing and the heir she needed to finally take the throne? If the queen had convinced Thak to prove her to be a fool, it would be one more nail in the coffin.

Everything is a test she reminded herself. She's be damned if she was going to fail this one.

He grinned, and there was nothing—absolutely nothing— malicious in it. For a moment she thought she could make out dimples, not one but two, beneath the neatly trimmed hair of his beard.

"All right. Fair is fair, Princess. Maybe not a devil exactly, nor specifically an angel, but close enough in the scheme of things.

"In the lore of our people, they're referred to as the Divine and the Cardinal. What you might think of as a Maiden and a Creator."

Mila nodded. In Gildernosh the Maidens were stars fallen to earth. Not quite goddesses but infinitely more than human.

"Eons ago, when the mountains were young and the land was unsettled, a band of raiders fled the mines in the western realms—what is modern-day Yallring and Gildernosh—their packs laden with stolen gems and stolen promises. Like many others both before and after them, they'd been made promises of riches for hard work and a job well done. But after years of toil and little reward under the heels of cruel men, the band of four made a bid for freedom and fled back toward the east.

They swiped what gems they could along with their master's daughter—a fair lass with hair the color of sunrise and eyes the hue of the moon.

"The young woman was as brave as she was beautiful, but also cunning and just a smidge sympathetic. She understood the men had little choice. She was the shield they needed to escape unscathed. She didn't fault their hunger for a better life, but one of the men in particular was exceeding hateful and two others indifferent to his depraved abuse. With time her sympathy evaporated. She found herself despising the men, save one."

Thak stopped and studied the mountains in the distance. Mila studied Thak. He had a far away look in his eye as if he could see exactly what the abducted woman saw. Feel what she felt. Or perhaps it wasn't the lass at all. Perhaps it was the men he was thinking of.

When she could stand the silence no longer, she waved her hands, urging him to continue.

"I was just getting to the good part." A slight grin formed on his lips.

Mila walked back toward her friends and their mounts.

"The youngest of the riders was a lad not much older than the maiden herself, but more a man than his older cohorts. When the travelers reached the foothills of the mountains you see here in the distance, the young man released the maid and convinced her to run. The lass did as he bade her, though it pained her to do so. She knew he would suffer for the act. She didn't make it far before the sounds of his screams drew her back.

"Enraged by the young man's actions, his companions ran him down and drove spikes of sapling wood through his shoulders, pinning him to the dying shell of a great tree. Blood flowed from his wounds as his companions circled him. The lass returned and, upon seeing the fate of the lad, wailed in fury as well as dismay. Armed with only a stick, she placed herself between the young man and his tormentors. The scent of his blood combined with the maiden's cries awoke a great devil who dwelled within the mountain. The creature burst from the granite boulders a hair's breath from where the young man lay dying. It was a thing born of terror and madness with great horns and plated scales, hooves and spikes, wings and claws. When it caught sight of the lass defending the dying man, it lashed out and killed the others in little more time than it took her to blink."

"I still don't believe in devils, and I'm not always in favor of carnage, but I am happy they got what they deserved," Mila said.

"I agree," Thak responded. "Sadly, bloodshed is occasionally needed."

"But that's not how it ends," Mila guessed.

"The devil was instantly enamored with the angelic creature it found weeping next to the dying man. Knowing it would never win her love directly, it did the only thing it could. In an act of pure devotion, it pulled the stakes from the man's shoulders and breathed life back into his lungs. The maiden couldn't believe her eyes. As she watched, the skin knitted back together and the grey pallor of death was washed away by the flush of life. His wounds healed and his eyes opened.

"But as with all good stories, the resurrection didn't come without a price. The once handsome lad now bore the horns and hooves, scales and teeth of a monster."

"Let me guess. The maiden didn't care? She loved him nonetheless?" Mila had never cared for fables and morality tales. The happy ever afters weren't real, and the truth was often much more unkind. Still, she didn't mean for it to sound quite the way it did, not mocking exactly, but far too close to it.

Thak stopped and when he spoke again, his voice had lost a touch of its warmth. "Yes, Princess. That is correct. She didn't see a monster. Only the love of a man who would die to save her. The pair—the Divine and the Cardinal—remained in the mountains, and from their love sprang the people of Thornscarp. The devil returned alone to his lair under the mountain and he was not seen again."

They'd returned to their mounts. Puddi and Glow had ceased their frivolity and were ready to move on as well. Any ease Mila had gained with the guard had evaporated in a rush at her careless tone. He didn't smile as he mounted his horse, but he didn't shy away from her either. Mila could feel the challenge in his gaze as he held her eyes and finished the tale.

"The old nannies say if ever a *worthy* young woman is in distress within the borders of Thornscarp, the devil will once again hear her call. Only then will his undying devotion pull him from his slumber to defend her." He spurred his mount into motion and looked back over his shoulder at her. "*If* she needs defending, that is. "

6

That Prince Is a Fool

THEY RETURNED TO THE CASTLE IN TIME FOR MILA TO FRESHEN up and change for the dinner revelry.

The event was much as the night before, with Mila, Puddi, and Glowildeen sitting and chatting with Thak, Ograt, and the sibling soldiers. Thak was back to his reserved self, and Mila couldn't help but think her inconsiderate words had everything to do with it. The last thing she wanted was to make an enemy of one of the only people to show her kindness since she'd arrived, and she vowed she would offer an apology if she could only think of how to word it without making matters worse.

Puddi, dressed in yet another new gown, flirted with Thak, and Glow, dressed in barely anything at all, nearly bit Ram's finger off at the knuckle when he thought to brush her hair from her shoulder to keep it out of his mead. Ograt continued to openly pine after the feather-headed guard, and Mila was pleased to meet Nox's husband, a slender royal guard named

Dawson with grey-green scales and long drooping wings bursting from the back of his tunic. Dawson's identical twin brother Wren, Petra's husband, was currently away with his Corps regiment guarding the southern border with Evansband.

Once again, the prince asked her to dance, stared at her with ill-concealed boredom, made one or two rude observations, and bid her farewell without further conversation. Once again, Mila had to avoid the gaze of the raven-haired, claw-fingered woman as she danced perilously close with her partner. Once again, she ended the evening feeling like the entire idea of coming to Thornscarp for a marriage alliance had been nothing more than a pile of dragon droppings, much as her father suggested it would be.

Thak walked them back to their chambers, said goodnight after lighting their fire, and suggested Mila tell the queen she was unable to sleep well, should she ask.

Mila, still confused, fell asleep thinking about the day and the odd behavior of both Thak and the royal family.

When she walked into the dining hall the following morning, the queen was waiting for her and asked how she'd slept.

"I feel it's impolite to say," Mila responded.

"Impolite?" the queen asked.

"Yes, Your Majesty."

"And why would it be impolite, Princess?"

"Well, because you all have been so welcoming to me, and the accommodations are more than adequate. But I have not been able to rest as I would at home," Mila answered.

"I see." The queen turned to Thak. "Please make sure the princess has all that she needs to rest comfortably tonight. And do take her out again today, if you would."

Thak bowed. "Yes, my queen."

The queen rose and wiped her hands on a napkin. "Before I go, there is one thing I'm curious about."

Mila looked at her blankly.

"Gildernosh still follows the same line of succession, does it not?" She dropped the linen onto the plate before her.

"It does, Your Majesty."

"So you'll take the throne as soon as you produce an heir?"

"Yes." It was as it had always been in Gildernosh. The monarchy had succeeded down her mother's line, and her mother had been queen for only a handful of years before she'd met an untimely death when Mila had been a toddler. Her father had been ruling as the Lord Protector in the interim, but as soon as Mila had an heir—preferably a daughter—she would take the throne and her father would serve as advisor to the throne.

"It's a shame your first marriage was so short lived."

"One could argue it was for the better. Were Gideaon still alive, I wouldn't have had the opportunity to forge this union with your realm." The potential union was one blessing that had come with the death of her husband. There were several others. Others she was unlikely to discuss with the queen any time soon.

Augustina twisted her lips as she studied Mila over the rim of her mug. "At least not under this pretense, I suppose."

Mila set down her fork and placed her napkin to the side of her plate. This conversation was going to have to happen at some point, so she might as well get on with it now. "I do truly want what is best for both our peoples."

"Do you? Ruling a realm the likes of either Gildernosh or Thornscarp comes with immense pressures, Princess. Often in ways and from directions we cannot fathom until we are being crushed under its weight. Believe me. I know all too well what that feels like. Do you think you'll be able to withstand the strain?"

Mila raised her chin and looked the queen in the eye. "I do. With all respect, Your Majesty, you have no idea what I am capable of or what I would endure for my people."

The queen's lips turned down as she dipped her head. "You're right. I don't. But think on this. How difficult will it be not to bow under the weight of the Gildernosh populace, the weight of your father's hatred, the weight of your own fear, when you get with child by my son? As the babe grows within your belly, how will you *endure* not knowing what 'attributes' the child might have? Will it cause you to fold under like a slip of parchment left out in the rain? Best to be honest with yourself now rather than regret your decisions when the weight of the entire realm is resting on your shoulders."

The queen moved away from the table as Mila rose to her feet, hands clenched hard enough to send her nails into her palms. She could just make out Thak from the corner of her eye, standing rigid beside the door.

"Again, Your Majesty. You know nothing of me save what you choose to see."

If disdain wore a face, it was Queen Augustina's. "I've seen enough to know not every lump of coal will one day become a diamond."

THEY VISITED SEVERAL NEW SPOTS THAT DAY. A SCHOOLYARD filled with babbling children. A weapons forge coated in soot. A small chapel with beautiful windows. She found it oddly comforting that despite her poorly chosen words the previous day, Thak welcomed showing her a myriad of small treasures around every corner and hill. After a day in the saddle, she found something even more peculiar happening. She found herself opening up to the guard about Gildernosh, something she would never have dreamed of doing with a relative stranger from a neighboring realm. Despite Glow's glowering and Puddi's nervous giggling, the horned man listened as they rode and never treated her like the pampered girl so many others did. He asked smart questions and smiled at odd customs. He furrowed his brow at things he didn't understand and scratched at his beard as he contemplated the many similarities and differences between their people. On occasion he would ask her to elaborate on something but wouldn't push for invasive information. In short, he treated her like a friend and confidant.

They were resting by a small stream, Puddi and Glow playing in the water, when Thak informed her that they needed to head back soon to make it to the night's revelry.

"I don't understand why I should even attend. I'd much rather retire to my room and have a quiet dinner there, rather than get paraded around by the prince for one dance and then be cast aside like rubbish under his boots."

Thak stilled. "Is that how you truly feel? Most women find Gregor captivating."

She grimaced. "I probably should have kept that to myself, but for all I know, Edonier may be just as bad, if not worse."

"And yet you'd still marry him?"

"You don't understand." She plucked a small white flower from the clover where she sat and rolled it between her fingers. "It's what my people need."

"But wouldn't you rather marry for love?"

"Of course I would, Thak. But it isn't that simple. I. . ." She shook her head.

"Go on," he prompted quietly.

"I'm not sure it's appropriate to have this conversation with you, but seeing as you're my only friend here aside from Glow and Puddi, I suppose there's little harm. You'll think I'm rather silly."

"I doubt that very much."

Thak lay back on his elbows in the clover next to her, long legs tipped in beastly paws spread out before him. His posture was relaxed, but Mila sensed the big guard could roll into motion at even the slightest threat.

"When I came here, I had this notion that as soon as I saw

the prince, I'd know my decision had been the right one. Despite all of the stories I'd heard, he would be not only handsome but also charming and full of integrity. Like you, I suppose." Mila felt Thak stiffen beside her, the conversation clearly making him uncomfortable. She'd only known him for two days. That idea was beyond ridiculous, but she could sense it in him nonetheless. She sighed. "He'd see me and know my offer of marriage was honest and pure and, maybe, he'd even find me pretty enough and companionable enough to want to marry me as well. But seeing as I have yet to meet him, well. . ." She sighed again. "I guess if he's like Gregor, my hope is lost."

"That prince is a fool," Thak said casually. He sat up and pulled a handful of grass from the ground, sprinkling it between his bent knees.

She watched the absent gesture, focusing again on his wonderful hands. They were a safe place for her eyes to land. Not tipped in claws or covered in scales. Imperfectly perfect with their clean short nails and patchwork scars.

"You are more than pretty and your companionship is more than any man—prince or not—could hope for."

Mila's chest fluttered at Thak's words. Her eyes darted from his hands to his face, but he continued to stare out over the meadow. She placed her hand over his and squeezed.

"Thank you," she whispered.

Thak turned his head. He studied her for a moment and swallowed. "We really should be getting back."

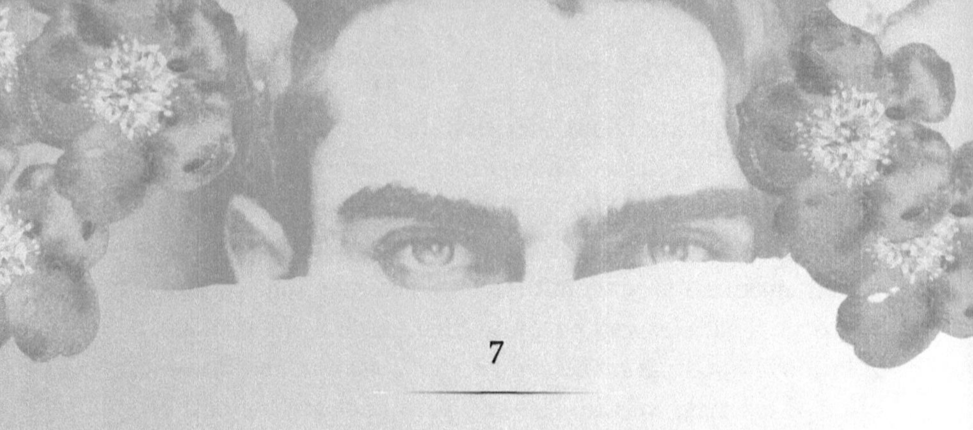

A Bracelet Made of Furious Gnome

No mass gathering, no musicians, and no lavender stags greeted Mila in the hall later that night. Instead of cramped tables and scantly clad woman, Mila found the same table she sat at for breakfast spread with simple place settings and sparse candles. A lovely arrangement of slender wildflowers rested in a simple wooden vase at the center. Queen Augustina sat at one end, Prince Gregor to her right. A third empty setting was placed to her left. Mila assumed it was for her.

She was suddenly glad she'd relented when Puddi insisted she arrange her hair and apply kohl to her eyes. She was wearing the last of her three dresses, but it was clean enough. She might need to talk with Quince about getting another gown or two for the remainder of her stay. She wouldn't complain if it was in the soft light fabric Puddi was wearing.

As ever, Thak had escorted her from her rooms, Puddi and

Glow trailing behind. Mila was pleased to see another small table shoved into an unobtrusive corner for her companions to take their meal.

She felt the force of the prince's eyes on her as she approached the table and dipped into a slight curtsy to the queen. Thak too dipped his head and pulled out her chair.

"Will you be joining us?" Mila twisted to ask him as she sat.

He gave a curt shake of the head.

"Oh yes. What do you say, Mother? Shall we have the guard dine with us this evening?" The prince's voice dripped with sarcasm.

"Enough of that." The queen chided her son and addressed Mila directly. "Thak is on duty, Princess."

As soon as the queen uttered the words, he moved behind her by several feet. Close enough to protect the monarch but far enough away to afford them the illusion of privacy. Mila knew he would hear every word. Clearly he'd proven his value and discretion to the crown in the past.

A young woman with cropped black hair, dark dainty hooves, and a beautiful face entered the chamber carrying a tray with several elegant silver chalices and a matching carafe. She placed a chalice before the queen and filled it with a rich amber liquid before moving to the prince and finally Mila. She placed smaller, plainer cups on the table for Mila's companions. As she was leaving, the woman shot a furtive glance toward Thak. It seemed Quince wasn't the only young woman in the castle to be rattled by the guard's presence.

Augustina rested her elbows on the table and placed her chin on her laced fingers. "I thought it might be best for us to have a more subdued meal this evening. Get to know one another."

"I appreciate that, Your Majesty." It was no stretch of the truth. Mila had felt she was on her back foot since arriving in Thornscarp, never knowing what to say to whom. The fact that she, as much a royal as the two sharing their table with her, was only getting information and conversation from a royal guard was off-putting to say the least. And after the—was hostile too strong a word?—conversation with the queen earlier, she needed to deploy every bit of diplomacy she could muster.

The queen continued to study her. "I feel as if we left on bad footing this morning."

The pretty dark-haired woman returned with plated meals of roast pheasant for each of them.

Mila waited until the woman finished before replying to the queen. "Not at all. Disagreements and misunderstandings happen all the time. I've already moved past it and hope you feel the same."

The queen didn't have time to answer before her son was addressing Mila. "Tell me, Princess. What do you suppose you'll do when your father finally sends for you? I gather your little adventure here was not entirely sanctioned by the crown." He swirled his chalice, studying the amber liquid within.

"No. It wasn't. But in time, I'm sure he will see how important it was that I made the journey."

Gregor picked up his knife and sliced into the thick slab of pheasant on his plate. "Indeed. And if he doesn't?" He swirled the chunk of meat in the bloody juices pooling around it and popped it into his mouth.

Mila picked up her own knife. The pheasant was a bit rare for her taste, but the roasted root vegetables, walnut and berry dressing, and buttery freshwater trout were all divine. "Then my hope is it will be a moot point."

"You mean to marry before you leave." His expression spoke volumes, and he burst out laughing, going so far as to wipe his eyes on his napkin.

Mila would not be made to feel small by this man. "It wouldn't be unheard of. And as short a time as that is, I am acting under a certain amount of urgency."

"Do you feel a military action is imminent?" the queen asked.

"I feel the threat of invasion is not far off. But in full transparency, it's more than that." The tension in Mila's shoulders was near unbearable, but she refused to roll her shoulders or stretch her neck. She sat, head held high. "Prior to the marriage with my late husband, one other suitor made a case to my father. He was declined in favor of a man closer to my own age from a wealthy southern family. It had more to do with finances than anything. My father sought to bolster the treasury via business contracts. Since his passing, the Lord Protector has been once again entertaining the idea of the previous suitor. It is not a match I wish to happen."

The prince snorted. "So if you're married before you return, that poor bastard is out of luck."

"If I am married before I return, it will be union of *my* choosing. Not my father's and not his advisor's."

The door at the side of the room opened again. Mila assumed it led to the kitchens, though she hadn't been in that part of the castle. Thak cleared his throat.

The queen glanced to the same serving girl where she waited at the door. "That will be all, Eloise. I'll send for you when you may clear."

The young woman looked from the queen to Mila. The princess thought she caught a flash of something like defiance in her dark eyes before those eyes flicked uncertainly to Thak. It must have been a trick of the light as it was gone in an instant. She turned her face to the floor and exited the way she came in.

"How many women do you think have presented themselves to Edon and me in the past half year?" the queen asked.

Mila hadn't a clue. She knew it was well known Edonier was to marry, but she hadn't given much thought to other families looking for the connection.

"I couldn't say."

"Thirty-seven." The queen leaned farther forward over her hands to pierce Mila with her eyes. She hadn't taken a bite of her food. "Thirty-seven lords' daughters or barons' nieces. We've had widowed ladies older than me and children not old enough for their first bleed dragged in here on offer. Each and every one looking to seal one alliance or another. Even a general from that hellscape Evansband bent the knee thinking to wed my son. The very same general who only months prior attempted to put an arrow in his back in an ambush."

Mila took a deep breath, set down her knife, and placed her hands on the table to either side of her dish. "I had no idea."

"Of course you had no idea. Gildernosh never has an idea what goes on here because They. Don't. Care." Her voice was mild, but the point was clear. The queen was not impressed by Mila, her title, or the realm she was to one day rule.

"I cannot speak to the wrongs of our past, only the hope I have for the future. I mean it when I say I desire nothing more than an advantageous alliance for both our peoples." She took a deep breath. "May I speak plainly, Your Majesty?"

"By all means." Augustina picked up her goblet and leaned back in her chair.

Mila's eyes flicked to the prince seated across from her. He once again had the half bemused smirk on his face, waiting for her to say something to dig her own grave deeper still. For no particular reason, she glanced past the queen's shoulder to Thak. He was the perfect guard. No interest whatsoever on his face as he stood at attention.

"First she wants him to dine with us, and now she wants his approval to speak."

The queen looked at her son and raised a single eyebrow. The fire in her eyes was enough to have her son quelling any other snide comments. With deliberate care, she turned her attention back to Mila, signaling she should continue.

"I tend not to agree with my father on several important aspects of state. As you have all clearly surmised, my coming here is one of them. But I assure you there are others just as important to me. Things which I believe will be important to my people. Not only now but for generations to come. For far too long we have relied on our wealth and position among the realms. It can't continue." Mila could feel her voice gain a slight wobble as she spoke. It was embarrassing. A fault she'd be reminded of on more than one occasion by her father as he chided, *soft, just like your mother.* She should be able to control her emotions, be regal and calm like the queen before her.

"And marrying my son will solve all of your problems?"

"No. But it might afford me the room to begin to solve them myself."

"And keep you out of whatever political marriage you wish to avoid." The queen continued to study her. "Interesting."

"You won't be solving anything." The prince swirled the wine in his goblet. "You might give Evansband pause for all of a week or two. But soon they'll realize there are other ways to gain a foothold in Gildernosh. Ways that don't involve simple brute force. Until you produce that heir you need to ascend the throne, you'll be in the same position you are now. Possibly even a worse one. You'll no longer be the beloved princess of your people."

"And why is that?" She chose not to comment on the *beloved* bit.

"Because they will know you've gone to bed with a beast. I don't for a moment believe you to be naïve enough to think it won't matter to them, but if I'm wrong, let me set the matter straight. Despite what you think, it will cost you. In the eyes of the realms, it will cost you."

"I'd hardly call you a beast, Your Highness. Why refer to your brother as such?" That flash of worry scuttled across her mind once more. Gregor was the embodiment of male beauty, but that didn't mean his brother was. Thak had made it clear. Traits could be prominent in some family members and not in others.

But, if they had similar personalities, she wasn't sure she'd refrain from calling him a beast either.

"Wouldn't call me a beast?" His eyes grew dark. "Perhaps you are that naïve."

Mila frowned, but before she could ask him to explain, the queen spoke.

"Despite your differences with the Lord Protector, my son does have a point. I know my words earlier were harsh and ill received, but they weren't completely without merit."

Mila could feel the blood rush to her face and was preparing to defend herself yet again when the queen held up her hand in a placating gesture. "Let me explain."

Mila nodded and kept her eyes on Augustina.

"Unlike you and your mother before you, I was not born into the crown. My husband, King Edon, carries the blood of royals in his veins. For seven generations, his line has ruled. My son will continue that rule when it is his time."

"I am aware, Your Majesty." Mila did in fact know the basics of Thornscarp succession; however, her tutors had not given much history on Augustina before she married the king.

"Were you also aware that he was king before I married him?"

Mila shook her head.

"Thornscarp does not share the same tradition as your realm. It is not required for a sovereign to have an heir or even be wed to ascend the throne. Edon's father died when he was in his prime. Struck down by fever. Edon was only nineteen years when he took his father's place. Although we knew each other for a time before, it was another six years before we wed.

"It isn't written in any history book or talked about by those outside this family, but I will tell you, I turned him down more than once before I agreed to be his queen." She smiled slightly, apparently lost in the memory. It was the most human Mila had seen her.

"I loved Edon, but I did not want to rule. And it wasn't just that the idea was unappealing. It was terrifying." Mila's breath caught. Queen Augustina did not seem the sort to be terrified of anything. "But I loved him, and eventually he wore me down. My love for him led me to gift my firstborn with his name. It led me to a throne I did not want but now proudly sit upon. It led me to be a better person than I was before I met him."

Mila did not want to speculate on what she'd been like before if this was the better version of her.

"I tell you this for two reasons. The first, because I want you to know I understand. Ruling is no easy matter. It is made all the more difficult when you want what you think is best for your people. Even if they don't agree with you. What the prince said is true. Despite your good intentions, many will not look upon you with kindness for marrying a prince of Thornscarp."

If the queen thought she was imparting something Mila hadn't already thought about, she was mistaken. The very idea had plagued her from the moment she rode out of Yallring. It was a gamble. She might very well return home to a populace who despised her even if she was sacrificing for their safety. It was a risk she had come to terms with and an outcome she would worry about later.

"And the second reason?" When Mila saw the shuttered look on the queen's face, she was suddenly sure she didn't want to hear the second reason.

"I am nothing if not fair. I understand the strain you are under just as I understand the strain my son will face when he one day becomes king. It is a strain that needs to be balanced with joy and gratitude." She flicked her eyes to the prince and looked over her shoulder at the guard standing behind her. Thak moved forward on silent paws and pulled her chair out while she stood. "I hope you make good use of your time with us, because if you think I'd let my son marry for anything other than love, you are in for a painful reality."

Gregor snorted a laugh and followed his mother from the room.

As the prince and the queen left, Thak looked to Mila. "I'll be just a moment, Your Highness."

Mila nodded as he followed the royals out of the hall.

The queen would not let her son marry for anything other than love? How in all the five realms was she supposed to make him love her if she hadn't even met him yet? It had to be a jest.

Or a test. *Everything the queen does is a test.*

Mila dropped her head into her hands. A soft thump was followed by pattering feet.

Puddi's small hand came down on her knee. "That might have gone better."

Mila chuckled, but the sound carried no mirth. "Indeed."

"Do you really need him?" Glow asked, no bitterness or anger in her voice for once.

"I'm afraid I do. Unless you want to travel to Evansband and hold off your countrymen."

"Not my countrymen. You know I make no claim to them."

"I know. But any other brilliant ideas would also be welcome."

The door opened. Mila had expected to see Thak returning to escort them back to their rooms, but instead, the woman with the cropped dark hair had returned. Mila was momentarily confused when she saw what was in the woman's hands. No serving platters or jugs of wine. It was a set of twin daggers, thin and delicate, one in each hand. The look on her face was positively feral as she advanced toward the table, light dancing off the polished metal glinting in her hands.

Mila stood quickly, pushing her chair back and stepping in front of Puddi. She was trying to place as much of the table between her and the advancing woman as she could while still protecting her friend.

Glowildeen snarled and lifted on her damselfly wings to

hover protectively in front of her princess, her own small dirk drawn and needle teeth gnashing.

"You shouldn't have come here. You all think you are above us. But let me tell you something. You and every other man, woman, and child in Gildernosh are nothing but dressed up trash. You aren't fit to lick his boots much less wed him." Twin daggers flashed as she rushed toward the table.

Any pretense Mila had of keeping it a barrier between the serving girl turned assailant and herself and Puddi melted away as the girl elegantly leapt atop it and stalked toward them. Her hooves made the softest of clicks as they landed on the wood.

Mila had just enough time to realize how completely absurd the entire situation was. She was heir to the throne of Gildernosh, and it seemed she was to be killed by a servant—Eloise, Mila remembered. Her name was Eloise. And Eloise felt Mila wasn't good enough for the prince of demons. How had this become her life? She might have laughed if she wasn't too busy pushing Puddi to safety under the table while trying to dodge the kick headed toward her head.

The woman's hoof would have connected and possibly sent Mila to her death had it not been for Glow. The attack the vicious little sprite launched was both endearing and vaguely terrifying. Mila knew Glow was skilled, but to witness it at such close distance was something she'd never expected. Glow moved with rapid artistry. Her dirk, no larger than a trout bone, left a series of wicked slashes over the attacking woman's face and neck, causing her kick to swing wide and propelling her off kilter. She tripped on a chair back and would have toppled to the ground if not for her own skill. The dark-haired woman cried out and swung her righthand dagger at Glow, but she was no match for the sprite's speed.

"Go," Glow commanded Mila, but there was no world in which the princess would abandon her friend to save her own skin. Instead, she picked up a wine chalice and smashed it onto the woman's head. The impact sent pain up her hand and into her elbow. Unfortunately, rather than slowing the attacker down, it only served to make her more savage.

Glow was also none too pleased. Magenta hair flying wildly, she swooped down again. "For the love of the Maidens, Mila. Get out of here."

Still holding the chalice, Mila back up several steps, but she did not flee.

Puddi remained hidden under the table.

Eloise continued to fend off Glow but was unable to land a blow to the menacing sprite.

The queen had spoken to the serving girl as if she knew her. Like she'd spent time bringing dinners and wine, breakfasts and tea, to the royals. But she fought like a trained soldier. Was it possible she had served time in the Corps? Or were all young people brought up with a killer's instinct in Thornscarp?

Mila had no idea, but it wasn't the time to ponder such mysteries.

Silver flashed, and Glow narrowly avoided having her wings severed from her body. She dodged in time, but the movement sent her farther down the table and opened a space for Eloise to advance further on Mila. Blood dripped from a dozen small lacerations to her face. It trickled from the side of her head where Mila had struck her with the chalice. Her teeth were stained red where it dripped from a slice on her upper lip. A chunk was missing from the tip of her nose. She was no longer beautiful, though in Thornscarp maybe it wasn't a concern but a badge of honor.

In one perfectly balanced leap, she closed the distance to the Princess of Gildernosh. Mila raised the metal chalice in time to block the dagger coming at her neck. Eloise grunted as she swung her other hand up, but the motion was sluggish and awkward thanks to the gnome dangling from her wrist.

The dagger in that hand clattered to the ground as Puddi's

teeth sank into the flesh of Eloise's forearm. The woman screamed and tried to shake her off. Puddi held tight, a bracelet made of furious gnome.

Eloise did the only thing she could; she tuned her attention away from Mila and swung her remaining dagger, clearly intending to slash it down on Puddi. Glow shouted as she flew to her friend, but she was still several feet away. Mila knew the sprite would never make it in time. Using all her strength, Mila shoved the dark-haired woman in the chest.

The dagger descended and would have connected with Mila's arm if not for the sword blade that appeared out of nowhere.

Eloise looked up at the same time Mila did—from the tip of the sword to the hand holding it—a very human hand with neatly trimmed nails and strong fingers and speckled with a myriad of various sized scars—and finally to the face of the guard both the hand and the short sword belonged to.

Thak frowned down on the woman, his sword aimed directly at her chest.

It was quite the sight. The failed assassin bloodied, her own countryman keeping her still with a sword to the heart, and a gnome, golden braid swinging wildly, dangling by her teeth from the woman's wrist.

Only when Eloise dropped the dagger did Puddi remove her teeth from her arm, spitting blood onto the floor at her side. Glowildeen, however, seemed less inclined to be charitable. She flew directly to the woman and pressed her dirk to the pulsing artery in her neck.

"I should end you now." Magenta hair was plastered to her flushed grey skin, but her words were even and steady.

Thak nodded. "If what I gather happened here is true, it would be within your right." Eloise drew a sharp breath, betrayal etched on her features. "But I would ask that you not, Lady Glowildeen Rosewink."

Something in the way he said the words was vastly different from his normal quiet grace. A note of command. A blush of nobility.

Eloise's face relaxed a fraction until Thak spoke again. "I'm sure the queen would rather deal with the matter herself."

"No." Eloise breathed, panic clearly setting in.

"You can't have thought your actions would be without consequence."

"I was only. . ." The panic was now mixed with confusion. The woman clearly thought her actions were justified and was surprised Thak did not agree.

Sword still at her chest, he asked, "Do you deny what has so clearly taken place here?"

"Never." Despite the blood which dripped from her damaged face, she raised her chin in defiance. Whatever she suspected the queen would do to her, it wasn't enough to take the righteousness from Eloise's expression.

"So you did intend to cause grievous harm to the princess? A guest in this place? A guest of King Edon and Queen Augustina?"

"I have served them well. In all things. This is no exception."

"That is not what I asked."

"You can't mean to choose this Gildernosh filth, You—"

Whatever she intended to say next never passed her lips. Thak dropped the sword from her chest and brought his other wonderfully strong hand around to connect with her jaw. The woman was knocked out cold.

8

Whip 'Em Out and Measure

After that night, Thak rarely left her side. They ate together, strolled the grounds together, and sat quietly in the shade together. On more than one occasion she accompanied him to training, where she and Puddi sat on benches observing the guards and soldiers run through their drills. Glow, on the other hand, participated with the men and women jabbing and thrusting weapons of every conceivable form.

Edonier remained absent. Prince Gregor continued his cycling between open hostility and casual indifference toward her. The king chose to ignore her completely. And the queen continued to be terse whenever she was in their presence. This went on for more than a week, so no one was more surprised than Mila when at breakfast one day, Her Majesty the Queen of Thornscarp had insisted Mila join her for a day of amusement in the village.

She was no longer shaken by the events of the night she'd

been attacked. Thak had done his best to reassure her, but in reality, if he hadn't shown up when he did, she might have worried his disappearance was by design—his absence a cleverly timed gap in which the assassin could strike. Despite her recovering, she still wasn't sleeping well. The bed that had been so comfortable the first few nights was growing progressively worse as the days drew on.

Puddi had been fretful for much of the first night after the attack, sure that any number of would-be murderers were primed to strike while they slept. She'd gone so far as to kiss the door and make promises to bring a jar of wood oil and rags to polish it should it remain steadfast and keep any unwanted visitors safely on the other side. The door hadn't answered; therefore, Puddi hadn't slept.

Glow was her typical surly self, but Mila noticed the way she took care to reassure her gnomish friend and give her an extra pillow and first turn in the bathing chamber. Although she'd never admit it, Mila was sure the sprite was proud of Puddi for doing what needed to be done to protect Mila rather than hide out under the table as the attack took place.

The princess wondered what exactly would happen to Eloise. Clearly the queen invoked a good amount of fear in the woman, and the thought sent shivers down Mila's spine. Was she even now being punished for her crime or was she simply in some holding cell awaiting judgment? Could she have been quietly and unceremoniously executed? It was yet another thing Mila had no idea about—how justice was meted out in this land of warriors.

Mila was edgy and tired and thought a day of distraction was a fine idea.

According to Quince—she and Glow seemed to be hitting it off quite well and the maid enjoyed filling the sprite in on all sorts of local gossip—that day was an annual event full of the locals competing in all manner of things. From typical archery and horsemanship, to pie baking and eating contests, to something called horning (Mila didn't even want to consider what that might be) and a completely lunatic-sounding sport involving embedding one's claws into a large tree trunk which was then rolled down a hill, seeing who could remain both attached and conscious the longest. It all sounded both quaint and a little barbaric. Mila wondered if the queen had invited her simply to see if she could stomach the more brutal games.

Thak had said everything the queen did was a test, and Mila was sure this was just one more in the long line of them between her and her realm's future.

Rather than show any trace of discomfort, Mila squared her shoulders and followed Thak down the road from the castle to the heart of the village. He'd informed her the king and queen had a royal box settled amid the stands and the grounds—the elaborate crimson and gold tent she'd seen during their previous jaunt through the village made so much more sense.

Mila was surprised when Thak had arrived wearing thick leather armor with polished bronze plates over his shoulders and wrists. It wasn't full battle regalia, but it was much more protective than his standard tunic and trousers. Under one arm he carried a bronze helm with long wedges cut from the temples. After studying it a moment, Mila realized the slots were to accommodate his horns. She could only imagine how terrifying he'd be if he ever faced an enemy wearing the thing, and she wondered how often the castle guards were called into service.

"Did you rest at all, Princess?" he asked.

"Enough. Thank you again for—"

He held up a hand. "We've been over this dozens of times. Do *not* thank me. You should not need to have a guard within those walls." He pointed an angry finger back at the hulking castle behind him.

Mila dipped her head in agreement. "Be that as it may, I still appreciate your actions."

Thak grunted through his nose, clearly not happy, but he didn't argue further.

Glow and Puddi were both beyond excited about attending the festivities. Puddi because any social outing was one to be celebrated and Glow because the promise of bloodshed always lifted her spirits.

If Mila'd been impressed with the variety of chimera and other creatures who partook of the nightly revelry in the castle, she was dumbstruck by them now.

The rain that had plagued their arrival was gone, and the sun was a beautiful ball of glorious happiness in the deep azure sky. The ladies wore loose silk skirts and delicate tops, tied and twisted in intricate ways that left skin and scales exposed in the gorgeous weather. The men were clad in variations of the same baggy trousers and soft fabric vests or the clothing of warriors, leather pants and padded armor. Mila imagined their winter garb would be much less revealing, given how high in the mountains they were, but in the spring sunshine, she envied them their comfortable clothing.

The sheer number of people on the grounds was staggering, but that was nothing compared to the differences in them. Bat wings and bear claws. Enormous tusks and flowing tails. Scales and fur and smooth alabaster skin. There were pixies and centaurs. Multihued horses and bands of goblins. Even a troll or two.

Gildernosh welcomed the fae from other lands. It was thought good luck to have the fair folk about, and their presence was sought after. Puddi and Glowildeen had become her ladies when she was just a child for that very reason. But it was nothing compared to this. Thornscarp seemed to embrace the creatures not as unusual visitors, but as part of the fabric of the place. Glow and Puddi belonged here as they never truly had in

Gildernosh, and for the first time, Mila felt like more than an outsider. She felt like a fraud.

"Will Prince Gregor be joining us in the box, do you suppose?" Puddi asked nervously.

Before Mila could speculate, Thak answered. "He won't be in the box. He's competing."

"Competing? Oh, how thrilling," the gnome trilled. "In which events?"

"Archery, swordsmanship, and the equine races. They're the only events the queen will allow her sons to compete in."

Sons. Did that mean Edonier would be here and competing as well? It didn't seem like something she should ask Thak, however. He was certain to make an entrance at any rate. If he was here, she'd finally get the chance to see him with her own eyes. The thought both excited and terrified her.

"Those all sound like noble sport. I'm sure Mila will be cheering him on the loudest. Won't you?" The gnome's eyes prodded Mila into giving an appropriate response.

"Certainly." Mila fought to control both the tone of her voice and her deep desire to roll her eyes. Thak must have picked up on something regardless.

"Not a fan of those particular events, Princess?"

How could she tell him it wasn't the events but the idea of swooning over a man whom she'd not had a single decent conversation with? She'd save the unearned accolades for after he proved he wasn't a complete bag of dung. She could marry his brother because she had to, but she'd be damned if she allowed herself to become one of those vapid women who fell at any handsome man's feet.

"Quite the opposite. I believe I'll enjoy them." Oh, balls and bastards. She might as well fish a little. "But perhaps I should cheer for Edonier. Or if he isn't in attendance, one of the lesser known contestants. If the festival is for everyone, don't the princes have the others at an unfair advantage?"

Thak tilted his head, one horn dipping slightly. "Perhaps. It's good to note, however, most of the participants know what they're in for and a good many of them could knock a prince on his ass, royal upbringing or not."

"Truer words were never spoken." Ograt approached them with a wide grin exposing his canines.

Mila didn't miss that he neither confirmed nor denied Edonier's presence for the games. Perhaps the day might get interesting after all.

Glowildeen at least thought so. She had a wicked grin on full display and a hungry gleam in her eyes as she flew past.

"I hate the idea of leaving you unguarded for even a moment, but I trust you can make it to the box without finding too much trouble?" Thak tossed his horns toward the bright red and gold canvas perched atop elevated pylons. "Niri should be close at hand at least."

The box wasn't more than twenty paces away. Mila had learned a few days after her arrival that Niri was the golden-feathered guard who'd so terrified her the day she'd made her proposal to the king and queen. She hadn't seen the fierce woman yet that morning, but Thak seemed to think it was safe enough. If Mila and her chaperones couldn't make it that far without disaster striking, they had little chance of surviving in Thornscarp another two weeks.

"I imagine we can," Mila answered through her smile. "Are you both competing as well?" She imagined Thak would do very well and Ograt perhaps even better.

"We are, and if we don't get a move on, we'll miss our first heat." Ograt clapped Thak on the shoulder, and the pair turned and headed into the crowd, Mila and Puddi watching them go.

"Maidens among us." Puddi sighed. "The buns on that man. They look good enough to taste, Mila."

"Puddi!"

"I know you've proposed to the prince, but tell me I'm wrong."

Mila smirked. "It would be very inappropriate for me to admit, but . . . you're not wrong."

The gnome waggled her eyebrows and licked her lips. "How far up his legs do you think the silky pelt goes? Like, all the way up?"

Mila snorted. "Enough of that, you wicked thing."

The pair set off for the royal box, but before they reached the impressive canvas, Mila caught a glimpse of bright golden feathers and the tips of elegant horns as the queen and her guard moved to ascend the steps. Hurrying away from them, a scared-looking woman with a long vulpine face tugged a child behind her. The boy was no more than three with fluffy orange hair. He seemed oblivious to the woman's urgency in the way only adorable children can get away with. She looked around furtively and snuck an ear of roasted corn and a hot jacket potato from a nearby stall. She quickly tucked them inside her cloak.

Glow was already flitting into the box, and Mila had no desire to call her back and raise attention to herself. "Go on ahead, Puddi. Let the queen know I'll be along shortly."

The gnome gave Mila an uncomfortable look but climbed the step alone as instructed.

It might have been foolish, but Mila refused to cower and live in fear. She took off after the woman and her charge. If she or the child were so desperately hungry, Mila would be more than happy to provide them with a lunch not stolen.

Was that why the woman had looked so scared? Had she asked the queen for charity and been turned away? Was it survival of the strongest here in this warrior realm? She had no idea.

The woman tugged the child away from the stall and into the throng of festival goers. For a moment Mila thought they were lost to her, but then she caught a flash of the child's orangey hair not far off. He ran over and plopped down on a blanket with several other children ranging in age from the tot she'd followed to a girl of perhaps twelve. Each of the lot had variations on the same features—long fox-like faces, tufted triangular ears, reddish coloring or bright amber eyes. They shared the ear of corn and hot potato between them. The woman must have deposited the food and blended back into the crowd.

Looking around briefly, Mila spotted another food stall. After a quick exchange of coins, she returned with a stack of steaming meat handpies, warm baked apples, and two more ears of corn.

"May I join you?" she asked the children.

Eyeing the goodies, they eagerly agreed.

"My name is Mila."

Off in the distance, she could hear the crowd going wild as the first set of competitions began. She'd missed which event it was and hoped the queen wouldn't be too angry over her tardiness to the box. She tried to listen for names of the participants but realized each was competing under a coded banner—color and animal—as several chants rose from the stands. It explained why so many of the people around her were waving strips of cloth in varying colors. There was an overabundance of red and gold in equal measure with others ranging from white and black to every shade of purple, blue, and green. When both red lion and gold stag were chanted, the crowd went wild. Clearly one of these two must be Prince Gregor. She had no idea if the other was in fact Edonier.

As Mila looked around, an odd thought struck her. These people were happy. The idea that the warrior realm could have citizens who seemed at such peace within their borders was jarring. It went against everything she'd ever been told about this place.

The oldest girl studied her and slid over, allowing her to sit beside them on the blanket. As it turned out, the group was a family of cousins, all visiting from the countryside south of the village. They'd traveled in for the festival in support of the eldest cousin, a girl of sixteen who had entered the soldiering sports, hoping to make an impression and gain an invitation to join the royal guard.

"I'll be sure to cheer her on then. What's her name?" Mila asked.

The eldest girl said, "Liark, but she's competing as black fox. Just look for the one with the secondhand armor, fox tail and ears."

"I'll do just that. Now I'm afraid I need to get back. But before I go, can you tell me where I might find the lady this adorable one was with earlier?" She ran a hand down the tot's orange head.

"Kit's mum? Aunt June?"

Mila nodded.

"She's right over there." The girl pointed off behind Mila.

It took Mila only a moment to spot the woman. While her features suggested a fox, Mila thought her expression more of defiant fear rather than cunning. To her credit, she didn't so much as balk as Mila rose and walked over to where the woman waited in the shade of a towering oak.

The sprinkling of fur over the woman's nose bristled as she said, "I didn't steal it, if that's what you think." Her eyes shifted to where the children still sat gathered on the blanket, remnants of food scattered about them. "But thank you for that."

"It was my pleasure. They're an adorable lot." It was true. Mila had enjoyed the company on the grass much more than she suspected she would in the royal box. Not expecting much more from the woman, she added, "And if you need provisions for the rest of your stay, or the journey home, I'm more than happy to help."

The woman opened her mouth to reply, but her eyes flicked over Mila's shoulder and widened. She snapped her mouth shut once more. She dipped her head, not to the foreign princess but to whoever stood behind her. Mila was almost too frustrated to look, but she sighed and turned nonetheless, finding the golden-feathered guard not two paces behind her, her moss-colored scales glimmering in the sun.

"Your Highness." Her words were clipped and direct. "Her Majesty the Queen awaits your company."

Mila set her lips in a firm line and followed the guard.

On their way back to the box, the pair passed a small group of adolescent girls. Two of them had matching black braids and small antlers atop their heads. The third had the majestic wings of some great bird of prey—all golden brown and tawny yellow. The girls tittered and giggled, and Mila heard the one with the wings exclaim merrily, "I can't wait to see Edonier compete. If we stand in the front, maybe he'll notice us."

The other two nodded, and the three pushed their way toward the fencing along the field.

Mila's pulse quickened. He was here and he was competing. She'd finally get to see the man she hoped to wed. *If* she could figure out which one he was.

"WHAT DO YOU MEAN YOU BOUGHT THEM LUNCH?" PUDDI'S LOW voice matched her wringing hands perfectly. "Oughtn't you tell someone? About the stealing?"

Glow's voice was pitched just as low, but rather than fretful, she sounded suspicious as she mused. "It could be one of the tests. Her minuscule eyes flicked to where the queen lounged on her elevated pedestal two rows behind them. There was a break in the competition, several heats apparently having gone while Mila was distracted earlier.

"If it is, it's one I'm happy to fail," she grumbled back. "A just society should look after all of its people. Not just the strong. No child should go hungry."

"Perhaps a just society should also refrain from indenturing the impoverished from neighboring realms to toil away in its mines."

Mila's head whipped around, and she stared at the queen, who stared right back, a single eyebrow raised in challenge. Beside her was the green-eyed beauty with claw-tipped hands who'd been glaring at her as she'd danced with the prince her first night in Thornscarp. To be seated there, she must have a connection or be from a prominent family. Augustina didn't seem the type to suffer fools or ass kissers. Edon, she couldn't say. He was more mystery than anything.

If Lady Claw Hands had looked at Mila with hostility before, it was nothing compared to the murderous scowl she wore now. Mila studied her a moment longer. It might have been the effects of the previous attack mixed with the woman's obvious dislike of her, but Mila saw quite a resemblance between the claw-handed woman and Eloise. They had the same coloring and delicate facial features.

While Mila hadn't thought she was speaking loud enough to be heard over the din of the crowd, it wasn't what caused her gut to roll. It was confusion. Clearly the barb was meant to implicate Gildernosh in some great wrong, but it was so completely off base. She couldn't fathom why the queen would think such a thing. It was true Gildernosh often recruited from both Evansband and Yallring, even occasionally from the far reaches of Krith, but those workers came willingly. They volunteered for the posts and were well compensated for their labor.

Everything the queen does is a test.

Obviously this was her way of seeing if a spoiled princess could keep her composure under the slightest provocation. Mila refused to take the bait and fail so simple a challenge.

"Agreed, Your Majesty." Mila turned forward and paid closer attention to the amusement before them.

"I asked Quince about that one." Glowildeen flicked her head backward in the direction of Lady Claw Hands. Maybe it wasn't just Mila who thought she might be related in some way to Eloise. "Name's Annissa. She bears watching if you ask me."

Annissa. It fit. Even her moniker sounded unpleasant. A hiss of air through gritted teeth.

Mila couldn't argue. The woman did seem the type to keep an extra eye on.

Directly in front of the royal box, a tall man with tusks—not unlike the king's— the inky wet eyes of some large ruminant, and thick scaly skin the color of frost announced the continuation of competition. More archery heats. It would be impossible for others farther away to hear over the raucous noise, but the crowd reacted to his words all the same. Perhaps more than one announcer was spread through the festival grounds or perhaps they all had preternaturally good hearing. It would explain how the queen had heard Mila's earlier comment. The thought sent a shiver down her spine, and she vowed to watch her surroundings more closely.

A pair of large straw-stuffed targets were set up on one side of the field, and a long length of rope blocked the other. As the first pair was called, Mila was pleased to see Ograt march out under the flag bearing a green leopard. He stopped short of the rope and turned to the box, dipping his head to the royals. With a good bit of swagger that had Mila smiling, he threw a quick wink to the golden-feathered guard. Mila desperately wanted to turn and see the fierce woman's reaction but didn't dare for fear of catching the queen's glaring eye once more.

Ograt wore what Mila presumed was his standard military uniform—a dull grey tunic over matching leather pants. A series of red and gold badges and bars adorned the left side of his chest. His opponent was similarly dressed, though less decorated, and after three arrows from each, it became clear the cat-eyed man was the far superior marksman. He left the field to booming applause.

The next pairing was called. Mila's pulse quickened ever so slightly as Prince Gregor strolled onto the field. The crowd reacted with a wave of thundering approval. The wood frame of the stand shook with the vibrations of hundreds of stomping feet, and high-pitched whistles pierced the festive atmosphere. Red and gold ribbons continued to fill the air around her, but she couldn't decide if the gold of his tunic indicated his banner or not. Unlike Ograt, he'd entered the stadium without one. Mila understood the crowd's enthusiasm as she occasionally received similar welcomes in Gildernosh. In her experience, the populace either loved or loathed the sovereigns.

The man cut a dashing figure in his tight-fitted tunic and crisp black pants. His boots were polished to a near blinding shine, and his face was the epitome of male beauty—all sharp cheek bones and slightly mussed hair. Too bad his temperament toward her left so much to be desired.

The prince made quick work of his opponent, never even glancing toward where Mila—and his parents—sat watching from the box.

Several more pairs went until the last group finally took their places. Mila was thrilled to see a girl with a thick foxtail and ears to match win the round. She was cheered on whole-heartedly by most in the stands, Mila included. It was only after they'd left the field that Mila realized she'd not seen Thak compete in the single elimination rounds. She'd assumed he was in the event, and she felt a touch of disappointment at having missed him. She also hadn't seen anyone receive the same sort of welcome from the crowd as Gregor. If Edonier had competed, she must have missed him too.

A portion of her regret was short lived, however. As the second round commenced, Thak, having divested himself of the armor, strode onto the field for the third pairing. He'd clearly bested his first opponent. The crowd welcomed him with as much enthusiasm as they had any of the previous contestants. Even the prince himself. It was no wonder he was such a favorite. Not only was Thak well liked around the castle, he was extraordinarily skilled with a bow and arrow, making short work of his opponent. The prince, Ograt, and Liark, the fox girl, all won their respective matches, and Mila wondered who she should hope would emerge victorious. Glow and Puddi had no such qualms. Puddi was firmly team Thak, and Glow called for Ograt to "crush them all."

The crowd, including the king and queen, were loving every minute of it. With each pairing and elimination, the denizens of Thornscarp grew rowdier and rowdier. As if the universe had crafted it, the competition soon saw just the four of them remaining—Gregor, Thak, Ograt, and young Liark.

The announcer called the first match, and Ograt smiled and chomped his teeth at Thak as the two of them walked up to the rope. Ograt's arrows found the center of the target, but Thak's buried themselves nearly atop one another. As the crowd erupted, gold banners waved from nearly every outstretched arm until the stands were an undulating sea of tarnished cloth—golden stag. The prince must be the scarlet lion. Thak clapped his friend on the shoulder and stepped back against the fencing, arms resting atop the long bow standing in front of him, becoming a spectator for the penultimate match.

Much to Puddi's dismay, as the remaining two approached the rope, Mila found herself clapping loudly for Liark. It was as if the gnome's displeasure fueled her cranky sprite friend and made Glow join in and cheer all the louder. She shot into the air to get a better vantage.

Why shouldn't a young girl from the outskirting countryside best a prince and earn her place protecting said prince's family? It seemed perfectly appropriate to Mila.

The prince seemed less inclined to appreciate the romantic aspect of the match. He didn't sneer but neither did he smile. Once again she wondered how Gregor fit into the warrior culture. Since Edonier was often with the troops in battle, it wasn't impossible to imagine the spare brother inheriting the throne one day. Leading this realm of soldiers didn't fit the persona he gave off. Mila'd had her fill of entitled peacocks, her late husband being top of the list. The thought made her want to see how he would handle defeat. Sitting up straighter, she cheered even louder for Liark, going as far as snatching up a discarded black ribbon and waving it in the air.

"Mila," Puddi hissed, "you're supposed to be getting him on your side." Puddi nervously threw a look over her shoulder to the queen, but Mila didn't care. She waved the ribbon more exuberantly.

Not surprisingly, the prince took no notice of her. Within moments, all three of his arrows were buried true, scattered mere hair's breadths from one another in the center of his target.

If Liark was nervous, it didn't show. Her first two arrows also found the center, perhaps even closer to one another than the prince's had been. The crowd settled and the atmosphere grew heavy in the silence. A collective breath was being held to see if this slip of a girl could best the mighty prince. Mila too held her breath as the teen drew back her bow and let her last arrow fly.

The crowd released its breath as one. A collective "Ohhhh. . ." sounded as the arrow hit just outside the center circle. The prince smirked as he bowed to the crestfallen teen, and applause rippled through the field. Liark retrieved her arrows, head held high, and turned and bowed to the king and queen. She made her way off the field as the crowd settled.

It was the last round. Six arrows would decide who walked off the field as victor. The prince who had been born and raised with a full belly and an army at his back or a simple royal guard who grew up Maidens knew where. Like everyone else in the stands, Mila was on the edge of her seat. She'd tucked the wayward black ribbon into her bodice, hoping to get use of it again later in the day. She didn't have a gold ribbon, but even if she did, she thought it might be pushing her luck to openly root against the prince a second time. She was no fool and knew how these things worked. A teen girl was one thing, but a royal guard was something else entirely.

Even so, it wasn't only Mila who was rooting for Thak—publicly or otherwise. She couldn't be certain, but it felt as if the massive guard with his shining horns, enormous paws, and graceful presence garnered more admiration from the spectators than the prince in all his chiseled jaw perfection.

Glow floated down next to her. "The big man seems to be causing your future brother some discomfort." She folded her arms over her chest and nodded to the field.

She was right. Maybe Mila hadn't imagined the crowd's enthusiasm for Thak. The prince stood stiffly with his brows drawn and his lips in a tight line while Thak was all serene indifference and relaxed posture. Just a man enjoying the fine weather and adoration of the crowd.

"Maybe they should just settle this the old-fashioned way," Glow continued. "Whip 'em out and measure."

"Glowildeen," Puddi shrilled as Mila stifled her chuckle. If she was already failing in the queen's estimation, Glow was sure to see them kicked out before the day was done.

"What?" the sprite asked the gnome. "Not like you of all people haven't been thinking about it. Your money's clearly on the big man as much as you pretend otherwise."

"Enough, you two," Mila admonished. "They're getting ready to start."

The contest was close, but in the end, it was the guard's arrows buried one atop the other that sealed the victory. Mila couldn't contain her smile as Thak approached the box and dipped his head to the king and queen and dropped to one knee before them—the prince doing the same at his side. Neither royal seemed surprised by his triumph, and both gave him indulgent if somewhat guarded smiles.

It was only when Mila caught the ugly look in the prince's eye as he turned to her that her merriment was quelled. The look spoke volumes. If he'd been anything less than vile to her before, that was about to change. Perhaps she could attempt to cheer a little louder for him in the coming events. Likely it would be too little too late, but she had to try.

Thak rose from his knee, his eyes flickering from the prince to her and back again. Reading the situation perhaps a bit too well, his own lips turned down and his brow creased. Mila could only hope for his sake he'd keep his displeasure to himself. She would be livid both with herself and the entire royal family if he got into trouble on her behalf, but she knew better than most how petty and jealous some entitled people could get, and it was clear to anyone with eyes there was some history between the two men. She was left to wonder what it might be as they both turned and left the field.

The morning went by in a whirl. Mila was entranced by each new and exciting event paraded before them. Her favorite was watching the children of Thornscarp compete in a tug o' strength contest in which the victors received accolades nearly as loud as Thak's archery win had garnered. It was second only to a pageant of sorts, where many of the same children donned warrior garb—paper mâché horns and claws, artificial fangs, and bulky straw muscles—and paraded around the field haphazardly filled with fallen enemies composed entirely of branches and red dyed cloth. It was both macabre and delightful. Inspiring even, if Mila thought about it. Gildernosh had children's pageants as well, but they were so dissimilar she could barely compare them.

The queen hadn't been wrong. In Mila's world, beauty and elegance were favored over just about everything else. The pageants reflected this. They were more about pomp and perfection and less about the realities of daily life. These children were learning young what Thornscarp needed them to learn, and while the brutality of it wasn't lost on the future queen, it was somehow reassuring. The realization left her more than a little unsettled.

"Mila?" Puddi's voice was laced with concern.

Mila shook her head and turned to the gnome, a small tight smile on her lips. "Sorry. Just thinking."

"It is all rather barbaric. I'm sorry you have to do this." But that was just it. Mila did have to do it, and it wasn't the children with the horns and the fangs that bothered her. It was the man with the perfect face who set her nerves on edge. Him and his missing brother. The brother she had offered herself up to as wife and future queen. Gregor would fit in perfectly back home. Perhaps Edonier would too. She couldn't bring herself to acknowledge whether that was a good thing.

The gnome returned her small smile and handed her a water jug. "Take this. It's warmer today than I would have expected."

A grateful smile softened Mila's face. She drank deeply, enjoying the faintly mineral taste as the cool water washed down her throat. It was just what she needed to clear her mind as the next competition began.

Men and women in full battle gear streamed onto the field. Half wore red arm bands and the others gold. Thak's form, once again clad in the armor he'd worn earlier in the day, was easy to spot, a gold sash wrapped snuggly around his bicep. His horns rose viciously from the custom-made helm he wore, but from where Mila sat they looked elegant and mesmerizing. Even so, she imagined from across the field, his opponents would chose a different descriptor. He stood taller than many in his cohort, but even still, two or three men equaled him in stature, if not in grace and fluidity. Perhaps one of these was Edonier?

Mila's eyes flicked through the horde of warriors. There was Liark—red sash. Ograt—gold. Petra—red. Ram—or maybe it was Nox, they looked so much alike—also red. Finally, her eyes fell on Prince Gregor. Red.

All of the people she would want to cheer wore the same color as the prince. All save Thak and Ograt.

On cue from the man with the tusks, the group divided. Red sashes to the eastern side of the field and gold to the west. Without any outward instruction, the latter group encircled Thak, but the team in red milled about, only a handful lingering close to Gregor. Without much warning, a deafening blare sounded from the royal box, and Mila flinched, turning toward the king standing with what appeared to be a ram's horn tight against his pursed lips. As startled as she was by the noise, she was more startled by the immediate clashing of metal on metal and the savage sounds of fighting from the field below.

Puddi gasped and buried her face in Mila's sleeve as the princess looked on in some combination of thrill and horror. It was a full-fledged battle between the two teams. Men and women ran at one another in a chaotic frenzy just mere feet from the roaring crowd. After a moment Mila realized it wasn't actually chaos. Not fully. Anyone wearing a gold sash moved in a regimented way—in clumps and formations. Small groups covering and advancing as units, targeting members of the red team and advancing with skill and precision. The goal became immediately clear. Engage the opponent and slice the band of colored fabric from their arm. As soon as the material was free, the person wearing it would exit the battlefield and wait on the sidelines. And while the warriors were using metal weaponry, the blades themselves appeared to be dulled and blunted. Even if they hadn't been, the ease with which they were wielded and the exacting movements led Mila to think not much blood would be shed in error.

While many of the red team members—Liark among them—had no direction in their advances or opponents, a few did. Gregor had a small group around him, but rather than acting as one, they seemed eager to sacrifice themselves to allow the prince to escape armband intact. Nox and Petra had gathered a small band of soldiers around them, and they moved in similar formation to those on the gold team. Thak's team members easily dispatched all of the red squad save these two groups while losing only a handful of warriors themselves.

There were injuries. A few men went down after taking blows to the head however inadvertent. Lips were bloodied and limbs were broken. The occasional grunts of pain mingled with the sharp orders coming from several of the soldiers as well as the prince. But still it was invigorating to behold.

Red was clearly outmatched, and even the skill of Nox's and Petra's blunted swords and Gregor's military training failed them in virtually no time at all. A grueling half an hour after the combat began, it ended with a slew of red sashes littering the field and more than half of the gold team standing proudly among them. The injured were assisted from the field.

The king blew his horn once more, and the victors stood before the box. At a sharp bark from Thak, the entire group dropped to one knee in unison, heads bowed to the royals before them. Just as smoothly and as one, they rose and trailed off the field.

The conquered red team moved forward and followed suit, though not nearly as elegantly or as synchronized.

Mila was captivated by the entire scene. She'd never seen such skill with weaponry and could only imagine what it would be like to witness the real thing—a real battle—from such close range. Her father would soil himself if he thought she'd entertained such an idea. Or more likely, he'd find some way to punish her for the mere thought. It was much too base an idea. Much too ugly for a princess of Gildernosh.

Puddi finally lifted her head from Mila's shoulder. "Is it done now?"

"Ah, for dung's sake, woman. It was just a bit of fun." Glow's grin stretched her small round cheeks, her mood the best Mila had seen it since they'd arrived.

"Yes. It's over," Mila reassured her gnomish friend. "I think I saw a stall down there with citrus punch. Let's go get you some."

"Oh, that sounds divine, Mila. Truly."

As they stood, Mila dipped her head to the king and queen.

"The racing is next. You'll want to get a spot along the gates," the queen called as they descended the steps.

They ventured away from the stairs, aware of the box emptying behind them. The royal entourage was making their way to the fencing where the last event of the day could be viewed.

As Mila drifted toward the stalls and the promised refreshment, she caught sight of the queen and Niri. The pair of woman were standing just off behind the box—the queen looking more approachable than Mila had seen her thus far. The queen watched the citizens of Thornscarp as they meandered by, a serene and almost loving look on her face. The moss-colored guard was watchful and ready to defend her queen if needed, but truth be told, Augustina appeared just as able to defend herself should the need arise. In fact, now that Mila thought about it, the royal family always seemed to blend in with the people around them. There was little doubt they ruled the land and a certain amount of deference was always palpable when Edon, Augustina, or Gregor was about, but they didn't separate themselves from the populace much at all. It was vastly different from the way Mila and her father were kept apart from those they ruled.

Mila stood in a short queue with her friends, waiting for

their punch, repeatedly stealing glances toward the woman she hoped to one day call mother-in-law. It hit her then. The fierce woman might one day be more to Mila than simply Her Majesty the Queen of Thornscarp. What a strange notion.

It was as she was contemplating the unusual path her life was taking that the fox-faced woman approached the queen and her guard. Mila's spine stiffened. She glanced around to see if anyone else was watching, but the festival goers all seemed to be enjoying themselves and no one sensed the danger June might be in. Surely she'd been dismissed by the queen once already, and her Her Majesty didn't seem the type to welcome repeated badgering. Because of this, Mila found her mouth dropping open when Niri not only didn't turn the woman away harshly but rather stepped aside for the queen to embrace her. The queen's smile was genuine as they parted, and she pushed a heavy purse of coins into June's hands.

Why on earth would the queen be giving June coins now? If she'd been generous earlier, the fox-faced woman wouldn't have needed to steal food for the children in her care. Unless, of course, she'd told Mila the truth and she hadn't stolen the treats at all.

"Mila." Puddi's voice broke her thoughts, and the princess turned to where the stall keeper was handing over two earthen mugs of sweet-smelling citrus punch. Mila nodded her thanks and placed a coin of her own into the woman's hands.

The trio made their way to the fencing as another horn sounded, and the air was immediately filled with the thunder of hoofbeats. A pack of thirty riders tore up a track which looped around the outskirts of the festival grounds. Obstacles and jumps littered the lane, and the horses and riders were forced to negotiate tight turns and perilous traps.

As the riders approached the stretch where Mila and her friends waited, she wasn't surprised to see the prince in the lead. Several other riders were quick on his heels, Nox and Ram included, as well as another auburn-haired young man with a muscular build and long sharp tusks. The unknown rider was fluid and sharp. Prince Edonier perhaps? Thak and several other participants from earlier in the day were in the thick of things just behind the leaders.

As they flew by, mud was kicked up and splattered several spectators, Mila being one. She laughed as she wiped muck from her chin and reached down to the gnome at her side and dislodged a large clump from Puddi's golden hair. Surprisingly, the gnome was equally thrilled.

The racers completed the first circuit and soon were barreling toward them again. Gregor still maintained his lead. Nox had dropped back a bit, but Ram was holding strong as was the man with the tusks. Thak was several lengths back, his mount showing little strain under the massive form of her rider. Glow zoomed up and whistled loudly as they approached. Puddi and Mila had the good sense to step back from the rail slightly and were able to avoid another dousing of muck.

As the race drew away from them, the field stretched out even more. As they came to the end of the circuit the distant horn sounded again, this time in three short bursts signaling the last lap of the race.

The prince had maintained his lead but only by the smallest margin. Ram's face was set on victory, but he'd not only need to overtake the prince but also fend off Thak who had gained on them. The fourth man—the possible Edonier—had lost quite a bit of ground and trailed the others by a fair margin.

Mila couldn't see well enough to make out who came across the finish line first, but Glowildeen could. The sprite floated down beside her, arms crossed over her chest and a scowl on her face. "That prick Gregor has finally won today. I'd have liked to see him get his ass handed to him one more time, if I'm being honest."

"Good for him. Perhaps he'll be in a better mood now," Mila said.

"If a man needs to win at sport in order to be in a good mood, he isn't worth it."

"Yes, well, try to remember we need this, Glow."

"Don't worry. I remember. If I didn't, I would have drug you out of here after the first night. But you remember it isn't him we need." Her damselfly wings slowed as she settled on the fence.

"Here they come." Puddi's voice was full of glee as the riders walked their mounts around the track and stood before the king and queen. "Did you see who came in second, Glow?"

"Big man. Though it wasn't by much. He overtook the quiet one at the last."

"Oh, poor Ram," Mila said. "He was doing so well."

"I'm sure he'll get over it. He's a soldier. Not a prince."

Mila flinched at the jab, but couldn't argue with her friend. The crowd clapped as the prince in question dipped his chin to his parents and the remaining riders followed suit. As they led their horses off, Thak clapped the prince on the shoulder, a wide and genuine smile on his face. It was so familiar Mila wondered once again what sort of history the pair shared.

Gregor's face relaxed as he looked at the guard. It came as a bit of a shock when his expression was closer to a smile than a scowl.

9

A Worthless Excuse for a Husband

The hall was packed with more people than the visitors from Gildernosh had seen in the previous nights. Clearly with so many in the keep for the festival, the king and queen had gone all out to welcome more citizens of Thornscarp to their table. Harried serving girls bustled from table to table, and the walls were lined with more royal guards than Mila had seen at one time since arriving to beg for Edonier's hand in marriage.

The cramped space was near to stifling, and not for the first time, Mila was envious of the preferred fashion the ladies around her wore. While she was perspiring in her long-sleeved gown, most of the women around her appeared comfortable in the loose-fitting and rather revealing halters and skirts.

Thak hadn't been at her room to escort them down, instead sending Dawson with his drooping grey wings and pleasant demeanor to make sure they arrived safely, before taking his place against the back wall overlooking the king and queen.

They sat at their normal table and waited among the overly loud revelers for their regular dining companions to arrive. After the enjoyable day they'd had, Mila allowed herself a rather large goblet of wine. It was oddly beautiful, a pale teal color with a dry light flavor that danced on her tongue. It was perhaps the best wine she'd ever tasted, and it was half gone by the time Thak and his small group of Corps friends joined them.

"Here's our band of supporters!" Ograt grinned and clapped as they approached. He took up his preferred spot and immediately downed a large mug of mead. Nox, Ram, and Petra quickly followed suit.

Ograt wiped a hand across his mouth and asked, "Enjoy the festivities today, ladies?"

"It was sublime." Puddi tilted her head back and closed her eyes, lost in the memory of the day. "Who knew such brutal sport could be so agreeable? And stimulating!"

"I did." Glow flashed her tiny teeth in a grin. "I actually *watched*." Puddi chose to ignore her friend's jab.

"Never a doubt about it, my tiny savage friend." Ograt raised his cup to the sprite in salute.

"And you, Princess?" Ograt asked. Thak turned toward Mila, obviously interested in her opinion as much as his friend was. "You certainly seemed to be enjoying yourself. Cheering louder than most in fact."

Mila waved a hand as if to bat the idea away. "It was something I wouldn't mind experiencing again."

"Hollering rather loudly for our Thak here." Ograt winked at her. "Wonder how the prince feels about that?"

Mila took another large gulp of wine. She hadn't thought she had been so obvious. And in the royal box too. Balls and bastards. She needed to get her head together.

In an effort to salvage her dignity, she pointed out that she'd been cheering just as loud for the rest of them as well as Liark.

"The girl did well," Petra said. "I, along with several others, was duly impressed. She'd be great in the Corps."

Mila shook her head and swallowed a bit of cheese. "She wants to join the castle guard."

"You spoke with her?"

"Her family. It's a long story, but they told me she was here to show her skills and hope to get picked up as a guard."

"She's young, but I might be able to ensure that happens." Thak leaned back in his chair, hands clasped at the back of his neck as he relaxed into a stretch.

Mila averted her eyes. Edonier. Think of Edonier. The prince she had yet to meet.

Playing with the rim of her goblet, she said, "You've got enough clout on the guard to ensure a girl with no other connections gets picked to serve here?"

Ograt snorted. "Something like that, Your Highness."

Thak threw him a look Mila couldn't interpret and called a serving girl over, asking her to bring several pitchers of water to the table.

The hall was filling up even further, and Mila wondered if every person with a title from the entirety of Thornscarp had been invited. The laughter was getting louder and the people freer. Several couples took up places on the dance floor, and even the sternest of the soldiers seemed loose and less inclined to scowl. Just as she noted earlier in the day, the denizens of the mountain realm seemed happy.

She still felt overdressed compared to the other ladies. Even Puddi with her newly acquired clothing and Glow in her scant diaphanous gown blended in better.

The table adjacent was occupied by a group of men in rich brocade tunics cut off at the shoulder to expose their arms. Mila didn't recognize them and surmised they must have been visiting for the festival. She could feel their stares as she took another sip of her wine.

"Don't mind them, Your Highness." Thak didn't look to the men, but rather kept his eyes on the food in front of him. He, along with the rest of the soldiers, ate ravenously. It was no wonder after the long day of expending energy, even if it was just for sport.

How they maintained their diet while on the battlefield she couldn't guess. Military strategy and troop maintenance wasn't something she had needed to know in Gildernosh. For far too long, the crown there had relied on buying their way out of trouble, and now they were paying for their folly. Evansband, Glow's home realm, in particular seemed more than eager to take the mines by force, and Gildernosh could barely muster an army to surround the capital. Securing the borders was going to be impossible. Unless, of course, Mila was successful.

Her father's chief advisor had suggested mercenaries, and to Mila's utter horror, it seemed as though the Lord Protector was planning to move in that direction. Buying loyalty didn't feel right. Then again, was she not doing the same just under a different guise?

Thak had washed and changed out of his armor before coming to dinner. His hair was still damp and his face rosy. Mila took in his crisp clean gold tunic as she replied, "It doesn't bother me. I'm more than a little accustomed to men studying me and finding me wanting."

The light caught the guard's thickly lashed eyes as he slowly blinked at her. Mila caught herself before she leaned forward to count his freckles. She needed to slow down on the wine.

"That surprises you?" she asked, a hint of disdain in her voice. "I suppose no one in Thornscarp dares to scrutinize Her Majesty."

"Not openly, though she has her detractors. The king as well on occasion. It comes with the position, I suspect. But the vast majority support her."

"Things don't work that way for me, I'm afraid. You may

find it strange considering Gildernosh is by rights a queendom. My father is not king, nor will he be. He is Lord Protector, but that does not mean he is without power or that he is in any way cowed by the fact I will one day outrank him."

A round of sniggers rose from the adjacent table, and Thak took a long deep breath, still not looking at the men behind him.

"Forgive my boldness, Princess, but I can find very little in you to be lacking."

She chuffed a laugh.

"I tell her this all the time, Thak," Puddi interjected. "I blame Gideaon."

"Gideaon?"

"Her slimy, ass faced, ball licking, worthless excuse for a husband," Glow piped up. Perhaps she'd been into the wine as well.

"Late husband," Mila corrected. "Although it's hard to argue with the other descriptors."

"And her father. Though since he's the Lord Protector *for now*, I find it difficult to say this openly." Puddi had a thoughtful look on her face.

"Maybe we should all slow down with the wine," Thak said.

"I've had wine before, Thak. Despite what the queen insists, I am not a child. Neither are Puddi and Glow."

"I am well aware you aren't a child." His face flushed, but he shrugged it off. "It's just, you can't mean both your father and your husband found you wanting in some unseen way." Thak leaned forward with a flash of intensity he rarely showed.

Once again she wanted to count his freckles. *Enough wine* the voice in her head admonished, but rather than listen she took another deep sip of the cool teal liquid.

"I fear you may say something you'll later regret," Thak said.

"I appreciate your concern. Now, let me see. Where shall I begin?" Mila raised her hand and ticked off on her fingers. "My hips are too wide. My ass slightly too large in general and certainly in comparison to my relatively average breasts." Mila pretended not to notice how not only Thak's but every other member of the table's eyes dipped to her chest. "I have one dimple on the right but no twin to it on the left. I'm slightly too tall, and don't forget that my hair is neither curly nor straight." Here she lifted her other hand and continued extending her fingers. "I spend too much time in the sun, preventing my skin from being porcelain, and worst of all, I have the unforgivable tendency to speak my mind and voice my concerns for the well-being of my people. Going so far as to encourage a change in how we perceive our station and how we are perceived by the other realms."

Thak sat back, his eyes wide and lips turned down, crinkling the soft hair of his beard. Or at least she *assumed* it was soft. It *looked* soft. Forget the freckles. She wanted to run her hands over the red-tinged facial hair to test the texture and satisfy her curiosity.

She shook her head. Perhaps Thak was right. It was the prince she was meant to be thinking about. "What kind of wine is this?"

"You should take it slow, Your Highness. That's gloomberry wine. It's a tad stronger than what you're probably used to," Ograt said. "A passion of the king's. He makes it himself. He serves it when he sees fit. It isn't often."

"Now you tell me." Mila looked longingly at the goblet. It tasted divine, but she couldn't afford to slip up now.

"Your father told you all of this?" Thak asked, genuinely affronted.

"Yes."

"And your husband agreed?"

"Yes. Quite emphatically, I'm afraid." Against her better judgment, Mila lifted the goblet to her lips and had to keep herself from choking at Thak's next statement.

"Well, that's all a load of goblin cock." He shook his head as Puddi gasped and Glow cackled. "My apologies, Princess."

She grinned at him. "None needed." It was nice to see the guard loosen up a bit, and something in the way he looked at her with such unbelieving eyes made her continue. "In fact, he needed help in the bedroom before he could perform. And not from me. He made sure I understood that all too well. He was vocal about which of my maids in particular could provide the service." The last words came out slightly more bitterly than she'd intended. The table had grown quiet, all eyes on her. It was a fact she'd kept secret from even Puddi and Glowildeen until then. "Some days I'm more than a little relieved he died before I bore the heir I need to ascend the throne."

"Fucking Saffron." Glow hissed, knowing without missing a beat of her wings which maid Mila had referred to. "Nixie tits. I hate that woman."

"Nixie tits and goblin cock!" Puddi giggled behind her hand. She had a far off glassy look in her eyes. "They should be introduced." Mila reached over and pushed the small goblet away from her friend.

"Did you kill him?" Ograt asked with mock seriousness.

"No. But some days, I wish I had."

The bald man's eyes widened. She took another long drink of her wine.

"Well, Princess, I can tell you this," Ograt said, a smirk on his face. "If you should happen to land Edonier in your marriage bed, there'll be no need for a maid in your chamber." His cat eyes flicked to Thak, and Mila thought the soldier was trying to get another laugh. But when Mila looked at the guard, all she saw was fury in his soft brown eyes.

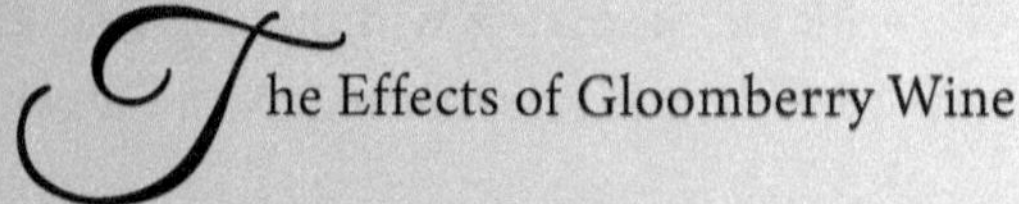

The Effects of Gloomberry Wine

THE WINE MADE HER DO IT. IT WAS THE ONLY EXPLANATION. OR maybe it was the memory of her terrible first marriage. Maybe it was both. The combination convincing her nothing could be worse than the humiliation she'd endured with Gideaon.

She needed to meet Edonier, and if no one was going to point him out to her, she'd find him herself. The best place to start was with his brother, and if the prince wasn't going to invite her into conversation, she would damn well invite herself.

The ground was more or less stable under her feet as she approached the table where he sat—this time not with his parents but rather with a large group of young women and a handful of important-looking men. None of them she noted, save Gregor, had competed in the earlier games. If she found this odd, she pushed it away. Who was she to say whom the prince should socialize with?

A lovely young woman with tawny brown skin and large doe eyes sat perched in Gregor's lap. As Mila approached, the woman blinked at her and smiled as she whispered in the prince's ear. He smirked back and muttered something that had the woman laughing out loud, the movement causing her breasts to rise and fall a hair's breadth from the prince's face.

Mila smiled benignly at the pair. They could make as much a spectacle of themselves as they saw fit. She refused to allow it to interfere with her mission. The doe-eyed beauty leaned farther back into the prince's chest, and Mila noted her legs ended in the slender hooves of an ungulate.

"Your Highness." Mila poured as much sickly sweet venom into the words as she could. These people valued bravery and aggression, didn't they? She would show the prince aggression for once.

His lip quirked up in a smirk. "Can I help you, Princess?"

"I'd like a word. Care to dance?"

"By all means."

He stood before the woman on his lap was prepared, and she nearly spilled to the ground, catching herself on the table at the last moment, her hooves clattering on the hard wood floor. Her lip curled as she took in Mila. The heir to the Gildernosh throne tried to stare down her nose at the pretty young woman, but as the room swayed and turned, it made standing straight a tad difficult.

"Having trouble holding your wine, Your Highness?"

"Not at all, *Your Highness*."

The prince snorted in either disgust or disbelief.

"Do try not to vomit on my boots." He grabbed her arm and swung her out onto the dance floor.

Her head swam in a dizzying loop.

"Well?" he asked.

"Well what?"

"Now is your moment to speak with me. What is it I can do for you, Your Highness?"

"Why is it you find it so difficult to be civil to me?"

"*This is* me being civil. I'm sure they fall all over you in Gildernosh. If you plan to marry into this family, I suppose you'll need to give up on being the pampered princess."

"I don't expect to be pampered." Mila was seething. "But a certain amount of respect would be nice. I will be queen one day. And you are also in line for the throne. Should something happen to your brother, that is. Surely someone will expect manners out of you at some point." They had swung and twirled their way to the edge of the dance floor. She might vomit on his boot after all.

"For you to be queen you need to produce an heir, correct?"

Mila nodded.

"And what makes you think a union between our people will result in such a thing?"

Mila's head swam. She hadn't thought that far ahead. The sole reason for her proposal was an alliance through marriage. That alliance would ensure the troops of Thornscarp would aid Gildernosh in its defense. Some neglected part of her mind had never really taken into account that the marriage might not result in an heir.

"Your first marriage was a failure in that regard, was it not?"

The words stung, but only a little. She hadn't wanted a child with Gidaeon, despite what it meant for her ascension.

But did she want one with Edonier? She didn't know.

Her stomach turned over. She was a fool.

It didn't matter. Her people's safety needed to come first. Her ascension to the throne was a problem for down the road.

The prince seemed to sense her miscalculation. "Are you unwell, Princess? You've gone the color of rancid pond water."

"I'm fine. Thank you. Perhaps it's the altitude."

"Hmm? Well, nothing has been decided as of yet. You still

have a handful of days to make your case. How about this, *Your Highness?* The day you are queen and I am king, I'll treat you with the respect you may or may not deserve." The prince stopped abruptly and dropped her hands, walking off in the opposite direction. Mila looked after him, no longer angry.

The day he was king? He couldn't possibly mean. . .

The idea was far too outlandish. Was this the test? Was Gregor actually Edonier? He couldn't possibly be. Was she expected to get *him* to fall in love with her? All this time she'd assumed brutal Prince Edonier was just death on the battlefield. She'd underestimated how the moniker might describe him as a person as well. Was the entire journey a waste? Even if the queen agreed to the proposal, Mila wasn't certain the prince would.

Her head was swimming and not just from the wine.

She tamped down the nausea and told herself it didn't matter. Even if the horrid man was Edonier and this was all some stupid charade, she would rise to the challenge. She'd been in a loveless marriage before, and she would do it again.

For her realm. For her queendom. For her people.

11

Who Says It's a Sacrifice

THE LIGHTS SWAYED DANGEROUSLY. OR WAS THAT MILA'S HEAD? Damn the king and damn his gloomberry wine. Damn Prince Gregor, or Edonier, or whoever he was and damn his perfect cheekbones and shitty attitude. Most importantly, damn herself. She thought she'd been doing something remarkable. Something a true leader would do. Remarkably stupid seemed a better fit.

Ahead, Glow bumped into a sconce and cursed viciously then belched and continued to fly on. Her friends had enjoyed their share of the drink as well.

The hallways weren't exactly crowded, but more people were out and about in the castle than had been there previously. Glow and Puddi ventured ahead, arguing over the merits of daggers versus poisons. Mila thought she might have heard a slurred version of Gidaeon's name come up more than once during the exchange. She couldn't blame her friends in wishing him dead all over again, and a flush of shame ran through her. She should have told them before, but it had been something she wanted to hide away and forget about.

Mila had been twenty years old when she was told she would marry by the end of the summer. She hadn't been naïve enough to think the man her father had arranged for her to wed would fall madly in love with her at first sight. She hadn't expected him to love her at all. She certainly hadn't loved him. It was her duty to marry. She knew that. And just as coming to Thornscarp had meant doing what was needed for her people, she had agreed to the marriage without so much as a backward glance.

Gideaon came from a respected family from the far south of Gildernosh. His father ran a lucrative trade group and shipping port on the idyllic western coast. Gideaon, eldest of six boys, was due to inherit a good chunk of the business, but his political aspirations had overshadowed even his drive for coin. He'd been handsome in the thin polished way many young men were. Slight and pampered, waxed and perfumed. Most days he took longer in front of the mirror than the soon-to-be queen of Gildernosh herself.

Glow had disliked him instantly. Not surprising. Puddi had loved him. Also not surprising. Until that is, he'd dismissed her as a servant. Then? *Then* Puddi had loathed him.

Mila hadn't cared about him one way or the other, but she *had tried to* make things work. She went to the dinners and the balls and the teas. She'd complimented him and his family. She'd talked of things they could accomplish and never once implied he would be "less than" when she was queen and he was her consort. In short she thought she had treated him with respect. Because that was what future queens did.

Gideaon for his part had seemed—if not interested in her— at least *tolerant* of her. At first.

And while Mila had suggested restraint—it was just a

wedding after all—her father had spared no expense in the weeks leading up to the nuptials. The realm celebrated their engagement with overblown festivities. Years after her mother's untimely death, a queen would finally be back on the Gilder-nosh throne. All she needed was a babe in her arms. Then the real celebration would begin.

Fine dresses were made. Exotic flowers shipped in. Gifts of gems and gold for the guests were arranged and the best bakers and chefs brought to the capital. There was even a two-week trip from Gidaeon's town to the capital, complete with village gatherings and stops for the couple in all the finest hotels. In short, money was spent as if it flowed from the ground like water from a spring.

She didn't want the fuss, but she got it. She didn't want a husband at the time, but she'd gotten that too. But in the beginning, what she wanted least of all was the marriage without the heir. To make an heir, she needed a willing husband. Which she assumed she had. So it came as more than a shocking slap in the face when on their wedding night, her pompous, arrogant, power-hungry husband declared her undesirable. She waited on the bed for him, certain she must have misheard. When she stood and approached him, resigned to doing whatever she must to seal the marriage, he'd pushed her away with a sneer.

At first she thought him possibly incapable of performing in the bedroom, but when he called for her pretty young maid and asked the girl to get on her knees for him, Mila was mortified. He consummated their marriage in only the strictest sense of the word, plunging into her at the last moment and leaving her confused and ashamed. She'd thought the maid would also be mortified, but it soon became clear they'd been enjoying each other's company for the better part of the past month, and rather than shamed, the maid had looked smug as she rose and left with the new prince consort in tow.

Mila had long since gotten over the memory of that night,

and thankfully she'd endured similar episodes only a handful of times before Gideon left on a trade trip one day and never returned. In the fourteen months and three days of their union, they'd spent very little time together, and she was thankful for that, even if it meant the chance of producing an heir was bare to none.

It was only after he'd died and she'd taken the time to examine her feelings that she'd become more than hurt. She'd become angry. She might not have been the most stunning woman in all of Gildernosh, but she wasn't exactly a hag either, mismatched dimples not withstanding. More than that, she was a decent person. She deserved a decent person in return.

The fact she was a princess and might one day be a queen seemed almost irrelevant.

"Princess, are you unwell?" Thak extended one of his large hands and steadied her elbow before she careened into a wall that seemed to appear out of nowhere.

Are you unwell, Princess? Nearly the same words the prince had used. *You've gone the color of rancid pond water.* But where Gregor had been snide and mean-spirited, Thak sounded only concerned.

"I'm fine. Thank you. Perhaps it's the altitude." She repeated the same answer.

"Don't let him get to you. The prince, I mean. He isn't worth it."

"If only that were true."

She could feel his body tense where he still connected with her elbow.

"He hasn't been himself of late." Not himself. Was Thak inadvertently confirming her rising suspicion? He sighed, scratching absently at his beard with his free hand. "The prince, in general, means well. He is loyal to his family but on occasion lets the strain get the better of him."

"So he isn't always fractious and rude?"

"Often. But not always."

The day she'd arrived at the castle, she'd been terrified of Thak. His imposing stature, his paws and horns. Now she was clinging to him like an old friend. A lifeline in this unchartered sea. He'd been honest with her about the prince, said something a guard probably should not have said. She owed him a bit more truth.

"I am not unwell. Just a tad unsteady. And I'd really like to meet Edonier. I'm wondering if this is all a mistake." She took a deep breath and forced her eyes to focus. "*And* reliving old memories. *Pointless* old memories."

He didn't reply but continued to hold her elbow as they made their way up to the blue room. Puddi stood giggling and stoking the wooden door. As they approached, the gnome threw her head back and licked her lips in the most ridiculously absurd attempt at seduction Mila had ever seen.

Thak, ever the picture of chivalrous good intentions, smiled and dipped his chin to the gnome. "Lady Puddi, I'd never forgive myself if I took advantage of you in your current state." She crossed her arms and pouted at him. "Trust me. You'll feel differently in the morning," he assured her.

The door bade them enter.

As they walked into the room, Quince appeared to turn down the bedding, spending more time than usual fussing over the mattress and arranging the layers. She left as Glow and Puddi disappeared into the bathing chamber and Thak moved to set the fire in the hearth.

"There is no need to pity me," Mila said to his back. He hadn't spoken about what she'd revealed to them that night, but still it hung heavy in the air. She was sure of it. Or maybe it was just the wine and her maudlin thoughts.

"I feel no pity, Your Highness. I'm impressed by your dedication. And truth be told, I am also conflicted at the moment."

She tilted her head silently, encouraging him to say more. He didn't.

"I didn't love him, and therefore his feelings toward me were easy to bear. It isn't unheard of. Royal couples are often arranged. Not many truly care for one another."

"Sad but true." He continued fussing with the kindling, not looking at her as she spoke.

"I mean, it isn't so different to what I'm doing now. Arranging my marriage. For the good of my people."

He nodded but did not reply.

"I dismissed the maid, not that it was entirely her fault. He was in a position of power and she was just weak enough to enjoy the feel of that washing over her. I still feel mildly guilty about it, but . . . I couldn't exactly dismiss my husband."

"You don't need to explain."

She tilted her head, and the room spun. Closing her eyes, she took a deep steadying breath.

"True. I don't, but. . ." Why was she discussing this with a guard? She rubbed at her temples, knowing the morning would bring unpleasant things.

"May I ask you a question?" Thak had the fire going and stood, dusting his hands on his pants.

"You'd take advantage of my inebriated state?" She raised an eyebrow at him, lips twisted to one side. "Do you intend to get more ugly secrets from me? Feed them to the queen?"

"No!" His cheeks flushed a slight pink. "You're right, I shouldn't ask."

"Relax, Thak. I'm only joking." She swung her feet back and forth over the edge of the bed and finished in a sing-song voice, completely out of character. "Of course you may ask me anything you wish."

Loud splashing and giggles erupted from the bathing chamber, and a small puddle of water crept beneath the door.

He pinched the bridge of his nose, and Mila could sense the

guard trying to decide if he liked the drunk versions of Mila and her companions or if he'd rather they all ride back to Gildernosh and leave him in well-deserved peace. "Maybe this is a conversation better suited for another time."

"Another time and I may not answer as honestly." She grinned at him.

"You admit to not being honest with me unless you're drunk?" The words were teasing, but something in his eyes spoke of a seriousness Mila couldn't ignore, even in her intoxication.

"I admit I am more guarded. I've not lied to you. Not once. But I also don't tell you everything." She flopped back on the bed and closed her eyes again. It was a further step away from royal behavior, but at this point, she couldn't bring herself to care. "As evidenced by my companions this evening, I rarely tell *anyone* everything. Puddi and Glow are like sisters to me, but even some shames are too much to burden them with."

"The only person in your earlier tale who should feel shame is the man who dared call himself your husband. And perhaps your father. What else you could have to hide, I can't imagine."

"Nothing earth shattering I can tell you. But I haven't exactly been forthcoming with the number of times I've wanted to run my fingers over your beard or count the freckles on your face." She heard his breath leave in a rush as she groaned and rolled to her side, burying her face in the crook of her arm. "I shouldn't have said that. I'm sorry. Please don't tell the queen. Or the prince. Or the other prince, for that matter."

"Ah, Your Highness. Your secret is safe with me." His voice was lower. He swallowed and chuffed a laugh. "But you may not want to tell Lady Puddi. I saw her teeth in Eloise's arm."

Mila chuckled, the tension once more broken. "You've no need to worry on my behalf there. I've seen her take down mightier foes than me. She may look the picture of innocence, but trust me. She could make Glow look tame at any time of her choosing. So what is this question?"

"I just wonder. You clearly sacrificed your own happiness for your people once before. Why do it again?"

"Who says it's a sacrifice?"

"So you'd be happy to marry for alliance alone?"

She peeked up from her arm and found him standing in the center of the room, arms crossed over his chest and watching her with interest. Between the horns and the legs tapering into paws, he cut quite the intimidating figure. It was so at odds with his calm presence and open questioning eyes, she was momentarily speechless.

When she found her voice, it came out tired and not entirely self-assured. "I meant what I said before. My people need this."

"That isn't an answer."

"No," she agreed. "It isn't." She groaned and tried to push herself up.

"And if it were, you could marry whoever this other suitor is."

Ah, so he had been listening as he stood watch over the queen. She'd thought so. Again she wondered why the royal family chose to trust this guard so much.

"*That* would be more than a sacrifice." A shiver ran down her spine. "And with no benefit to my people in exchange. Perhaps an heir, but nothing else. I don't wish to ascend just for the sake of myself."

"Here." He extended his hand down to her, and she once again grabbed onto him like a drowning woman.

"Have I told you how much I like your hands?"

Amusement twinkled in his eyes, and his lip quirked to the side in a lopsided grin. "First my beard and freckles, now my hands. I'm starting to question your judgment a tad, but no, Your Highness. I don't believe you have."

"Well, I do. They're perfect."

He shook his head in bafflement and tugged her upward. His pull was graceful. The way she came to rest against his chest was not. She bounced into him, and only his hands under her elbows kept her from tumbling sideways.

He cocked an eyebrow at her wobbly form. "Your father is wrong. You're the perfect height. Although you are entirely too easy to manipulate."

Ignoring the subtle compliment about her stature, she scowled at him. Was the manipulation referring to Eloise again? His earlier mention had her pondering for a brief moment what had become of the serving woman.

"Physically, I mean. I'm certain your character is much more stalwart." One corner of his mouth twitched. "I wonder if someone shouldn't give you defense lessons, Your Highness."

"I'd be happy to be your pupil."

"I was thinking Petra, but if you insist. I'm becoming rather partial to your solitary dimple." The twitch blossomed into a full smile. Without thinking, she ran her fingers over the side of his cheek. The hair of his beard was just as soft as she'd thought it would be.

"Princess." His face stilled, the smile evaporating.

"Yes?" Her voice was no more than a whisper as she stared up at him.

He stepped back from her and gently released her arms.

"Just as I told Lady Puddi, I'd never forgive myself if I took advantage of you in your current state."

12

*Y*esterday's Rubbish

MILA HAD BEEN WRONG. THE BED WASN'T COMFORTABLE. IT WAS lumpy. It tilted at the wrong angle. It stank of feet and the sour smell of sweat. She would be sure to tell the queen at breakfast how truly horrid it was and for once not be lying about her lack of sleep. All she had to do was calm the banging in her head and she'd rise and head to breakfast.

She cracked an eyelid, and the stabbing in her head tripled. Maybe it wasn't the bed that stank at all but the small gnomish foot that had found its way into her face during the night. She removed Puddi's heel from her chin and buried her head in the pillows. Still the banging persisted.

"Your Highness." That was Thak's voice. Had he stayed the night in her room?

Surely she would have remembered that. Wouldn't she?

More banging at the door. "Your Highness? I'm afraid I'm going to need to open the door. Are you decent?"

"Define decent," she grumbled.

"I've got Quince out here, and unfortunately I'm going to need for her to come in."

Mila sat up and squinted at the door. No more gloomberry wine. Ever.

Oh, Maidens. Last night.

Last night she had been dangerously close to kissing him. A guard.

How was she going to look him in the face when she'd practically thrown herself at him when he knew she'd proposed marriage to the prince? And this was after she'd spilled the horrid secrets of her first marriage. He'd said he didn't pity her. She remembered that much. But what could he possibly think of her? That she was desperate for attention? That she would welcome any man to her bed? That she would use him as Gideaon had used Saffron?

Shame flooded her. A fine sheen of sweat coated the back of her neck and pooled below her breasts.

It was hard to tell from the other side of the door, but if he was embarrassed on her behalf, he was doing a good job of hiding it.

She felt like yesterday's rubbish.

Puddi and Glow didn't seem to be fairing much better. The sprite was curled up, knees to chin at the foot of the bed, her delicate wings folded over her face. The gnome had her feet on the pillows, loud snores erupting from her open mouth. Mila knew she would never be forgiven if she let Thak see her friend like that.

"Puddi, come on. Rise and shine." She jostled the woman's arm and was rewarded with a curse that was more suited to Glow than Puddi. Maybe she could let Thak see her like this after all.

"Princess?" Thak called one more time.

"I'm coming, Thak." She stumbled across the room, wondering what could possibly be so important. Thak never woke her, simply waited for her to rise at a respectable time and would be there waiting when she emerged dressed and ready for breakfast.

Opening the door, she was ready with the question on her lips, but one look at the guard's face and she stopped.

Something was definitely amiss.

"What is it?" At the hard set of his lips, her flush of shame was replaced by a frown.

"Quince is going to help you get dressed." His eyes flicked down her body, and he tensed. Maybe he wasn't embarrassed for her. Maybe he was *angry* with her.

Suddenly, standing there in her thin silk gown seemed horribly inappropriate. She crossed her arms over her chest. "I can dress myself. Or Puddi can help me."

Thak dipped his head to the bed and the snoring, drooling gnome crumpled atop it like a sack of laundry. "I'm afraid we don't have the luxury of waiting for Lady Puddi to get her wits about her."

"Can you at least tell me what has happened? How presentable do I need to be?"

"Presentable enough for an audience with your father's emissary. He's waiting in the breakfast hall and seems none too pleased to be here."

Her father's emissary.

Her time was up and she still hadn't met Edonier. Or she had and he was that ass Gregor in disguise. She was doomed either way.

She should have known.

Mila's stomach lurched, and she raced to the bathing chamber, sure she was about to be sick. Thankfully, she was able to keep the contents of her stomach contained. She splashed some cool water on her face, and Quince entered carrying her teal dress. Mila groaned but allowed the maid to help her look as presentable as was possible given her state and the short timeframe.

Walking with Thak to the hall, she steeled her spine and pulled back her shoulders. If she was lucky, it would be one of the younger emissaries she favored and more importantly who favored her. She'd been spending the past few years carefully cultivating a group of advisors she trusted. Men and woman who did any number of jobs in and around the capital. But the number was small. For the most part, the advisors were older men. A handful of them had been advisors to her mother and were still in her father's good graces, but most of his inner circle served only him. As much as she hoped for an ally, she was sure he'd send one of his most loyal.

"Your Highness?" A small divot had formed between Thak's brows, his lips set in a firm line.

Mila was sure no matter who stood on the other side of the door, the conversation would be unpleasant. There was a real possibility she would be leaving Thornscarp later in the day, but she did not want to go with Thak being angry with her.

Yes, he was just a guard. But he was also a good man.

"I'm sorry," she said. "About last night."

"What?" Had she not been standing outside the door with Maidens knew which of her father's trusted men—he had no female advisors—was on the other side, she would have laughed at the utter look of confusion he wore.

"I can tell you're angry. I'm sorry for putting you in an awkward position last night. It was wrong of me, and as much as I'd like to simply blame the wine. . ."

He released a short breath. "Your Highness, you have nothing to apologize for."

"I'm not sure that's true."

"Regardless. As it happens, I am very much not angry with

you. As I said, I am *conflicted.* But I also don't think this is the best time to discuss it." He tilted his head to the door.

"Yes. Right. I'm fine. This is fine." She took a deep breath. "Maidens help me. You'd think I was some adolescent girl, not the future queen." She rolled her neck and stepped forward as Thak opened the door.

Balls and bastards. No luck then. Not one of hers. It was the Lord Protector's favorite.

Seated at the same table as the queen was Joaquine Sturgess. Oily. Slimy. Ass-licker.

She should have known. Her father's lapdog would be the first to volunteer to make the journey if he thought he could drag her back to Gildernosh kicking and screaming. Mila knew her father was trying to do the right thing by holding the country together until she could ascend, but she was more than certain Joaquine would be happy if she never took the throne. Unless, of course, he was the one married to her when she did. She'd sell herself to just about any noble before she let that happen.

"Goodness, Princess." Not even bothering to rise fully from his chair, the man dipped his head as she walked in. When he righted himself, the hungry gleam in his eye was beyond evident. "I realize you left in a rush, but could you not have packed a decent gown? You look . . . quite disheveled. Otherwise, I'm pleased to find you alive and unscathed. I can assure you, you've given your father quite the scare."

"He wouldn't be in distress if he'd listened to me when he had the chance." Ignoring the barb about her attire, Mila walked in and turned to the queen who was watching with a slightly amused expression. "Your Majesty. I do apologize for any inconvenience the Gildernosh representative may have caused. I assure you, I would have given word had I known he was coming."

The queen's lips twisted in distaste. "No need for apologies, child. As it happens, Joaquine and I have met before." She popped her lips apart and her brow rose, and Mila knew instantly that whatever that visit had entailed, it had not left the Queen of Thornscarp with a good impression of the man.

"Yes. Still. I am a guest in your home, and I hope to remain as such until the conclusion of our agreement."

"And what agreement might that be?" the emissary asked.

"An agreement between the princess and myself and one you will be informed of in due time, should it be necessary." The queen pulled her tea mug to her lips and took a long sip. "Now, Your Highness, why don't you have some breakfast?"

Mila sent a small smile toward the queen, trying desperately and failing miserably to decipher if Gregor's mother was being kind to her of her own accord or if she just detested Joaquine so much she wanted to make things difficult for him. In the end, it didn't really matter so long as Mila got what she needed out of the exchange—to hear what the man had to say and then send him on his way without having to inform him of her proposal. Her father had to know why she was there, but the longer it was before she needed to confirm it, the better.

Mila filled her mug with tea and grabbed a small delicately crafted bit of flaky sweet bread to nibble on. She didn't think her stomach would tolerate anything more at the moment.

Thak had moved from his place behind Mila when she sat and stood a step behind Queen Augustina. He was the only other person in the room, but the mere presence of him looming there, hand on the hilt of his sword, was enough to dissuade any possibility of violence against the crown. Moreover, having him in the room helped Mila settle.

"Your Majesty." Joaquine turned his attention to the end of the table. "Is *His* Majesty King Edon to join us?"

The queen tilted her chin and studied the man. She might not have been born into the crown, but that didn't mean she hadn't been born to wear it. Mila took immense pleasure in watching Joaquine squirm under her gaze. A bead of sweat escaped his hairline and traveled the length of his jowl, disappearing under his chin.

"I'm afraid the king is otherwise engaged this morning. You did arrive at our gates rather early and without an invitation. But seeing as I am here"—she swept her hands to encompass the room—"it should not be an issue."

Mila knew the king and queen were likely both aware of the emissary's timeline. Just as she was sure the crown's sentinels had tracked her progress through the winding mountain roads the moment she'd entered the realm, she knew Joaquine's route would have been watched and reported on. If the king was *otherwise engaged*, it was by his choice, not an unfortunate coincidence.

"Of course." Joaquine cleared his throat but didn't continue.

Mila took another sip of her tea and looked at the man her father had sent to retrieve her. The man who would very much like to make her his wife. A man twenty years her senior and a man who made her skin crawl. A man with pale stubby fingers tipped in nails too long to ever be considered appropriate.

Even as a child, always among the powerful of the realm, she'd been perceptive enough to know Joaquine wasn't as he wanted people to believe. He was manipulative and vile, always taking liberties under the guise of serving Mila's father. Although she had only the barest glimmers and flashes of memories of her mother, and never had the chance to know her as an adult, Mila wanted to believe that if she'd lived to rule as she should have, this man never would be in the position he was. The idea made her stronger somehow.

"Joaquine. Why has Father sent you all this way? He very well could have sent a courier to inquire on my behalf."

"He did. Send messengers, that is. Several. All through Yallring. To Evansband. Even one to Krith. The general feeling was you'd either decided to travel home—Jonas was sent there—or had been abducted. I knew it was a waste and tried to convince the king that you wouldn't have left without word of your own accord unless. . . Well, abduction was looking more likely, but there was the small matter of your companions. Do tell. Where are Lady Puddi and Glowildeen?"

"Unless what?" she asked. The emissary looked confused. "You said I wouldn't leave of my own accord *unless?*"

The corners of his mouth turned down in distaste as if the very room around him smelled of rotten flesh, mildew, and feces. "Unless you planned to act on your own with the ridiculous—" He cut himself off, a beat too late for calling a marriage alliance with Thornscarp ridiculous while the queen sat mere feet away enjoying her breakfast.

Mila wanted to ask him to continue, but there was no need. Judging by their expressions, both Augustina and Thak knew what he'd been about to say.

"We did not receive word asking for ransom, and it became clear to me that perhaps my time would be well spent making the journey here."

"You do realize I am fully capable of leaving my father's side when I see fit. I am not a child." Mila's eyes flashed to the queen as if reminding her as well.

"No, but you cannot disappear on a whim and expect there would be no repercussions."

"It was not a whim. I can assure you." Mila's hand rose to her cheek of its own accord, the sting of her father's slap still faintly echoing.

Joaquine snorted a laugh. "A queen must learn many lessons, Your Highness. That will likely not be the last or most brutal of them." The hunger was back in his eyes, and for a moment, it seemed he'd forgotten where he sat.

Not taking her eyes from the man, Mila stiffened at the veiled threat to violence, and she felt rather than saw Thak take a step closer to the table.

"It's not only queens who deserve brutal lessons." Augustina rose from her chair, and Thak took a step backward, drawing Mila's attention. His face was schooled into one of blank indifference. *His "guard" face*, Mila thought.

Standing as well, Joaquine flushed a bright crimson, whether from embarrassment or anger, Mila wasn't sure. He was travel worn. His clothes were rumpled and stained with sweat under his arms. His dark blond hair hung lank to the edge of his collar. It always bothered Mila that he wore it long in the back while it was thinning on top, giving him the look of someone trying and failing to look younger than his years.

"You still have failed to address the princess's question. Why exactly are you here?" The queen's voice demanded no argument.

"She, and her companions, are to return with me immediately." He raked a hand over his forehead, pushing into the greasy pate.

The queen didn't hesitate. "I am afraid that isn't possible."

Mila's heart stumbled over itself. Perhaps she could hope still.

"With all due respect, Your Majesty. This is not negotiable. The Lord Protector demands it. Even now, Evansband is priming for an attack on our southern border, and it is not safe for the heir to the throne to be away from the capital where she can best be protected."

"Evansband is attacking?" Mila asked at the same time that Thak said, "Then she is safer here."

Joaquine ignored Mila completely as he addressed Thak. "You'll forgive me if I don't take the word of a guard."

The queen looked over her shoulder and shot Thak a look that told him to keep his mouth shut. Anger flared in Mila. She dropped the uneaten bit of pastry from her hands and rose.

Perhaps taking Mila's movement as acquiescence, Joaquine continued, "Our forces on the border are stretched thin." They were always stretched thin. It was why Mila was there to begin with. "And we believe they will be overrun within the week. If we leave today, we should be able to get back to the capital before they make it that far west."

Mila's heart sank. If that was true, she was too late. Once Evansband's clans breached the borders, there would be little to stop them from rolling all the way to the capital. The citizens of Gildernosh had relied on wealth and comfort for decades. They were not a fighting people, and resistance to an all-out invasion would be little to none.

As if the queen could hear her thoughts, she said, "Your Highness. I will not prevent you from leaving. As you stated, you're able to make your own decisions. As future queen, those decisions are not always easy. If I might offer a word of advice, however?"

Mila nodded.

"I'll speak with my Master Covert. His network should be able to gather a bit more information in a short time. Wait until you have those answers before you decide."

"You'd do that for me?" Mila was wary of the offer but relieved nonetheless.

"I do it for many reasons. War rarely stays within its own borders."

"Thank you. Yes. I'll wait."

Joaquine's face turned an unpleasant shade of puce.

The queen turned to Thak. "Have your men escort the emissary to a room where he might get some rest. I might suggest somewhere in the eastern wing."

At that, Mila did feel relief. She'd learned the castle well enough to know the eastern wing was the farthest from the blue room she was occupying.

"And make sure whatever men he brought with him are taken care of as well."

Thak bowed as the queen headed to the door. Mila walked

around the table and stood next to the tall guard. Despite her earlier shame at her own behavior, she'd much rather be near his hulking form when she was left with just her father's man in the room.

"Don't wander too far today." The queen directed this to both Mila and Thak. "I'll expect we should have some information soon."

Joaquine had the decency to wait all of a minute after the queen made her leave before he turned and spat at the heir to the Gildernosh throne. "I've always known you'd be a disgrace to your father, but this is too far. Whoring yourself to these people? It's disgust—"

The remainder of the word was cut off as Thak's hand closed around the man's throat. Mila gasped as Joaquine's feet lifted from the ground as Thak pressed him against the nearest wall.

"I'm not sure how things are done in Gildernosh. But you'd do well to remember you are in Thornscarp now. A little respect for your future queen is expected."

Without waiting for a reply that surely could not come via Joaquine's compressed airway, Thak opened his hand and let the man fall from his grasp. Joaquine hit the ground and crumpled to his knees.

He drew in a ragged breath and sputtered, "You filthy demon scum. How dare you?" He scrambled to his feet and raised a trembling hand at the guard.

"I'd think very long and very hard before you say another word." Thak took a step and placed himself between the emissary and Mila. The motion or the words or the combination of both caused rage to flicker in Joaquine's eyes.

"I'll have you beaten for this." Spit flew from the man's lips. Mila flinched at the words.

"I doubt that very much."

"I wasn't talking to you." Joaquine sneered. "A repugnant

beast such as yourself would likely relish in it. It'll be death for you."

She could feel the moment Thak registered the meaning of his words. They seemed to settle over his form with the weight of a thousand chains. He stilled under the threat. This man. This emissary for her father was threatening to have Mila beaten. The future queen of Gildernosh. Beaten. Because she dared to align herself with a man he deemed beneath them.

She couldn't bear his silence, his judgment, or his pity. She stepped around Thak and stared Joaquine dead in the eye. His face was flushed, his breaths coming quick.

In the coolest voice she could muster, she repeated Thak's words to him. "I doubt that very much."

The guard behind her let out a slow breath. Much like a trout hauled from the river, the man before her opened and shut his mouth several times, apparently at a loss for what to say.

"I'd better rouse Puddi and Glow. They'll need to know what's happening." She tightened her lips as she looked from Thak to Joaquine. "I'm sure the emissary would be happy to rest for a bit as well."

Thak dipped his head, the light catching on his horns for the briefest of moments. "Yes, Your Highness. I'll show him there now."

He extended one hand to the emissary, directing the man out into the adjoining hall. The other never left the hilt of his sword. Mila watched as he padded away on his large elegant paws, the trembling form of her father's advisor stumbling along beside him.

$\mathcal{S}$omething to Think About

THAK STOOD BEFORE THE KING AND QUEEN OF THORNSCARP, Prince Gregor to his side. Edon and Augustina sat together on a small couch, and even though Thak was sure they were in disagreement, the love they had for one another still shone brightly.

Not many ever saw the monarchs' private chambers, but Thak was well acquainted with them. Many important meetings took place in that very sitting room. Thak had seen his fair share of those meetings.

"As much as I loath the idea of leaving right now, I agree with the king. It's the right thing to do." She'd told him she liked his hands. It was such an odd admission and she'd been suffering the effects of the king's gloomberry wine, but still it made his heart beat quicker and sent warmth flooding his body. They weren't the soft gentle hands of a noble from Gildernosh. Of that he was certain. In his lifetime of swordplay and violence, they had been nicked and bruised. Beaten and battered. Fingers dislocated and nails torn off at the quick. And if the king and queen agreed to his plan, they might have a few more imperfections on them by the time the next weeks were through. But if it was in defense of Gildernosh, maybe it would count for something. Maybe she'd find the blood on them acceptable.

The queen crossed one hand over her midsection, grasping the king's waiting fingers. "You owe those people nothing. And we still aren't sure of the princess's intentions."

Gregor lifted an eyebrow and smirked. As much as Thak loved the prince, sometimes he wanted nothing more than to drive his fist into the man's pretty face. The past few weeks had been particularly difficult for him to keep his temper leashed. But once again, he kept himself in check as the prince spoke. "That is true, Mother, but some things seem to be falling into place. I'll be the first to admit, she isn't exactly what I'd expected. And the intelligence is sound. Evansband is primed for an invasion, albeit a small one. You could call it a feeler. Just enough forces to take a couple of the easternmost mines. Nothing big enough to make a push for the capital yet."

Edon angled his tawny head to the queen. "He's got to go, Augustina."

"Does he? Because from where I'm sitting, it would seem wiser to simply give this information to that prick Joaquine and send him back to his master. What they decide to do about it is up to them. Hire mercenaries or whatever."

"But war rarely stays within its own borders. You said so yourself. Sooner or later, it'll be knocking on our doorstep," Thak told the queen. "If we give the clans something to think about, we may be able to stave it off."

"Or we risk bringing it here all the sooner."

The king took a deep breath and squeezed his wife's hand. "Why did you let the girl stay if you had no intention of making the alliance work? This could be just what we need to finally end what's been happening there. I think it's best we let him try."

She blew out a long breath and dipped her horns the barest inch toward her husband. "You've always been too good for this world, Edon. But if you all are in agreement, I won't try further to dissuade you."

"That's settled then." Edon stood and clapped Thak on the shoulder. "I wish you good speed and strength. May the Cardinal fortify you and the Divine bring you victory." The king said the words in a formal tone and embraced Thak quickly before stepping back and allowing his wife to do the same.

"Thank you, Your Majesties." Thak dipped into a shallow bow and turned to ready himself for the journey south.

14

A Fair Trade
Or
Two Promises

"Are you certain you wouldn't rather go back inside, Your Highness?" Dawson's voice revealed none of the distraction Mila was certain he must be feeling as he watched the troops across the yard.

His eyes never left the men and women of the Corps as they readied themselves. They'd been out there for the past hour, trying to escape the confines of their rooms, Dawson doing his duty to escort them in Thak's absence. It wasn't until they reached the grounds and the flurry of activity that she'd realized the Corps was moving out.

It had come as a surprise to Dawson as well.

Mila didn't see Nox among them, but she'd caught sight of both Petra and Ograt carrying saddle packs toward the stables. If they were leaving, it was a safe bet Ram and Nox were too. Dawson might not know when he'd see his husband again.

"If it's no bother, Dawson, I'd like to continue our walk." Mila, Glow, and Puddi had made several loops around the grounds, Dawson never leaving their side. The weather was sublime, and she had no interest in locking herself up within her rooms worrying over what the coming day might hold. She could delay the decision until she had all the information and then hope to delay it even further.

"Of course, Your Highness." His eyes were tight.

"If we promise not to move from this spot, will you please go and find Nox? I'd hate for him to leave without you saying goodbye."

He shook his head. "We each know our duties. His is to the Corps, and today, mine is to you." When she opened her mouth to argue, he cut her off. "He'll come and find me before he goes. This certainly isn't the first time he's been called away, and it won't be the last. We've done this countless times."

"At least he'd got his siblings with him."

He chuffed a laugh. "That he does. Not sure if that's good or bad, mind you. Maybe they'll get lucky and meet up with Wren's division. That'd at least bring Petra some joy."

"You're identical? You and Wren."

He nodded.

"Does it ever get hard for her, to see you and think of him?" Mila asked.

He titled his head and quirked his lips. "Perhaps."

"Have you ever pretended to be the other and swapped?" Puddi asked excitedly.

At this, Dawson looked downright horrified. "No."

"Hmm. Shame." Then she shifted gears so swiftly, even Mila was confused. "Where do you suppose they're going?" The gnome looked only slightly worse for wear after the night of sipping the strong spirits.

Mila had relayed the morning's conversation to her friends —at one point needing to physically restrain Glowildeen from taking off to the other side of the castle in the hopes of slitting Joaquine's throat. But even with the knowledge of her father's instructions, she couldn't think why the Thornscarp Corps would need to get involved. The most likely scenario was that while gathering whatever intelligence the queen could on the situation, a threat to Thornscarp had simultaneously been uncovered.

She was mulling it over as they continued their loops. The sun had risen high into the sky, and once again Mila felt herself envious of the women of Thornscarp and their flowing silk pants and breezy loose tops. If she ended up staying, she would ask Puddi to arrange for some new garments with her source.

"I'm the last person to speculate." Mila looked to Dawson.

"I have my suspicions, but I'm afraid I can't share them."

"Then what good are you, pigeon?" Glow grumbled as she flew past.

"Good for watching your backs, bug." He continued scanning the grounds as they moved along. After a few minutes of quiet he looked to Mila. "I'm sure Thak will tell you what he can before he leaves."

"Leaves?"

"He'll be moving out with the Corps, likely as not."

"Oh. I had no idea." Mila's heart dropped. She had no right to be upset by the news, yet she was.

"My apologies. I assumed you knew. He mentioned it when he asked that I take over his duties to you this morning."

"I see." But she didn't see. Thak was a royal guard, not part of the Corps.

She hadn't seen him since he'd escorted Joaquine to his chambers and Mila had gone off to wake Glow and Puddi. The queen had asked them to stay close for the day, but she'd assumed that directive was to keep Mila near should information on the Evansband attack on Gildernosh be correct. Maybe she was wrong. Maybe Augustina wanted Thak close so she could give him a different set of orders. What those orders were, Mila could only guess.

How long would he be away? And would she still be in Thornscarp when he returned? Or would she be riding home with Joaquine by that point, never to see the guard again?

Mentally she kicked herself. It was Edonier she was meant to be worrying over. He was, after all, the head of the military. Where they went, so too would he. If she was right, and Edonier and Gregor were one and the same, he would no doubt be leaving as well. And with him went any chance she had of securing the alliance she so desperately needed.

There was no sign of the prince among the troops, but that certainly meant little.

As they came around the long hedge separating the walkway past the stables, they were greeted by Quince.

"Her Majesty the Queen has asked me to fetch you to her, Your Highness." She turned and looked at Dawson. "Nox grabbed me along the way. He says he'll meet you outside the great chamber as well."

Dawson let out a relieved sigh and dipped his head in thanks. Perhaps he wasn't as convinced they'd get to talk as he wanted to let on.

"Is she in the hall, Quince? I can escort the princess and her ladies."

"Oh, would you, Dawson? I've still got work to do in the guest wing. So many visitors for the games and now the Thornscarp emissary and his men."

"He can fuck right off, Quince," Glow said. The maid's eyes widened as she looked from the sprite to the princess standing next to her. "Ah, don't worry about Mila. She'll tell you the same."

Mila suppressed a smile and kept her mouth shut.

"Anyway, whatever you've been doing to our bed the last few nights, double it up on him. I swear it's becoming more uncomfortable by the day." Glow stretched her back to emphasize the point.

At this, Quince looked downright mortified. "I'm sure I don't know what you mean," she squeaked.

Mila frowned. Had she been sabotaging the bed in some way? The sweet maid didn't seem the type, but her days in Thornscarp were proving she couldn't trust everyone as she would have liked.

Before Mila could pursue the matter of her mattress, Quince dipped into a courtesy and hustled off in the opposite direction.

"Remind me to check the mattress later," Mila muttered to Puddi.

The gnome yawned and nodded.

Dawson led them back into the castle and toward the hall Mila and her ladies had visited upon first entering the castle. The halls were full of activity, guests and courtiers alike bustling to and fro while soldiers dashed out toward the grounds, packs and weapons at the ready. No one stopped them and no one gawked or giggled. There still might have been the occasional side glance from snooty ladies, but her days in the keep had tempered the worst of the half-whispered jeers and ugly glances.

Just as they were nearing the small flight of steps that led to the hall's entrance, Thak jogged up to the group. "A word, Your Highness?"

"I'm to meet the queen. I don't like the idea of keeping her waiting." In truth, she was afraid the news of his leaving would show on her face.

"This won't take long, I promise. Dawson, you mind escorting Ladies Puddi and Glowildeen to Her Majesty? Let her know I captured a moment with the princess. I'm sure she'll understand." He gave Dawson a look Mila couldn't read, and the winged guard dipped his head in acknowledgment, disappearing into the hall with her friends.

"You're wearing boots," Mila said.

"I am."

"You were right."

"I was?"

"The cobblers of Thornscarp appear to be very talented indeed."

He smiled. "They are."

"Dawson says you're going today with the Corps."

He stopped smiling and gave a brief nod. "There is a matter I need to attend to, yes."

"How long do you expect to be gone?" It wasn't a question she had any right to ask and certainly not one most heirs to a monarchy as vast as Gildernosh would even consider asking a guard of an opposing realm, but what she really wanted to know was if she would see him again.

"It's hard to say. If things go as I hope, no more than a week."

"But it might be longer." It wasn't a question.

"It's possible, yes."

Mila set her lips in a hard line, wondering what he had wanted to talk to her about.

"Your Highness—"

She cut him off. "And the prince?"

Thak stiffened, his lips turning down as he looked at her.

A moment passed before he asked, "What of him?"

"I assume he will be accompanying you as well."

"No." He cocked his head, and his eyes narrowed. "The queen has asked that he remain here for the time being."

"I see." But once again the words were a lie. There was so much Mila did not see. The prince staying while a royal guard left with the Corps made no sense to her.

She could see from the twitch of his lips he didn't believe her. "Do you now?"

Putting on her most queenly expression, she remained silent.

"I understand it must be hard to believe, but the prince really is doing his best with the position he is in. You'll have to trust me. Don't be too hard on him while I'm away."

She wasn't sure she wanted to trust him, but she recognized the request for what it was. A guard doing his best to protect the man he served. "I wouldn't dream of it. One of these days you'll need to tell me what it is between the two of you. There's a history there. I just can't decide if you have hate or love for one another."

"Most days it's a bit of both. I will tell you. All of it. In fact, I'd hoped to unburden myself to you today, but now. . ." He looked toward the doors and stepped closer and grabbed her hand, pulling her along behind him out of the main corridor and into a small alcove.

While Joaquine's earlier comments about her appearance hadn't meant more than the air it took to speak them, Mila was suddenly aware of how disheveled she must look. The previous evening hadn't been kind to her complexion, and the morning was crueler still. Her dress was rumpled, and her dark hair had been pulled into a messy braid that hung wildly over one shoulder. She grabbed the end and toyed with the loose untamed strands. Thak's eyes trailed the movement of her fingers, and he took her hand in his, stilling the action.

"This. . . We shouldn't be here," Mila said. If the queen sent someone to fetch her, or worse came looking for her herself, and found them together like that, it would be bad for Mila and so much worse for Thak. Nothing about his posture suggested he was merely guarding her.

"I'll not take much time."

"But if someone sees."

"They won't."

"But—"

"If you don't let me speak, you will be delayed and then surely someone *will* find us."

She nodded and looked up into his warm brown eyes. *Those*

lashes. The memory of his face under her fingertips the night before brought a flush to her cheeks and her heart thumped wildly in her chest. She was certain he must be able to hear it.

She cleared her throat. "What is so important that you'd risk this then?"

"I have buckets of things I'd like to tell you, but today is not on my side. Time and circumstance are forever my enemy." He blew out a short breath and scrubbed a hand over his face.

"Is this about the prince as well?"

"In a way, yes."

She needed to clarify. "Edonier, I mean." She wanted to ask if he was actually Gregor as she suspected but didn't want to put Thak in a position where he'd be forced to lie to her.

"Yes." He closed his eyes. "I want to explain properly." He stopped, struggling visibly to find the right words to express whatever it was he wanted to say. "I— Never mind. This isn't the time or the way to do this."

"Thak, you are going to drive me mad. Just tell me."

"I will. I promise. If you will in turn make *two* promises to me."

"Hardly a fair trade."

He smiled "I know. But as you are a good person, I'm sure you'll indulge me."

"All right, Thak. I will trade with you in promises if I can."

"I've tasked Dawson to watch over you in my place. If I could pry Niri away from the queen, I'd have asked her, but as she is the captain of the guard and Her Majesty's confidant and friend, it would have been futile to ask. I trust Dawson nearly as much. I expect him to keep you safe, so I'll ask you to promise not to make his job harder than it has to be. Stay away from that emissary as much as you can."

"I'll do my best, but surely you understand how it might appear if the heir to the throne ignores her country's representative entirely. I don't plan to be an absent monarch, and sooner or later I'll have to deal with him, no matter how unsavory he is. And the men he brought. By rights, those are *my* men."

"I do understand. It just makes me . . . uncomfortable. Thinking about you in that man's presence."

"I may not be the queen of Thornscarp, Thak, but I assure you I am stronger than I appear."

"I've not a single doubt of your strength, Princess, and two of *your* men are going with me, if you'll allow it." He swallowed as she nodded her agreement. That certainly felt as if he intended to be back before she left. "At the very least, keep Lady Glowildeen in your company. She's a right little demon with wings." Despite the terminology, Mila could sense his words for the compliment they were.

"There you can rest easy. I'm genuinely shocked she's allowing me this moment out of her sight."

He gave her a half smile but his brow furrowed again. As if not wanting to look her in the eye, he stared at the end of her braid and gently grabbed it, running the wayward strands through his fingers. "Your hair is perfect, you know. It doesn't need to be curly or straight."

The world gradually vanished around them. Mila reached up and took his chin in her hands. Despite her inebriation the night before, she hadn't imagined how soft the copper-tinted hair on his face was. He continued to run her hair through his fingers, not speaking or breaking the magic of the moment.

Mila knew this was not only dangerous. It was wrong. She'd promised herself to this man's prince, but in the moment, standing in the tiny secluded area of the castle, all she wanted to think about was Thak. All she wanted to feel was Thak. All she wanted for herself was Thak.

She'd never felt that way about anyone before and feared she might not again.

She would sacrifice for her people and marry a man she didn't love eventually. But not then. It had been nearly two weeks and Prince Edonier still hadn't shown. Or, if he had, he was either openly lying to her, pretending to be his brother, or avoiding her altogether. If he or the queen wanted to fault her for this moment, so be it. She would be a queen one day too. When the day came to forge that path, she'd do as she must. In the hall with Thak she was not a princess or heir, not a queen or betrothed. She was simply a woman.

And so she acted rashly. Reaching up on her toes, she took a small piece of something for herself.

Her subjects and lands, her proposals and promises, her title and duty. All of it fell away as she placed her lips against his and kissed him softly.

Thak's hand stilled where it held her braid between them, and she knew she'd made a mistake.

Pulling back, she readied her lips to deliver the apology as her hands fell from his face.

"Princess." His voice was low and pained.

She'd crossed a line and immediately regretted it.

"I. . ." But what could she say? Nothing would be enough for putting him in this position.

"Did you mean that?"

"Did I mean to kiss you? Is it possible to kiss someone by mistake?"

He nodded.

"I. . ." She would not add liar to the list of her sins. "Yes."

He nodded again. She moved to step back, but he tugged on her braid, wrapping it around his fist and using it to simultaneously tilt her head back and anchor her to him. And then he was kissing her—not softly as she had him—but fiercely and with the same savage strength she'd seen him exhibit in training and on the games field.

Fire blossomed in her belly and radiated to every corner of her body. Her heart pounded even faster, and she felt her legs turning soft beneath her.

He was possessive and hungry, pulling at her lower lip and moaning into her mouth. She kissed him back with an intensity to match his own. She kissed him as she'd never kissed another man. None of the foolish boys she'd known when she was young. Certainly not as she'd kissed her husband.

She pushed the thought away violently. She would not let the memory of Gidaeon sully the moment.

Tugging her head back further, he trailed a line of scorching nips and strokes of his tongue down her jaw and to the crook of her neck. She shivered and ran a hand up over his ear and into his hair, resting it at the base of the horn there. He shuddered and moaned against the delicate skin of her neck. Her knees wobbled.

She wanted nothing more than to stay tucked away in the tiny space they'd claimed, but they were playing a dangerous game. If anyone saw. . .

She pulled back, her breaths coming short and fast.

"Thak."

He'd rested one arm against the wall over her head but continued to hold her braid hostage. "Hmmm?" He tilted his face forward and rested his forehead against hers.

"You asked me to make two promises."

"I did." His breathing was as ragged as her own.

"What was the second?"

He sighed as he exhaled and stepped back from her, dropping her braid back onto her shoulder.

"Promise not to hate me when I return."

15

Troll Ta-tas

For three days Mila floated about the castle, untethered and unsure. She'd done as Thak asked and kept mainly to her room, venturing out only for brief walks on the grounds or to see if any news of interest had arrived. Glowildeen never left her side and neither did Puddi. She could tell they too were growing restless, but there wasn't anything for it but to wait.

Dawson had just as much cause to be anxious. Nox had been dispatched right along with Thak, but if the guard felt it, he didn't let it show.

"As I've told you, Your Highness, Nox and I have been down this path many times before." His grayish scales reflected the orangey glow of the sunset as he escorted her around the grounds yet again. "It's a skill anyone who loves a soldier must learn. There's always a chance he won't return, but I choose not to dwell on it. He does what he's been called to do and I love him for it."

She smiled sadly at him. "He's lucky to have you and you, him. I wouldn't mind that sort of love one day."

"Oh, Mila. You will, just wait until—" Puddi's words cut off with a sharp look from Mila. She'd told her companions about the moment alone with Thak, but they'd sworn to keep her secret between the three of them. The last thing she needed was for someone to get word of it and ruin everything. She'd like to believe Dawson would hold the confidence, but there was no way to be certain.

When Thak had left her in the hall with the queen three days prior, his guard face was back in place. If she hadn't been a party to their moment in the hall, she never would have suspected he felt anything for her at all. After checking to ensure Dawson was there to escort her after her meeting, he'd dipped his head to the queen and left. She hadn't seen him since.

If she'd hoped to get any sort of answers from Augustina, she was sorely mistaken. The queen informed her that Thornscarp's intelligence was able to confirm what Joaquine had said, Evansband's troops were on the move. They had reliable information that a small vanguard had already been placed in Yallring but that most of the soldiers were still amassing within the Evansband border. She informed Mila that Edonier was already on the move with a chunk of the Corps. They would not act to do anything other than ensure Evansband could not cross via the land border with Thornscarp. Given its access to the sea, however, this did little to alleviate Mila's fears.

When she'd inquired if Thak had gone with them, the queen deflected and would only tell her he was on an urgent errand for the king.

"I meant what I said earlier," the queen offered. "Given how this impedes your original request, I will be happy to have you stay with us as long as you see fit. Alternately, if you choose to return home now, I would understand."

Mila had thought about it, and against her better judgment,

she informed the queen she'd like to stay. Augustina nodded and Mila had returned to her rooms.

Over the coming days she did allow Dawson and Glowildeen to accompany her as she checked in on Joaquine and the two guards who remained with him. She recognized both men. They were well respected in her father's household, and while they were seasoned enough by Gildernosh standards, they had little to no chance of fending off even the average Thornscarp warrior. She could sense they knew it too. There was a tension in them each time she spoke to them, perhaps because they'd heard what had happened to Joaquine or perhaps just because of their surroundings.

"I believe it would be wise for you to make your leave sooner rather than later," she explained to the emissary. "The men who accompanied the Thornscarp troops can be sent home once they've arrived back. You'll need every able-bodied man should Evansband make their move."

"And leave you here to your own devices, Your Highness?" he asked. "I think not."

"Suit yourself. At the very least, you should send word so the Lord Protector doesn't worry over your safety."

"And what shall I tell him of yours?"

"What you see. I am safe and well."

"Perhaps a closer inspection is warranted. I wouldn't want to mislead your father."

"That won't be necessary." She pulled her shoulders back and looked down her nose at him. "If you so much as breathe in my direction without an invitation, I will ensure when I leave this place, I'll carry your balls back to my father in a velvet box."

Dawson snorted and winked in her direction. "I'll be sure to assist Your Highness. Lady Glowildeen can as well."

She wasn't sure when she had stopped being fearful of the people of Thornscarp. The transition had been slow and incremental, so much so that she'd barely noticed it. But she knew now she would trust Thak or Ograt, Dawson or Petra without thought. Perhaps one day Edonier as well. She couldn't say the same for her father's man.

"Thank you, Dawson. It's my hope it won't be necessary."

"It didn't take them any time at all to corrupt you, did it?" Joaquine asked.

"I'd wager, by your standards, I was already corrupted. So I guess we are in luck."

"My standards, Princess?" He looked at her coldly. "My standards are your father's standards. And your father's standards are those of Gildernosh. So my standards are in fact exactly what should concern you."

"I don't give a—" She turned to Glow. "How do you say it? Troll ta-tas? Yes. I don't give a troll's ta-tas about *your* standards, and neither does the throne I will one day sit upon." Mila turned on her heel and left the man to write his letter.

16

*U*nannounced and Unescorted

DESPITE SO MANY MEMBERS OF THE CORPS BEING GONE, THERE was still much to do in the high valley where the keep sat nestled against the foothills of the monstrous mountains. The spring thaw had come, and while the denizens of Thornscarp might not have the same vast fertile fields as Gildernosh, they had enough space to plant crops to get them through the harder months ahead.

The men and women who weren't soldiers all pitched in. They brought their children and anyone old enough and fit enough to help with the planting. When the queen mentioned this the following morning, Mila immediately asked if she could participate.

Augustina tilted her chin and looked at the princess with barely concealed surprise. "As it happens, you can. Although maybe not in the way you suspect. You'll want something different to wear. I'll have Quince bring you something suitable. Meet me by the gates in an hour."

That was how Mila found herself dressed in lightweight trousers with a thin long-sleeved tunic made of fabric that felt as if she were wearing a cloud. She was pleased to find several new ensembles in the stack the maid had left in her room. They were designed for various occasions and activities, but all looked and felt delicious.

Her role was entertaining the youngest of Thornscarp's citizens. Augustina was there as well as several older women and a group of courtiers she recognized from the castle. Mila wasn't surprised in the least to see Lady Annissa, with her horrendous claws and equally horrendous disposition, not far from the queen's side.

Dawson had traded his guard duties for a hoe as Niri could easily watch over things in his stead, and Mila was momentarily hurt when he told her she wouldn't be allowed to assist with the tilling and planting. It soon became clear her role would be no less exhausting or dirty. Who knew watching wee ones could be so daunting?

Puddi was thrilled to play a game of ducks and dragons with the tots. Glow, however, was much less pleased. Crossing her arms, she found a branch to perch in and monitor things out of reach. Mila scowled at the sprite but couldn't really blame her when she overhead a boy of perhaps six tell his sister he'd like to keep the pretty bug as a pet.

Mila found herself sitting in the grass with a girl no older than four years standing behind her. The child had the most beautiful golden eyes to go with her feline features. She was twining stems of mountain thyme and wild blueberry buds into Mila's hair, humming and singing to herself the whole time. When she deemed the princess suitable, she patted her head and took off to run in circles with her friends.

As Mila rose, a leather ball went soaring past her face and

into the nearby bracken. With little thought to her trousers, Mila waded in after it. It took several minutes and many inpatient calls from the boys who'd thrown it before she could locate it. Once she did, she began the laborious process of extricating herself from the vegetation. She'd almost made it when a rather unruly branch caught her ankle and sent her stumbling forward. Unable to save her balance, she ended up on her hands and knees in the grass.

A snigger from above had her craning her neck to see who would rather mock her than lend a hand.

To no surprise, Annissa stood staring down at her, clawed hands tucked behind her back and an ugly smile on her otherwise beautiful face.

"Looks like you've finally found your place here then, haven't you, Princess."

Mila heaved a sigh and rose to her feet, not bothering to engage with the hateful witch.

"Heads up, boys," she called as she threw the ball back to their waiting hands.

"Surely by now you must know he'll never marry you."

Mila didn't bother with a response, but it didn't discourage the other woman. "You're not good enough for him and certainly not good enough for Thornscarp. You can try to charm him all you like but mark me, you will fail. And when you do, I'll be here. Waiting. To stomp on your precious face with a smile and a bow."

Who exactly was she meant to be charming? These people and their secrets and half truths. Everyone seemed to be in on it. It had been weeks of this nonsense. Either they believed her to be worthy of him or, as Annissa was all too eager to point out, they did not. Whatever the queen felt, Mila wished she'd just end the secrecy. If Gregor was maintaining this elaborate charade, Annissa was right. Her charms were failing. Why not just cut her loose to return to her people?

"Ah, I've hit a nerve, have I?" Annissa smirked. "Good. I hope it stings. Eloise had the right idea. Maybe it's best she didn't succeed. I'd hate for her to get put to death for something as noble as keeping you from the throne."

Mila couldn't help herself. "Enlighten me. Other than me not being 'good enough,' why do you care so much?"

Annissa shrugged, a clear taunt in the movement. "The throne has always been mine and no one, not even a princess, will keep me from it."

Mila had heard enough. It was no real shock. She'd seen from the start how Annissa looked at Gregor. If anything, it only reinforced her theory about Edonier's true identity. She closed her eyes, blew out a breath, and shook her head to clear it. Nothing she could say to this woman would change her opinion. Leaving Annissa standing in the sun, she simply walked away.

After several games of toss the toad—not a real toad thankfully, but a bean-stuffed bit of cloth—and a stint of rocking a series of cradles while their occupants cried whenever she slowed, Augustina called the children into a circle. The oldest children looked as if she'd offered them the moon and stars. With only a bit of jostling for the spots closest to the queen, they settled quickly and stared at her with rapt attention.

Mila too found herself beyond curious.

As soon as they found their spots on the grass, the group—elderly matrons, jam-handed toddlers, injured warriors, a princess and her attendants, even the haughty courtiers—all fell silent and waited for the queen to speak.

"Long ago when the mountains were young and winters were wild, a traveler from a distant land arrived searching for the waters buried deep in the ground." Augustina's voice was regal yet warm. Her eyes found those in the group around her as she spun her tale. "He was a simple man and had heard tales of the magic the springs could convey to the worthy. The guardians of the springs were happy to take him to the tunnels that led deep in the ground in exchange for a story. 'But I have no story to give you,' the man said. 'Everyone has a story,' the guardians replied. 'I don't,' the man told them.

"The guardians asked him why he needed the magic of the waters, and he explained that he had been traveling for years, hungry and tired, beaten and broken. He explained that he longed for a place where he could feel welcome and warm, and the waters in the mountain would provide such a place. 'I wish to lay down my head and feel the waters comfort me, to nourish me, to welcome me home. Then I may finally be at peace.' Sensing that the man intended to go to the springs and find his end after such a long journey, the guardians felt sorrow for him. 'We will take you to the waters, but we will stay with you while you feel their embrace. We will sit with you in fellowship while they warm your body and your soul. We will feed you so that your body may find nourishment just as your soul does.'

"The man accepted their offer, but just as the guardians had hoped, after a time he did not long for his time to end. After a time, he longed for more than the hot springs. After a time, he was content to sit with the guardians. And after a time, he was ready to leave the waters beneath the mountain and join those who lived above."

The queen stopped and looked around once more at the rapt faces surrounding her. Sitting there with her long auburn hair in beautifully intricate braids and her onyx horns shinning in the sun, she looked every inch the elegant queen, but when she spoke, her voice was more of a warm mother imparting shared wisdom to her children. "And what do we learn from this?"

"I thought it was a story. Not a lesson," a gap-toothed girl said.

"Every story *is* a lesson if you listen close enough." The

queen winked at the child, and the girl nodded, a sage understanding on her face.

The queen glanced at the other children. "No one? That's all right. I'll tell you. We learn that even from the beginning, way back when the Cardinal and the Divine still walked among us, Thornscarp has been a refuge for those who need it."

Mila might have imagined it, but she thought Augustina looked to Annissa as she said this. The dark-haired woman either didn't notice or didn't care.

"Now, what story shall we have next?" Augustina asked the children.

Annissa rose from where she sat and approached Quince and one of the other castle maids. "The queen will be parched, and there's little water left. Can't you do things properly without being directed?"

Quince dropped into a short curtsy. "I'm sorry, miss. I'll go and fetch some now."

"Be quick about it." Her lips were tight and her voice low, but little escaped the queen's notice.

Augustina stopped her story about the first warrior to defend the southern border. "Is there a problem, ladies?"

"No, Your Majesty," Quince squeaked.

"Annissa?"

"I was just ensuring the maids knew you'd be needing refreshments."

"While I appreciate your concern, I have no such need at the moment."

"You are too gracious, Your Majesty. But the princess looks rather uncomfortable."

The horrid woman was trying to use Mila as an excuse for her treatment of the maids.

Augustina didn't look convinced. "I see. Well, if she is in need, Quince, please fetch whatever she may want. Perhaps you'd like to walk for a spell with Lady Annissa, Your Highness."

"Actually, I'm happy to help Quince." Mila shot a pointed look at Annissa. She didn't wait for the queen to acknowledge her statement, much less approve of it before standing.

Glow lifted from her branch, but Mila waved her off. "Quince won't let me get lost. Stay here and keep Puddi out of trouble."

The sprite followed her gaze to the group of handsome soldiers who'd been put out of commission from various injuries. The sprite heaved a sigh but nodded.

The pretty maid wore her customary grey uniform, but the way the sunlight glinted off her scales in iridescent waves made her look ready for a night of frivolity rather than a day of work. She led Mila up to the castle where they entered via the lower level side door. It was the same opening the princess often used with Thak when they were headed to the stables.

The pair took a familiar path until they reached a simple yet solid oak door Mila hadn't previously paid much attention to. The maid pushed the door wide and allowed Mila to enter before her. She took the lead once again as they headed down a straight path toward what sounded like a busy kitchen.

As they came into the large open space, Mila saw it was in fact bustling. Several cooks and a handful of scullery servants moved in a well-choreographed ballet of knives and ladles, pots and fire. Cold soups were decanted into sturdy clay dishes, and roasted joints of meat were pulled from spits to be sliced onto massive platters. Bread cooled on a rack and pies bubbled on an wide ledge behind the preparation table.

Quince stopped one of the servants and relayed the message from the grounds. More provisions were requested, and Lady Annissa in particular wanted it done quickly. The harried man gave an epic eye roll and long suffering sigh that would have done Glowildeen proud and glanced at Mila. Immediately his face balanced and his expression transformed into unabashed mortification.

"Don't fret on my account. I thought we were doing just fine."

The statement did little to reassure him.

Mila looked to Quince. "I'd rather not cause any undue distress. Perhaps I'll just wait until you're ready to return?"

The dark-haired maid smiled, her long snakelike tail swishing softly across the ground behind her. "Yes." Her voice filled with relief. "Your Highness, that might be helpful after all."

Mila returned her smile and wandered out of the heart of the kitchen, leaving behind the cacophony of clattering pans and chittering voices. The farther she walked, the rich smells of roasting meats and simmering broths gradually gave way to the heady aroma of fermenting fruit and aged oak. Similarly the steamy air began to cool, and the farther she went, the stones lining the walls took up a not unpleasant dankness.

Despite the cool and dark stone, the wall sconces continued to illuminate a welcoming path. She wondered briefly if she should go back, but she was intrigued and it didn't *feel* dangerous. Though to be fair, she hadn't sensed anything in Eloise to make her think the girl would try to kill her either. Thak's plea to keep Glow with her at all times tingled in the back of her mind, but she shut it out, telling herself she'd run at the first sign of something being amiss.

Around a last gentle bend in the tunnel, an open door framed wooden casks in the room beyond. She halted abruptly when the hunched form of a man partially straightened from one of the closer barrels. He rested one hand on the lid, the other on his lower back. His long wavy hair—gold threaded through with grey—hung to his shoulders, and though his back was to her, Mila knew instantly who it was. King Edon.

She'd stumbled upon the king in his wine cellar. Unannounced and unescorted. That could not be good.

These casks were likely filled with the same gloomberry wine which had so addled her just a handful of days prior.

Mila hadn't had a single conversation with the king since the first morning she'd presented herself to him and he'd laughed at her arrival and proposal. She'd seen him since then of course, but he always seemed more inclined to let Augustina do the talking for him. And more often than not, he was simply absent. She hadn't sought him out and clearly he'd done the same.

She wasn't sure she wanted to break their streak of avoidance just yet.

She turned to slip away before he noticed her lurking in the entrance. She made it all of a step before his voice echoed through the cavernous room.

"I'd let you sample some, but I'm told one of my favorite vintages took you quite unawares recently." His voice was gravelly and deep, but there wasn't any malice in it.

She grimaced and turned back to the king, dipping her head as she did. "It's a touch stronger than what I'm accustomed to, I'm afraid."

"You could probably say the same about most things here in the mountains." His voice held a chuckle once again, but rather than let it rile her as it had the first morning, she chose to smile along. It was, after all, the truth.

"You'll get no disagreement from me."

Edon stood to his full height and placed both hands on his back, twisting and stretching to relieve whatever kink had settled there. When he was loose, he walked to a small cabinet and removed a tall glass flask and small wood and bone spigot. He reached up near the top of the cabinet and tugged on a lever affixed to the wall. Far in the distance, Mila heard the sound of a tinkling bell.

The king returned to the wall of casks. "I have an idea."

She raised her eyebrows and turned down her lips, studying the man.

The king wore the same loose-fitting pants favored by many of the men in Thornscarp. His shirt was simple but neatly pressed, and his boots were the shiny black of onyx washed by river water. His tusks gleamed as if recently polished, and though he held no court or audience, his beard was tended and his eyes shone in the flickering torch lights.

She watched as he inserted the spigot into a barrel at mid height. One turn of the bone handle and lush teal liquid flowed into the flask. In the dim light it was darker than she expected, not unlike the sea before a storm. He filled the flask a third full and turned to her, swirling it as he did. Closing his eyes, he put his nose in the top and waved a hand at her to come closer.

Reluctantly Mila approached. She suppressed a smile as she noticed his tusks sitting just to each side of the tall thin glass. Perhaps it was custom blown for just such a purpose and just such a man. When his lids finally rose, he smirked as he noticed her noticing him.

"Perk of being the king. The artisans can design anything I fancy."

He handed her the slim delicate vessel. "Swirl it and then sniff. Tell me what it is you smell."

Mila did as he asked, a quizzical expression on her face. This was not at all the direction she expected her first private audience with the King of Thornscarp to take. Dipping her nose forward, she delicately inhaled.

"Close your eyes. It helps."

Letting her eyelids drop, she continued to take small sniffs of the swirling liquid. At first, it just smelled like wine—tart and sweet and tinged with alcohol. But as she focused, she sensed other things there too. Faint traces of oak but also vanilla. A touch of cherry and maybe truffle? Strangest of all was a spicy smokiness that reminded her of roasted peppers. She opened her eyes and explained it all to the king.

He grinned broadly and clapped. "Yes. Yes. Perfect."

She handed the glass back as a kitchen maid entered with a

large earthenware pitcher filled with a luscious assortment of chopped fruit and bright persimmon juice.

"Thank you, Tolly. And thank Glan for me as well. I know she's got her hands full today."

The maid curtsied and left soundlessly.

Edon dumped his flask of wine into the juice and gave it all a good swirl. The blue and orange liquids combined to create a dusky purple draught. "You'll find this a pleasant alternative until you become accustomed to the full gloomberry proof."

He poured a small measure back into the slender glass and handed it to Mila.

"It's better when it's been sitting together for a spell. All that fruit does wonders with the wine." One lip curled up, revealing more of the tusk beneath as she studied the concoction dubiously. "Go ahead."

She took a small sip and nodded appreciatively. "Quite refreshing actually."

"It is. It is. You know, your mother enjoyed the same preparation quite a bit."

Mila's eyes jumped to the king's.

"You didn't know we were acquainted."

It wasn't a question, but she answered anyway. "No. I didn't."

He smiled sadly. So different from the king she'd met her first morning there. Looking back, however, she wondered if perhaps he was the same and it was she who was now different.

"I'd like to say I knew her well, but that would be untrue. We had a working acquaintance. One I respected. She was the first monarch of Gildernosh in many many years who seemed eager to strengthen our political ties. I was . . . *disheartened* to hear of her passing."

"Thank you."

"It was a wasting illness, was it not?"

"Yes. I was only a tot, but I'm told it came on fast. The

healers barely had time to make her comfortable before she was gone."

"And your husband too was taken from you. My condolences. That's quite a bit of tragedy for one woman to bear. Tragic for you as well as your realm."

Mila elected not to tell him one death had been much more tragic than the other. He'd hear of it all soon enough, she supposed.

She took another sip of the fruit-infused wine.

"You should take it outside with you. Enjoy the rest of the beautiful weather."

"I'll do that. Thank you."

Edon smiled, and she realized the tusks might be terrifying but his smile was actually rather kind. Not mocking. Not sarcastic. She wondered again if she'd been too out of sorts at their first meeting and had poorly judged him.

She picked up the pitcher, meaning to head back to the kitchens.

"I do hope you're enjoying your time with us, Your Highness."

"I am." She found it wasn't a lie at all. "Please, Your Majesty. Call me Mila?"

"All right, Mila. And things are clarifying for you a bit?" He fiddled with the spout on another barrel.

"Clarifying?"

"With Edonier."

"Oh, well, I've yet to meet him, soooo. . ."

"Hmmm." He frowned. "I see."

She opened her mouth, but he held up his hands. "I'd help if I could, Mila, but I know when to stay out of the way. I might rule this kingdom, but only a fool would think I rule this family. It's why I'm hiding in here after all." He winked at her. "Despite how little they need it, Augustina has always been quite protective of the boys, and I'm not fool enough to get on her bad side."

17

Bravo

Mila couldn't sleep. No matter how she positioned herself, her body simply wouldn't get comfortable. After flipping from her side to her back and rolling to her stomach for the hundredth time, she finally gave up and slipped out from under the thick covers. Her companions had given up on the mattress and elected to occupy the cushions on the floor instead. They were both sound asleep.

Slipping on a robe, she crept to the door. Now that she knew exactly where the kitchens were, it should be easy to slip down and pilfer something soothing to drink. A glass of warm milk if she was able to find it.

Cracking the door, she peered outside. Dawson had retired for the night, and whoever the young guard with the curling golden locks was, he was snoring into his chest as he leaned against the opposite wall. She almost felt bad about not waking him. There hadn't been another attempt on her life in the past days, and she wasn't entirely sure she needed a guard for the short jaunt to the kitchen. As long he didn't wake or get himself into trouble by telling someone she'd slipped out past him, all should be well.

The castle was strange in the darkness. Lamps flickered along the walls, but without the boisterous sounds of courtiers and guests bouncing off the walls, the shadows that flickered were less playful and more menacing. She quickened her steps and navigated the path in no time.

As Mila cut through the smaller dining hall into the passageway to the kitchens, she thought she heard footsteps. Slowing her pace, she listened again. Nothing.

Firelight danced ahead of her. She could hear the humming of a lovely melody. It sounded oddly similar to the songs she'd heard Glow sing from time to time. Just as glorious notes reached a crescendo a second voice joined the soft humming. While the humming was melodic and perfectly pitched, the second voice was all scratches and crags. Oddly, it didn't harm the tune but rather added a layer of dimension that had Mila smiling as she listened.

The princess followed the voices like a trail of breadcrumbs and found herself in the flickering firelight and heady heat of the kitchen. Floating above a large iron stove, a sprite with spiky chartreuse hair and the same stone grey skin as Glow-ildeen sprinkled something into a small cauldron. The black pot bubbled and steamed, producing an aroma sent from the Maidens themselves.

Mila's mouth watered.

She didn't see whoever the second harsher voice belonged to, but she could still hear the jaunty notes. They were coming from a cupboard at the back of the room behind a sturdy set of shelves.

Not wanting to startle the pair but definitely wanting to

sample whatever was in the pot, Mila cleared her throat and stepped farther into the kitchen.

The sprite looked up from his pot and smiled. "Hiya, Your Highness."

Surprised he'd recognized her so quickly, Mila smiled in return. "Hello."

"What can we do ya for?"

Mila wandered closer. "I was just looking for something to help me sleep. Warm milk or the like."

"Oh, I think we can do you one better," the sprite said as he sprinkled more of the brown flakes in and gave the pot a stir.

After spending nearly three weeks tasting all the delicacies the kitchens were capable of producing, Mila was pleased by the notion of something better than simple milk.

"I'm intrigued."

"As you should be." A short woman with pewter hair pulled into a tight coil between the twin ram's horns on her head shuffled in from behind the shelves. Her voice was just as scratchy in speech as it was in singing. "Hemply," she snapped. "Have you added enough chocolate, boy?"

"You know I have."

"And what about the cinnamon?"

"Of course."

"And what about—"

"Yeah, yeah, Glan. I've added the pinch of pepper and the touch of vanilla."

"Hmmm. Let me try?" The old woman ignored the smirk on the sprite's face and took up a small spoon. She dipped it into the pot and sniffed it before blowing on it for half a breath and shoving it into her mouth. Mila watched all of this with a bemused look on her face but broke into a full-blown grin when the horned cook closed her eyes and moaned.

"Told ya." The sprite crossed his arms and winked at Mila.

"Well, what are you waiting for then? Grab the mugs."

Hemply did as instructed. One at a time, he wrangled three crocks from a shelf, two almost as big as he was and a smaller one just right for a sprite. He paused and grabbed a fourth. He ladled the thick sweet-smelling concoction into three of the waiting mugs and handed one each to Mila and Glan. His moves were deft for his size, and not a drop of the sweet-smelling concoction was spilled.

The cook clicked hers against each of the other two and raised it toward Mila. "To your health, Princess."

"Thank you," she replied and took a small tentative sip. Immediately she understood the woman's earlier reaction to the drink. It was sweet and spicy. It was warm and comforting. It was a warm hug and a hot bath and the best dessert she'd ever experienced. It was like nothing she'd ever tasted before.

"If you look like that after just a sip of cook's cocoa, I can't imagine what you look like after. . ." Gregor had entered the kitchen. "Never mind. I shouldn't be imagining that at all."

Mila flushed to her roots. "It's just. . ." She had no words.

"Yes. I am aware." Gregor picked up the fourth crock and held it out as Hemply filled it to the brim. "Apparently we do some things better than Gildernosh after all."

"Apparently."

"But you've had cocoa before, Your Highness?" Hemply asked, disbelief flavoring his words.

She shook her head. "I've never had anything like this."

"The cocoa beans only grow in the mountains," Glan explained. "They won't have the chocolate there on the coast."

"No. But I wish we did." Mila took another small sip and sighed. "Do you mind if I take this back to my room?"

"Why would we mind? You take all that you like, Princess." The old cook offered to fill her mug again, and she happily obliged.

"I'll walk back with you," the prince announced. "I've been meaning to chat."

The admission startled Mila. What could he have to chat with her about? Maybe he was finally going to own up to being Edonier. She had heard one of Quince's friends giggling earlier in the day about how *dreamy* Edonier was and how *absolutely wretched* it was not to stare when he walked by. She could certainly see how the woman could be referring to Gregor.

"That would be wonderful." She tried to keep a smile in her voice. "Thank you."

It must not have been enough of a smile. "Someone's not her normal chipper self," the prince observed.

"No, I daresay I'm not," Mila responded.

"And why might that be?"

"I suppose I'm tired. I've not been sleeping well." Mila turned from the handsome face of the prince and took another sip of her cocoa. "Perhaps this will help.

"Perhaps."

They walked in silence for several more moments.

As they came to the same alcove where she'd kissed Thak, the prince slowed his steps.

She looked at him as he set his mug on a small low table.

Mila didn't like the look in his eyes. It was a mix of anxious fear and resigned determination.

"I should be getting back upstairs," Mila said as she took several steps back and away from the prince. He matched her progress with slow predatory steps.

"What did you want to speak to me about? I'm tired and would like to get some rest." Mila stopped near the entrance to the alcove. Folding her arms across her chest, she lifted her chin.

"I was under the impression you wanted to get to know me better."

"I do."

"But you want to ask me something, don't you?"

"I have been wondering about something, yes."

"And what would that be, Your Highness?" He took another step closer to her.

"Who are you really?"

He smiled but there was little joy in it. "I'm the prince of course."

"Yes. But which prince?"

"Which prince do you believe me to be?" He was toying with her. Laughing at her.

"Are you Edonier?"

"Why would you think that?"

"Because it's been nearly three weeks and I've yet to meet him. Your mother seems happy enough to have me getting to know you though."

"And if I say I am? What then? Will you welcome me to your bedchamber tonight? Strengthen your proposal? Get me to fall madly in love with you?"

"No." She spat the word more than spoke it.

"So, you think the first time we have a private moment will be after we're wed?" He cocked one eyebrow up.

"No. But. . ." She didn't know what to say or how to get herself free of the conversation. He was the prince after all. She was the one who'd thrown herself into his path.

"But? Do you not find me handsome enough? Not princely enough? Or perhaps you wish I had horns and paws?" The prince said the last with a taunt in his voice and a smirk on his face.

Mila's eyes widened. If she didn't know better, she'd think the prince was jealous of Thak. Jealous of a palace guard.

Well, he should be. Thak was everything the prince was not. She could just imagine the look on her father's face if she returned home with Thak. Not only a chimera—the descendant of a demon if the story was true—but a lowly guard to boot. Despite herself, the thought sent a flood of warm bubbles cascading through every inch of her, body and soul.

All traces of that warmth fled as the prince took another step toward her. Mila refused to step back again. She didn't want him to get the impression she was running from him.

"Of course you're handsome, Your Highness. I'm sure you're quite aware of it. And I *would* like to get to know you better. I'm simply having trouble understanding why you think this conversation is best suited for this moment." She looked down and grimaced at her thin night dress. Not that half the women in this place wore much more, even to feasts and festivals.

The prince ran his tongue over his lower lip and stepped around Mila, circling her where she stood. "I'm happy you find me attractive, and I find this setting more than suitable. Aren't you curious, little princess? I may have the face of an angel, but maybe my other bits are a little more *demonic*." He raised his brows and grinned. Gone was the resigned anxiety he'd shown earlier. Whatever had pushed him to make this decision, he was all in now. Still, something in his manner felt not only forced but also false—a player on the stage. "Not that the other ladies have complained, but I'd hate for you to get a fright on the night of your wedding."

"With all respect for Your Highness, I'm going to have to ask that you leave me to return to my chamber." A shiver ran down Mila's spine as the prince continued his circling. He was drinking her in as he walked.

"Oh," he crooned and drew a finger down her shoulder. "I don't think I will. We should get to know one another. After all, a man likes to know what he's signing on for." He was all but admitting to being Edonier. Suddenly she felt sick. She couldn't go through with marrying him now. Not when this was how he behaved. His cruel indifference had been one thing. This was something else entirely.

The prince stopped his perusal and placed one finger below Mila's chin. Taking her mug out of her hand, he absently placed it on another small table. She pursed her lips as he tilted her face upward. "Let's see how desperate you are to protect your people, Princess."

The prince wrapped one arm around her waist as his lips came down on hers. Mila tried to turn her head, but the prince used his free hand to dive into her hair and keep her facing him. His lips were brutal, and the more Mila tried to fight him, the more he seemed to enjoy the savage kiss. She opened her mouth to scream, and he used it to his advantage, tugging roughly on her lower lip and chuckling as she gasped.

Mila managed to get her hands up between them and pushed against his chest, but the effort was futile. He certainly wasn't built like Thak, but he was sturdy enough. Out of other options, Mila did the only thing she could think of. With a ferocity she didn't know she possessed, she grabbed the front of the prince's tunic and used the stability of the hold to her advantage. She stepped back on one leg and drove her knee up as forcefully as she could into the prince's groin. The silk of her shift ripped with the thrust. The prince grunted and dropped his hands from Mila's hair and body, then doubled over trying to catch his breath.

Mila thought about running, but as she turned the prince caught his breath and started laughing. It was wheezy and winded at first, but the longer she stood there watching him the heartier it became. His hands were on his knees as he drug in another breath, the laugh continuing. "Thank fuck for that, Mila. Thank fuck."

She had no idea what he could possibly find so funny.

Heart still racing in her chest, she stared at him. Heat and anger mixed with a good dose of humiliation. Confusion flooded her.

"Oh, Mila. Bravo. I knew you had it in you." He stood slowly and winced as he moved his hands from his knees to his hips, turning and twisting in an effort to relieve his discomfort. "I had no right to do that. It was disgusting, and I'm revolted by myself."

"Perhaps you'd care to explain."

"It was never my idea. Not this bit at least." He grimaced as he finally met her eyes. "Truly. It's no excuse, but I'll only say I did it with the best of intentions." He motioned between them. "I just wanted my nightly cocoa, and you presented the perfect opportunity for one more of my mother's famous tests. I nearly thought I had you, but thank fuck for you. If you'd let me go through with that, he'd have killed me."

She raised her eyebrows.

"Not literally of course. Although. . ." He twisted his lips and cocked his head. "Maybe."

"Who? Who would have killed you?"

"My brother. Edonier."

Mila flinched back. "Your brother? But I thought you. . ."

He grinned and shook his head. "Nope. I'm still just Gregor." He picked up his mug and raised it to her in much the same way Glan had earlier. "Sweet dreams, Your Highness. I hope one day you can forgive me." He started to walk away but paused and looked at her once more. "And for the record, I can't wait for you to join the family."

Hot tears threatened at her lashes, but she held them at bay. "How can I join the family when I've never even met your brother?"

"Haven't you though?"

"No. I haven't."

"I think we both know that isn't true."

18

Secrets No More

THE TREK THROUGH THE LOW-LYING FOOTHILLS AND SOUTH TO the border where Thornscarp kissed both Evansband and Yallring had been uneventful. The Corps had made this journey many times before and likely would make it many times again. The clans of Evansband were a restless bunch, war and discord their constant pursuits. Generally, they took their energies out on one another, but every few years, they'd come together with larger designs on their minds. The Corps had quelled two ill-planned attempts to invade at the southern border in the past five years. The battles were generally brutal but over quickly, the clansmen sent back to their homes, tails between their legs.

It was no surprise they'd found the time ripe for another potential conquest, and to be fair, Thak was more than a little surprised they'd waited this long to set their eyes once more on Gildernosh. As much as Mila might protest it, it was clear they'd grown lazy on their wealth, choosing to buy their way out of trouble rather than attempt to build a populace that could defend itself. Moreover, a populace that *wanted* to defend itself. When you had others doing all the dirty work day in and day out, you started to think the laundry was hung and the shitters cleaned by the wind and wishes.

Up until a handful of weeks earlier, Thak would have been happy to let the clans walk in and help themselves to the gems and coin that never ceased to flow from those mines. With any luck the invasion might even expose some of the more unsavory aspects of how those mines were run and who exactly the Lord Protector was supposedly protecting.

Now though? Now as much as he'd like to turn a blind eye, it simply wasn't an option.

They were camped in an elevated vale. It was a spot they often used when things began to heat up at the border. It gave the captains easy paths to multiple choke points. They could divide the troops and defend entry into the southern mountains with few casualties to the Corps. They'd never utilized the position to keep the clans from traveling into either Yallring or Gildernosh. Thak, however, was worried the Evansband soldiers would be able to flow right past them. Ograt assured him it wouldn't be so simple. Yallring hadn't needed much encouragement to realize they wanted what Thornscarp wanted. Together, they could seal the passes and keep the bulk of the invaders within the borders of Evansband.

Unless of course they chose to invade by sea. If that was the case, there was little Thak or anyone else could do. It would at least buy Mila and her people some time to set up basic defenses at the port cities.

Gregor had seemed confident it wasn't at that stage yet. A feeler he'd called it. But in case he was mistaken, the prince assured Thak they'd send word to Gildernosh. The king and queen had agreed. It would have to be enough.

"Come on, old friend," Ograt said as he placed a hand on Thak's shoulder. "It's time."

"No sign of the giants?" Thak asked.

"Thank the Cardinal, no. At least according to the scouts."

"Thank the Cardinal indeed." The intelligence was murky on that one point. Evansband had been trying to recruit giants from the wilds. If they had even a few with them, the Corps could be in trouble.

Thak grabbed his helm and mounted his horse. Affixing it to his head, he and the rest of the Corps streamed down through the vale and into the paths of the unsuspecting conglomeration of Evansband clansmen.

The invasion was over before it began. The bloodshed almost nonexistent. Once the Evansband vanguard realized what they were heading toward, *who* they were heading toward, they called an immediate retreat. Messengers were sent. Intentions made clear.

Thak wasn't fool enough to believe it would end there. Gildernosh was just as ripe with coin as ever and just as reviled. The clans would regroup or Yallring would step in. For all any of them knew, the giants would be swayed or even Krith would realize an alliance with the clans could be to their mutual benefit. The feeler had failed, but once the smell of war was on the wing, it took more than one rebuke to quell it completely.

A battalion was left to camp in the vale. It would be enough for now to keep things in check, but a larger strategy would be needed.

Thak was running through options in his head when he saw the men Joaquine had brought with him from Gildernosh. It had been the queen's idea to have them accompany the Corps. A gesture of goodwill she'd called it. Thak could appreciate sarcasm when he heard it. If they could see how the invading forces quelled at the might of Thornscarp's warriors, it would remind them why it was better to be Thornscarp's ally rather than enemy.

Now the men sat on a log, well back from the bulk of the Corps. They had bowls of stew in their hands, but their heads were bent together, whispering and grumbling. Every now and then, they'd shoot a furtive glance in his direction, and he could guess what exactly the topic of conversation was. It made no difference what they said. Let them speculate. Let them wonder. The moment he set foot back in the castle, all of his secrets would be secrets no more. He would make sure of that.

Later, when he was wiping the blood of one of the Gildernosh guards from his hands and face, he realized it might make a difference after all.

19

Nothing Scandalous

Everything the queen does is a test.

The words had never felt truer to Mila than in the days following her strange encounter with King Edon and even stranger encounter with Gregor. It was as if several more layers of ice had melted off the royal family. Their hearts might not have been completely warmed to her, but they were certainly on their way to thawing. Augustina was more apt to engage her in conversation, and while Edon remained hidden away more often than not, when she did see him, it was easy to return the smiles offered to her. Gregor, while still aloof and at times brash, was no longer downright hostile. He seemed almost *friendly.*

That hostility was left to both Lady Annissa and Joaquine, although for different reasons.

It had become abundantly clear the claw-handed witch hadn't had her eyes set on the handsome Gregor at all. It was Edonier and the crown he was to inherit she wanted. The dark-haired beauty seemed to be everywhere. Lurking in the halls.

Strolling in the gardens. Casting nasty looks with her eerie yellow eyes over candlelight and dinner dishes. The fact that her cousin still sat in a cell awaiting the decision on what should be done with her didn't help matters.

As for Joaquine, Mila could sense he'd like nothing more than to grab her and forcefully drag her back to Gildernosh and her waiting father. Each day that passed seemed to ratchet his frustration into ever-tightening coils. On more than one occasion she'd suggested he leave, but he refused to return empty handed.

On some level, Mila could relate. She too wanted to return triumphant to her home. For her, triumph meant having a prince at her side. For Joaquine it meant her at his side alone.

"How much longer do you suppose?" Puddi lay back on the grass, twirling the end of her long golden braid. "I've heard the gossip. They say the prince was seen on the road yesterday. Surely it can't take that long to settle things and for him to come find you."

It was another glorious day in the scenic realm. The air perfumed with mountain blooming wildflowers. The light clear and unmarred by dust or unhappiness. It seemed most of the castle's occupants were outside enjoying the sublime atmosphere or else they'd heard the same rumors and were waiting for the Corps to return.

Sprawled out on a linen-covered chaise a little way down the lawn, Gregor was shirtless and holding court to a small group of rapt women, Annissa among them. His magnificent bare chest was still not enough to keep Annissa's attention solely on him and off Mila. Hate radiated from the woman in waves. It was surely a gift of some sort, that level of animosity.

A group of adolescent boys jostled and rammed against one another. All fussy horns and gangly limbs. A group of adolescent girls—all shiny scales and flowing locks—pretended not to notice them.

"I've no idea." It wasn't just that Mila was anxious to finally meet Edonier. She was concerned. Very concerned.

Promise not to hate me when I return. The words hung over her head. Why would she hate him?

She's always been protective of the boys. Surely the mighty Prince Edonier didn't need to be protected. Did he?

I can't wait for you to join the family.

The gradual warming of the family to her.

Everything the queen does is a test.

Why would a palace guard need to travel with the military to the border? Because perhaps he wasn't just a guard after all but the *head* of the military. The man the soldiers loved and revered.

Her head was swimming. She knew what she wanted it all to mean, but that line of thinking was foolish and would get her nowhere. She'd been wrong about Gregor, and surely she was wrong about this too. But if she wasn't? What then?

That would mean he'd been lying to her all along. How could she ever trust him after a deception of that magnitude?

Or worse, if she *was* wrong and Edonier suddenly materialized to take her hand in marriage while she had these feelings for Thak, she would be subjected to seeing him and his warm brown eyes and his battle-scarred hands and his imposing horns day in and day out. What if she had to live everyday pretending what she felt for him didn't exist? What if? What if? What if?

"You all right there, Mila?" Glow asked. The sprite had been practicing with her dirk, chasing bumblebees and slicing milkweed fluff out of the air.

"Just distracted."

"Mmm-hmm."

Puddi rolled and faced her. "You could take him as your personal guard and consort, you know. It's done all the time."

"I . . . what?" Mila gaped at her gnomish friend.

"Thak. Take him as your . . . I don't know. What's the word for a male mistress?"

"Puddi!" Mila scolded. "No."

"It's actually not a bad idea." Glow looked thoughtful. Her friends had no idea of the thoughts she'd been having, and there was no chance she would bring her suspicions to them at the moment. "We see how he looks at you, and after your little dalliance before he left, it's obvious you at least like him a little. Who would have thought?"

"I will not take him as a paramour or consort or lover"—she flapped her hand as she tried and failed to come up with the proper word—"or whatever. I just . . . I couldn't. I will honor whatever vows I make. It wouldn't be fair to Thak. Can you imagine what would happen to a guard found with the prince's wife?"

Glow snickered. "At least you aren't denying it."

"And it wouldn't be fair to Edonier."

"Or to you, Mila," Puddi said softly. "Maybe you should call the proposal off. After everything that happened with Gidaeon, you deserve some bit of happiness. Maybe it's with Thak."

"I can't."

"Why not?"

"Because we need this."

As if on cue, a door from the castle slammed, and Joaquine, accompanied by his two remaining guards, strode out into the gardens. The group of boys stopped their antics and sneered at him. The girls stopped their feigned indifference to giggle viciously as the men from Gildernosh walked past. Mila sat up straighter but refused to rise from her position as the man came to look down on her. Let him. It meant nothing.

"Your Highness. This has gone on long enough." No sense in being civil then. "I must insist we leave for the coast tomorrow with or without the men I sent along at the request of Edon."

Mila wondered what the two Gildernosh guards had

thought of traveling with the Corps. "As I've told you, you are free to go."

"And as I have told *you,* your father and your people expect more from you." The sunlight picked up on the scalp beneath the thinning blond strands atop his head. She wondered, not for the first time, if in his youth he'd ever met the ideal for physical standards he so willingly placed on everyone else. Or if he was one of those petty men who thought they could judge without being judged themselves. She leaned toward the latter.

"My people expect me to lead one day, Joaquine. That is precisely what I am doing."

"They would rather see you in a grave next to your mother and your first husband than to ascend the throne like this." He spit the words at her, disgust written all over his face.

Mila rose in one fluid motion, causing him to back up a step. "Be that as it may, I will honor my word here. If that means my people despise me as they rest safe and whole in their homes rather than bending a knee to whoever wishes to invade, then so be it. At least I will go to my grave knowing I did what must be done. For my people."

"Well, this is all rather exciting, isn't it?" Gregor had strolled over without Mila noticing.

What he'd done still sat in her like an ugly bruise. Part of her knew she'd have a hard time forgiving him for it, but another part, a curious and devious part, wondered if it wasn't really for the best. Sure, she hadn't openly invited his advances, but it was like the act had ripped back the curtains to allow the first rays of light into the gloomy secrets the family was keeping. He seemed different toward her now. Not the conspirator she'd once hoped he'd be, but not her enemy either.

"Hello, Prince Gregor." Puddi put a hand over her eyes to shade the sun as she smiled up at the form of the shirtless prince. Mila could practically see the gnome salivating at the sight.

To his credit, the prince didn't laugh or scoff. He simply dipped his head in acknowledgment of the woman lying at his feet. It was quite a shift from the haughty man she'd come to expect.

Joaquine turned to leave, but before he could go, Gregor placed a hand on the older man's shoulder. "Running off so soon?"

"I have nothing further to say."

"Perhaps you could tell me about life in Gildernosh. I've heard it's a feast of excess. Silk and gems and women and wine." Gregor didn't bother to glance at Mila as the face of the spoiled prince returned, and she was left wondering who the real Gregor was. The man cozying up to her father's emissary or the man who'd applauded her rejecting his advances. Either way, he was a master of the mask and she would do well to remember it.

Joaquine eyed Gregor shrewdly. By all appearances, Gregor was a suitable man for the likes of Gildernosh. Not a trace of chimera on him. No fangs. No hooves. No problem to associate with in public.

"Yes," he said slowly. "All of that is true."

"I'd love to visit one day. Your fair princess hasn't even offered the barest morsel of information. Not a drop." He frowned as he glanced at her. "And no invitation to visit your fair realm either. And yet she asks for much from us."

"That's not fair," Puddi exclaimed, all hints of her earlier admiration gone in a flash.

"Isn't it?" He turned fully to Mila. "What do you say, Your Highness? Have you offered up anything of real value in your time here? I don't mean your elegant hand in marriage."

Something in the way he looked at her over Joaquine's shoulder suggested she agree with him. Once again she was in a game she didn't know the rules to but felt it best to play along anyhow.

The men remained standing, so Mila did as well. She refused to lounge about while this conversation took place.

"I thought it wise to secure an alliance before I spilled state secrets, Your Highness."

"State secrets? Interesting. Is the death of your beloved Gidaeon a secret then?"

"I've made no attempt to hide his death from anyone." Surely Gregor would have heard the stories by then. She had neither the energy nor the desire to discuss it all again.

"Ah, such a tragic event," Joaquine crooned.

"So I would imagine," Gregor said.

"She hasn't spoken of it?"

"There is much she hasn't spoken of."

"Must I remind you both I am right here?" Mila looked from one to the other.

"No reminder necessary." Gregor looked at her flatly.

Joaquine smirked. Mila hoped this was all an act on Gregor's part. She was finally coming around to the idea of not loathing him, but at the moment he was making it difficult. If it was an act, however, it working wonders on her father's man.

"As you might know, Gideaon was handselected for Mila by her father, the Lord Protector. He was a fine upstanding member of a rather wealthy family in the south of Gildernosh. He had the temperament to deal with the princess and an unwavering loyalty to the crown. The union was one the people had no choice but to adore, and we were all hopeful it might result in the heir needed for the princess to ascend."

Glow grumbled something that sounded suspiciously close to troll shit and was rewarded with a scathing look from Joaquine.

"Sadly for all of us, Gideaon died in a tragic accident before such a thing could come to fruition."

"Accident? Nothing scandalous then."

Joaquine's brow creased, and he looked cautiously at the prince. "No. Why would you suggest it?"

Gregor hooked his thumb toward Glowildeen. "I can imagine this one offing a man in his sleep."

He smiled and laughed, and soon Joaquine was laughing right along with him. Mila wanted to defend her friend, but again, something told her to stay her tongue.

"No, no." Joaquine waved his hand through the air. "A merchant ship he was sailing went down off the coast, and there were no survivors. It happens. We tried to convince him he didn't need to continue to travel with his goods, but unfortunately the man had trouble relinquishing control."

"And he'd tired already of his new bride, I suppose." Gregor grimaced as he said the words, an apology etched on his face.

Joaquine took no notice of it. The emissary's smile was smug as he asked, "Can you blame him?"

Mila realized Gregor's apologetic expression wasn't for her alone when a smooth deep voice behind her answered, "Yes. I very much can."

 Bird in a Cage

IN THE PREVIOUS DAYS, SOMEONE HAD DELIVERED TO MILA'S chambers several more gowns and sets of loose-fitting pants with the intricately twisted bodices. She looked down at the ensemble she'd donned that morning. Made of shimmering lightweight material, the color of ocean mist, it was rather more revealing than Mila was accustomed to. Dipping low in the back and snug through her breasts, the decadent fabric set off both the deep ebony of her hair and her bright green eyes quite nicely. When Thak greeted her, his reaction to the gown couldn't be masked and Mila was forced to raise the back of her hand to her lips, effectively concealing her smile.

If she looked pleasing to him, it was nothing compared to how she felt at seeing Thak in the bright afternoon sunshine. His boots were scuffed and his tunic dirty. A long line of bruising traveled from his left temple to the corner of his jaw. Mila's hand moved to touch the tender flesh there. She stilled herself before anyone noticed. She had no inkling of who'd inflicted the wound, but she despised them all the same. He didn't carry his helmet—it was likely tucked away somewhere with the rest of his gear—but his magnificent horns were capped with tarnished silver sleeves. She assumed they were meant to protect the tips from shattering in combat, and immediately she wanted to know what sort of conflict they'd seen.

His eyes were red rimmed and spoke of days with little sleep. She wondered if it was from the travel, the conditions, or something deeper.

Promise not to hate me when I return.

He dipped those silver-tipped horns in her direction. "Your Highness." His voice was tired and worn. Whatever he'd seen, whatever he'd been sent to tend to, it had not been easy and it had not been kind. She knew this without asking.

"You're back."

"I am." He studied her face. "It suits you. The sun on your cheeks."

A tantalizing mix of relief and longing flooded through her.

She found herself wanting to tell him of all the odd things she'd experienced in the days since he'd departed. In the days since she'd kissed him.

She wanted to ask him about the children and the stories. About the king and his self-imposed banishment to the gloomberry wine cellar. About Gregor and Annissa and Joaquine and the queen. Mostly she wanted to tell him what she suspected about Thak himself and watch to see if his face shifted or tensed. If he'd deny it or laugh. She wanted to tell him she hoped she was right, because if she was wrong, she didn't think she could choose marrying Edonier and protecting her people over being with Thak and protecting her heart.

"Where are my men?" Joaquine's voice was ruthless, and she longed to shove some sort of rag in his mouth to silence him. Preferably one retrieved from the bottom of a latrine. "I meant it, Your Highness. Your father will be displeased if we linger any longer. Once I have a full report from the border, I expect to be on our way."

The guard turned his eyes on the emissary, and any hint of warmth evaporated from their depths.

"Perhaps we can continue our conversation about all the finer things I might expect on my first visit to Gildernosh while I help you locate them." Gregor was all smiles and good spirits.

Mila sensed Thak relaxing as Joaquine reluctantly gave in to the prince and the pair headed off in the direction of the stables.

Thak's gaze followed them, and a chasm formed between his brows. "You're leaving?" he asked Mila. Hurt laced his obvious fatigue.

"I've no intention to at the moment. No."

"No?" Slow realization dawned on his handsome face, and it was his turn to look relieved.

"I believe I've held up both of my promises, and I expect that conversation you owe me."

"Perhaps you'd like to go somewhere more private, Mila," Puddi suggested helpfully and winked. "We'll just be here enjoying the sun."

When Glow agreed with the gnome, Mila rubbed at her ears, not sure she'd heard correctly. "Make no mistake, big man, I'll hunt you down and slice off your balls should the need arise," Glow added.

Thak nodded. "Understood." It was only then, before he motioned for her to walk with him, that he looked around and bit out, "And where in the name of the Cardinal is Dawson?"

"He's around here somewhere. I told you I upheld my promise. And so has he. I've barely been out of his sight."

"There shouldn't be a barely. He should have stayed with you every second I was gone."

"Every second? That would have gotten a bit uncomfortable for both of us when it came to enjoying the ridiculous hot spring taps in my bathing chamber. Though, I suppose he needs to bath too at some point. Puddi would have enjoyed it, I'm sure."

She looked at him and was shocked to see he wasn't the least bit amused. "I'm only joking, Thak."

"It's not that." He pinched the skin between his eyes. "I just . . . when I left, there was quite a bit I wanted to say. Things you need to know. You're light and smiling now, but you won't be soon."

"Did something happen?"

"Lots of things happened. Nothing I couldn't handle, but I've been worried about you."

"Worried about me? As you said, the castle was far safer then venturing home and likely infinitely safer than wherever you've been." She glanced again at the bruising along the side of his face. "Dawson has done an excellent job, I assure you. Wait til you hear about our encounters with Joaquine and Annissa and your—" She stopped herself before she could finish that sentence.

Preoccupied as he was, it didn't seem to register that she'd cut off abruptly. "Annissa." He grimaced. "I hadn't thought she might give you trouble. I should have. What with Eloise. That was an oversight on my part."

"So they are related?"

"Cousins."

She nodded thoughtfully. "That does explain some things." She tore her eyes from the bruising on the side of his face and noticed they'd made it nearly to the castle entrance. "Where are we going?"

"I need to speak to the king and queen, but I was hoping to make a detour to my chambers first. I need to change."

Mila had never been to his chambers. She didn't even know where they were. But as they entered the castle and headed toward the stairs, another bit of certainty clicked into place. The direction they were headed didn't feel like a path to a guard's dormitory.

He'd stepped in front of her as he led her down the hall.

"Thak?" she asked as she studied the ridiculous muscles stretching across his back.

"Yes, Your Highness?"

"We're back to Your Highness again?"

His lips pulled tight.

"I see." She lifted her eyebrows and bit her lower lip. "Why does the royal family trust you so much?"

"How do you mean, Princess?"

"Well, for starters, you've been given the task of watching over me. No chaperone, no interference from others? I'm not saying you aren't trustworthy, but does it not seem odd you're taking me to your chambers alone? Anything could happen."

He looked at her over his shoulder, and Mila once again found herself wanting to trace each freckle. Feel the tickle of his thick lashes against her face. Kiss his full lips.

"Anything?" he asked, a hint of a laugh in his voice. Finally.

"Yes." She crossed her arms and slowed her pace. "I could make up any number of things to say, and who would be the wiser?"

"You and I both know you aren't going to make up an outlandish story. Lady Puddi, perhaps, though I don't know that I'd be the seducer in that tale."

Mila chuckled. That might have been true weeks before, but now her friend knew Mila might have feelings for Thak, she'd never dream of it.

"Even if you did," Thak continued, "I've known the king and queen a very long time. They'd certainly trust my word."

"I see. How long is a very long time?" she pushed.

"More years than I can say." It was an evasive answer. "Now, Princess, what happened with that odious emissary of yours while I was away?"

He was changing the subject. She wanted to push him more. His answers felt true but not entirely complete. She decided to try another tactic. Maybe he didn't want to speak openly while they could still be overheard.

She gave him the briefest of versions about her conversations with Joaquine. She told him of Annissa and her quest for the throne. At this the skin around his eyes tightened and his lips thinned. She told him an abbreviated version of her time with the king and mentioned that Gregor seemed to be warming to her, though she deliberately left out the details of how that came to be.

She recognized the route they were taking and was shocked to realize it was the same path that led to the blue room. To her room. When Thak stopped one door down from her own, something bubbled up inside of her. All this time. He'd been right next door. Right next door and she'd never known.

She couldn't find words as Thak placed his hand on the center of the pine door. His flesh was scarred and calloused, bloodied across two of the knuckles. Dirt and grime from the road marred the skin and sat embedded under his nails. The wood shivered and the pine muttered a subdued "enter" and swung wide.

He pushed the door open and stepped aside, giving her space to proceed before him.

The room was roughly double the size of the space she, Glow, and Puddi had been occupying. While theirs was done in soothing shades of blue, Thak's was all in rich browns and creamy caramels. On the wall opposite the door, large windows looked out over the training grounds and farther up onto the village. The purple-tinted mountains were a smudge against the deep cerulean sky. Long cream-colored drapes framed the glass and were tied back with thick golden ropes. Ropes also tied back similarly hued curtains on the massive four poster bed.

Mila had never, *never* seen a bed that large. It made sense, but still.

Where her bed was piled high with comfy pillows and thick comforters, his was sparse and neatly made. The sheets were tight and tucked in on all sides.

The fireplace took up one corner next to a door she presumed led to a bathing chamber like her own. Above the mantel a set of crossed battle-axes gleamed as if they'd been hewn and polished the day before. A desk sat in the other corner. Neatly stacked papers and a handful of books rested atop it. Above the bed hung a large oil painting of the same mountains the windows looked out upon—the colors just as vibrant, the lighting just as glorious.

It wasn't this painting that her eyes fell on, however. It was the one beside the desk. The one taken down from the wall and turned toward the wall.

"You asked me before if I felt like I was sacrificing myself, my happiness, for this union. Do you remember?" she asked.

"I do."

"And I told you, I'd do anything for my people. But even still, I didn't feel it was a sacrifice."

He nodded.

"I wasn't lying. It didn't feel like a sacrifice at the time. But now? I wonder if I could ever be completely happy marrying a man I don't know. I've done that once already, you know."

He dipped his head and blew out a breath, staring at the floor. He looked up and followed her eyes to the portrait facing the wall. "I need to tell you something." He gestured to a plush high-back chair, and she dropped into it wordlessly. He walked to the small table set with a carafe of ordinary wine and two glasses. He poured one and handed it to her and took a long pull from his own. He turned and walked back to the other side of the room.

Mila, not liking the tone of his voice, took a tentative sip of her drink and placed the glass on the ground near her feet. She turned her head, but from her position, all she could see was the thick corded muscles of his back. Sighing, she sat forward.

"Go on," she prompted.

"I. . ." He turned toward her and ran a palm up his forehead. "I don't really know how to explain this."

There was a tightening around his eyes. "I'm afraid—after everything you've gone through these past weeks—that when I tell you, you'll never want to speak to me again."

"Thak." She stood and crossed the room to him. "You were the first person in this entire kingdom to treat me with kindness and decency. Or at least that's how it felt to me. Now I wonder if I only saw what I expected to see. But that's not the point. What I'm trying to say is I'm sure it can't be all that bad."

He shook his head, pain etched on his handsome face. "Do you recall the first night we talked? I told you everything the queen does is a test?"

"Yes. I've thought about that statement no less than a dozen times since. And then you prompted me to lie to her about not sleeping well, of all things. I still don't understand why that would be important. Is there a stone under the mattress or some other ridiculous thing?"

"You've heard about that custom then?" He smiled faintly. She hadn't heard about the custom, but now she was even more resolved to pull the mattress from the frame when she returned. "No. The queen thought you a spoiled girl who only likes pretty things. You're from Gildernosh after all." He winced as he said it. "She listened to her Master Covert and was convinced you could never understand the people of Thornscarp and our chimera nature. You should be disgusted by us. By this." Thak raised his hand and indicated the horns protruding from his temples.

Mila's hand acted on its own. She watched as it lifted and gently stroked the vicious horn from the edge of the metal casing the tip down to the base where it disappeared into the loose waves of Thak's hair.

The big guard closed his eyes, and a shudder ran through him. "Mila," he groaned.

"Sorry," she whispered. "I shouldn't have done that."

Thak took her hand, which disappeared in his much larger one. "If you do that again, I'll not get this confession out of my mouth."

"Why does that make me very much want to do it again?" Mila smiled. "When I first came here, I didn't know what to expect. And yes, it was a bit unnerving when we first met. Not just you. When I first laid eyes on Niri. The scales *with* the feathers? She is terrifying."

Thak chuckled.

"But then I got over my initial shock, and I got to spend time with you. I realized that if *the prince* were half the man you are, I wouldn't care if he had a tail and a forked tongue." Mila wanted to outright ask him about her suspicions, but if he was going to tell her—and it seemed that might be where he was going—she wanted him to do it in his own way. "Just look at Gregor. I think we're starting to see eye to eye, but for the longest time. . . He's beautiful to look at, but he didn't make a good first impression." She wrinkled her nose, and Thak grunted in agreement. "I still don't know why I'm lying to the queen though."

"She dangled that handsome bastard in front of you. She was concerned. Thought maybe all you cared about was a shiny handsome prince. You should have been able to rest easy, even if you knew nothing about him. Perhaps you'd even give up on Edonier and make a play for Gregor. If you thought Edonier might *look* like Gregor and you could sleep easy without meeting him, you would have failed the test. If you were worried about marrying someone who was easy on the eyes but treats you poorly, maybe there's more to you. Maybe you'd pass the test."

Mila suddenly understood. The queen wanted her to fail, and what better way to fail than to agree to a marriage based solely on her desperation and what she saw on the surface?

"But what does that have to do with you?" She wanted to get him back on track.

"I'm part of the test, Mila."

"She wanted to see if I could put your appearance aside and still spend time with you?" she guessed.

"Yes, but it's a little deeper than that."

"Tell me."

"When you asked Gregor before if he had a say in the decision about the marriage, he told you a partial truth. In his own way, he has more a say than you'd think."

Mila nodded.

"He doesn't have a full say. But I do."

Mila's heart fluttered in her chest. A bird in a cage. Rose petals in the mountain breeze. Sprite wings in battle.

Thak looked away from the question in her eyes. "The royal family trusts me with you, Mila, because I am *part* of the royal family. Thak is short for Thakeri. It's a family name. My mother's family. My full title is Prince Edonier Thakeri Thorn. Otherwise, I'm known as Prince Edonier the Mighty of Thornscarp."

21

No More Tests

A STORM SWIRLED IN MILA'S HEAD, AND SHE WAS HAVING TROUBLE focusing. While she'd begun to suspect as much, hearing confirmation directly from Thak—from Prince Edonier of Thornscarp, she corrected herself—still rocked her. Maybe it was in the way he made it sound like he knew he was in the wrong, or maybe it was her own self-preservation, or maybe it was the reality that she was going to marry a man who had been disingenuous from the moment they'd met. Maybe it was all of those things or none of them, but suddenly she wanted him to take it back. She wanted to live in ignorance for just a while longer.

Memories rushed back to her from the previous weeks. Thak escorting her through the kingdom. His love for the villages and the people. The easy way the guards and soldiers interacted with him. The queen's trust in him watching over Mila during her time among them. All of them mixed and shifted and blurred in her mind.

Thak was Edonier. Thak was who she'd offered herself to in marriage. Thak was the one destined to be King of Thornscarp and who could help her protect her own people.

It was no wonder Gregor had laughed at her when she'd asked him if he was Edonier in disguise. It still didn't explain his terrible attitude toward her or why the queen thought to test her in this way, but she was beginning to see the pieces all come together.

Just hours ago she was so convinced she'd wanted this, but knowing it suddenly made her feel like a fool.

"Your Highness. Mila. Say something. Please." His tone was anxious.

"I . . . I don't know what exactly to say," she finally responded. Mila stood and walked a looping path around the room. "I was beginning to figure it out. That you were him. But the rest? I just can't see why you'd do it. I don't understand. You've been lying to me. All this time. You let me believe you were just a guard and that the prince was . . . away. Or avoiding me. And then Gregor and the kiss. If you're the prince. . ." She trailed off, remembering what could have happened if things had gone differently with Gregor. Her stomach turned.

Thak stilled and closed his eyes. Hands clenched in fists at his sides, his voice was calm. Quiet. "Gregor and the kiss? What kiss?"

She didn't answer. Couldn't.

"What kiss, Mila?'

"I. . ." She was at a loss.

"You just used my brother's name and the word kiss in the same sentence."

"It was. . ."

He slowly opened his eyes, and she felt his stare down to her very toes.

"It was?" he asked.

"It was nothing. A test. I don't know." The words came fast, and she was angry that he was angry. After all the lies and the deceptions, now he was angry about something she didn't want and hadn't asked for and had dealt with in the best way she knew how.

"Fucking Gregor. I'm going to throttle them both."

Throttle them both? Who was he referring to. Was he angry with Dawson as well for not being there?

"It wasn't Dawson's fault. The man needs to sleep sometime, you know." She wouldn't let the guard get into trouble over this. Not when Thak himself had quite a lot to explain.

"Dawson? I'm not angry with Dawson."

"But you're angry with me?"

"No." His eyes widened and the corners of his mouth turned down. "Not in the least."

"Well, you're clearly angry with someone."

He scratched absently at his beard, looking at her from under hooded eyes.

"I am. But not with you and not with Dawson. Why don't you tell me what exactly happened."

Mila wanted to do nothing less than recount the story. There seemed many, *many* more important things to discuss. Like why Thak had pretended all this time to be a mere palace guard and how in the love of all that was good, they'd managed to get an entire kingdom to go along with it. But she did as he asked and told him about her wandering to the kitchen, the bliss that was warm melted chocolate in a mug, and her run-in with Gregor. She admitted that the encounter was leaving her conflicted. He'd kissed her and attempted to seduce her, all without her encouraging him in the slightest. The queen in her wanted to punish him for the offense, but then he'd apologized which had at least seemed heartfelt. And he'd been more open and much less unpleasant to her since. Not in a way that she felt he wanted something from her, but in a way that felt his prior attitude had been no more than an act. She also mentioned how she'd suspected Gregor was actually Edonier. The admission was met with an expression Mila could only place somewhere between amused and repulsed.

"That bastard. He's not just a prince and not just my brother. And I think I might hurt him very badly after what he pulled."

"Not just your brother?" Mila was growing more agitated. "What is he then?" She'd known of Gregor of course. He had a very different reputation from Edonier. The feckless younger brother to the mighty soldier was known throughout the kingdoms as a young man who loved the drink and the ladies a bit too much.

"Gregor is what we call the Master Covert. Head spy. Keeper and finder of secrets. If I am the kingdom's brawn then he is its brain."

That was . . . surprising. Every bit she'd heard about him had led her to believe him to be a irresponsible and spoiled man, more interested in wine and women than in secrets and espionage. It seemed Gregor was a better actor than she'd given him credit for.

The entire time they'd been toying with her.

Thak ran a hand over his face again. "It was actually his idea. This whole stupid charade. When his men scouted you approaching from Yallring, we assumed it was for one of two reasons. Alliance—as my father had hoped—or seeking sanctuary. For a brief moment Gregor considered you were being sent here as some sort of official delegation, looking to recruit for the mines or as mercenaries. It was his idea to have me unavailable to greet you. My mother jumped on the plan and here we are."

She thought she'd been falling in love with him, was *worried* she was falling in love with him even.

"All this time you were playing with me. And what if I'd given in to him? Would you have laughed in my face and thrown me out? Was that your mother's test or yours?"

"No. Mila. I swear I didn't think he'd ever try something like that. That she would ask it of him. He is nothing if not loyal, and despite what you rightfully think of him, I can't believe he'd have taken it further."

"But this is all some big game to you and your family." Mila moved to put some distance between them and paced the room again. She'd been so sure she wanted Edonier to marry her and sure she'd wanted this secret revealed, but now that he was laying it before her she just felt . . . betrayed.

"Mila, please. I know you're hurt. You have every right to be incensed. But listen to me." Thak—no, Edonier. She needed to get accustomed to calling him Edonier—came to stand near her. "This wasn't my idea, but I willingly went along with it. It was the wrong thing to do. I realized that when you'd been here no more than a day or two. You deserve better. My father said the thing would crash down around us, and he was right. But while my mother may have gone about things wrong, she did it for the right reasons."

Mila spun to face him. "The right reasons? You can't be serious. What reason could possibly justify my humiliation like this?"

"She is protective of our kingdom. She is also rather protective of me."

"As if you need protecting! Everyone knows the stories of Prince Edonier. The prince, the man, the legend. Beloved by his soldiers and bane to those who oppose him on the battlefield."

"I am a force *at war*. I'll not deny it. But you have no idea how many lovely young women have walked through those doors claiming to be of royal blood. How many fathers from other realms have paraded their daughters in front of my parents, only to turn green when they see me and realize it's a monster they thought to unite with their precious daughters. How many nobles from within our own borders have presented themselves because they think gaining the seat at my side will somehow allow them to act in unsavory ways."

"Unsavory ways? This Thak. This is unsavory. You're no better than they are."

"You think I don't know that? I know what I've done. And it is killing me." His voice broke, and Mila's rage lost some of its edge.

"It's because they don't know you. The real you," she said.

"Some do. Some don't. Most—like Lady Annissa—don't care one way or the other as long as I give them the throne they want."

Gidaeon's face flashed in her mind, and she understood exactly what he was saying. Mila softened even further, making his next whispered words sting just that much more.

"And would you have taken the time to get to know the real me before you fled from my sight that first night?"

"Of course," she responded immediately but paused. "Or, at least, I think I would have."

She thought back to her arrival at the castle and how her tears had flowed once she was alone with Puddi and Glow in her chambers. Niri with her scales and feathers. The soldiers and courtiers with fur and tails. Even sweet Tryn and his tufted ears. And Thak. Thak with his massive horns and padded paws. It was only after being around his quiet confidence and gentle grace that she'd gotten past those things. Maybe the queen had been right. Maybe she didn't deserve him at all.

The prince—prince and heir of Thornscarp—must have seen the conflict on her face. He stepped forward and placed a gentle hand below her chin. He tilted her face upward and looked into her eyes. Mila felt that look all the way in her toes. "I understand if you can never forgive me. But I certainly hope that you might."

"It's a lot. I'll not lie. There are parts of this that hurt more than I care to admit right now. But I'll try," Mila said. "But I think it's only a fair trade for you to try to forgive me as well."

"And what do I need to forgive you for?"

"For being angry. For coming here, to your home, begging you to marry me. For treating you as I have been treated in the past, even though I know how that feels. It seems maybe being queen might change me from the sort of person I thought I was."

"Hmm. Not many of us are always the person we strive to be. But we keep striving nonetheless." He ran his hand from her chin up the side of her face and into her hair. "If it helps to sway you, Ograt considers you magnificent. He's called me an ass from the onset of this thing. He can barely stand to be in Gregor's presence, and they've always been practically brothers. Though I believe it's truly Lady Glowildeen he's overly fond of."

Mila chuckled and melted into his touch. She raised her hand, and once again let her fingers trail from the tip of his horn down to the base. He groaned in response.

"It's a bit comical when I think of it. I wasn't sure you didn't already know who I was. It seemed as if you were just playing along, trying to find the right moment to reveal you were on to us. You seemed so scared of me the first night. Like you were wedding yourself to the devil and trying to keep a brave face. It took a handful of days for me to realize it wasn't an act at all. I watched as your fear melted away and you stopped seeing all of this." He ran a hand in the air from the top of his horns cascading down toward his paws. "You were just seeing me. I was so close to telling you. At least a dozen times. But my mother wanted to keep putting it off. Just one more day. One more conversation. One more test. She can be . . . stubborn at the best of times."

Mila nodded and raised her brows. "Mmm-hmm."

Thak chuckled in response.

"What should I call you?" she asked. "Your Highness, as you insisted with me? Thak? Edonier?"

"My subjects call me Your Highness—so definitely not that. Edonier is my formal name, but my family and close friends call me Thak. If you wish to do the same, I won't object. But"—he closed his eyes as she stroked her hand down his horn again—"I'd really rather you call me your husband."

Mila started in surprise. "Are you agreeing to my offer then?"

"How can I refuse? You're courageous and kind. You're dedicated to your people, and I'm sure you'll be the same with mine. Add in your beauty, the way you look in that thin silk gown, and what you're doing to me right now"—he sighed as she stroked her hands down through his hair and over his shoulders—"and you certainly pass the test."

"You'll need to tell me where you went. No more secrets. I want to know who did this to your face as well."

"No more secrets," he agreed. "No more tests."

Her hands stilled. "But could you love me?" She hated the uncertainty in her voice. The vulnerability.

"I already do, Mila."

She released her breath on a giddy sigh. "That's unfortunate," she responded seriously. Thak frowned. "I can't marry a prince when I've already fallen in love with a royal guard."

She sent him a teasing smile.

Mila yelped when Thak wrapped his strong arms around her and lifted her off her feet. He carried her to the bed and cradled her as he climbed onto the mattress and lay down with her on top of him. Mila didn't wait before she stretched along his solid body and kissed him. He tasted like warm spiced wine, and Mila could envision herself getting just as drunk on him.

Thak shifted below her, and she pushed up onto her elbows.

"You know, I think my mother has done something to this bed," Thak grumbled and reached under the mattress, retrieving a large heart-shaped stone. He raised it and showed it to Mila.

"What on earth is that?" she asked.

Thak grinned as he shook his head. "I thought you'd heard the old grannies' tales. It's an old superstition in Thornscarp. If you place a heart stone in someone's bed, their true love will be revealed." He shrugged. "Knowing my mother, I'd be shocked it there weren't several dozen below your own mattress."

Mila smiled down at him. His expression turned from light and teasing to hungry and intense in a blink. Gone was the blank face of a guard. She wondered briefly if her own expression gave as much away or if he'd been able to read her better than she had him.

She ran her fingers up over the bruises in a featherlight touch. Then back down along his jaw. His beard was more unkempt than she'd seen before, the red tint darkened by days on the road, and something told her he'd be happy to get into a hot bath and wash the travel off soon. She'd let him. In just one minute more.

She trailed her fingertips over his lips and then to the cup of his ear until finally they ran through the tangled dirty mess of his short chestnut curls.

"I was so unnerved by these before. But they really are stunning." She ran a finger down the length of one massive horn." He didn't speak as she felt the smooth texture. "I know you need to clean up and see your parents." Her hand returned to his hair, her eyes never straying from his face.

"I do."

"Now?"

"Soon." He let her study him. He lay still beneath her body as she traced over his features again. She ran a finger around the base of the horn at his left temple, and he closed his eyes with a shiver.

"How soon?" She dipped her lips to his and kissed him gently.

"Soon."

"That's a shame." She kissed him again.

He groaned and lifted his head from the pillow enough to kiss her back. She asked and he answered.

He was gentle at first, but then the hunger that had been in his gaze unleashed itself and he was devouring her. He was her breath and she his. He was strength and steel and determination. Perhaps she could be those things to him in return.

She kept one hand in his hair and moved the other to his chest, tugging at the fastenings of his tunic. She wanted to feel his skin beneath her fingers. To know this was real and not another lie. Another test.

She was frantic now, grasping and tugging. Thak broke the kiss and placed his hand over hers, stilling her movements. "Mila, stop."

She groaned. "Why?"

"I don't want you looking back on this and regretting it."

She pushed back as if slapped.

"Why would I regret it?" Her heart pounded, and despite herself a cruel sort of suspicion crept under her skin, coloring her words. She hadn't been good enough for Gidaeon. Maybe. . .

Thak sat up and took her face in his hands. "Because I've just told you we've been deceiving you for weeks. You might be relieved now, but tomorrow, you may not feel the same. I'll not add to the confusion."

She was more than a little stunned. She was hurt. Hadn't he said he wanted her still? If she could forgive him, why wouldn't he let her? "I'm sure I know my own mind, Thak."

"I'm sure you do too. But let's just wait, hmm?" He grinned. "I'm not going anywhere. There'll be time. For all of this. I promise."

She felt color flood to her cheeks. "Of course." She pushed up from the bed and away from him. "I'll let you get cleaned up then."

"Mila. Wait." He was scrambling to his feet, but she was already out the door.

22

The Trap

HE'D KNOWN THIS ENTIRE STUPID CHARADE OF GREGOR'S WOULD end badly. His brother was incredibly smart but could be wildly stupid at precisely the same time. He'd argued against it, but his mother had thought it a brilliant strategy: get the girl to fall in love with him, not his title. Only then would he truly know if her feelings were real. Whether he would love her back was also taken into consideration. If she'd turned out to be a sniveling pampered dolt, he could beg off without it causing any ugliness. They'd simply say Edonier had never made time to journey back to the castle and the queen would refuse her on his behalf. If his identity happened to be revealed years down the line, they'd deal with it then.

Convincing the populace to go along hadn't been terribly difficult. Those in the castle protected him fiercely on most occasions, so having the days prior to her arrival to ensure everyone knew not to address him as the prince was simple enough. For those in the village, he'd simply keep himself apart as much as possible.

He hadn't loved the idea, but he'd not really fought against it either. Because he was a fucking fool.

There'd been that one brief glimmer of hope when she'd seemed to work past all the deception and half truths and tried to understand why his family—why he—had done what they'd done. That flash of what could be. It had shocked him. She was not at all what he'd expected from the heir to the Gildernosh throne just as he likely wasn't what she'd expected from a brutal prince.

The brutal part was true of course, but only when it was required. All the stories the denizens of Thornscarp helped to propagate, all the lore of demons and monsters, and the talk of devils and debauchery, it was a necessary evil. One designed to keep the people of his kingdom safe and protected. He wasn't ashamed of wearing that persona. When it came to defending his people, he'd wear it and live up to the title on the battlefield. He was, after all, good at killing. When he needed to be.

Of course he'd known what she'd thought about him the day she stumbled in out of the rain, all soaking wet hair and eyes as big as moons but trying for all the world to look as brave as she could. And he'd known what he'd thought of her as well. They were both wrong. It had taken only a handful of days for them to start peeling back the layers of preconceived judgments and long-held prejudices.

And he knew weeks ago he should have come clean. But he'd waited. And waited. And waited some more. It would have been easy. He saw that now. And when he'd finally told her, sure he would hurt her beyond repair, she'd been angry, but part of him could tell she'd already figured it out, and once she'd worked through it, there'd been that glimmer. That flash. And he felt so euphoric, he thought he'd continue to do the right thing—and he'd hurt her even more. Because for all his skill with an axe or a crossbow, for all his brilliance with strategies and formations, he was terrible with words. And because he hadn't thought about her past or how doing what he thought was the noble thing would make her feel rejected when it was the last thing he wanted to do.

He scrubbed his hands over his face and yanked the silver tip protectors from his horns.

He was overdue to report to the king and queen. The delay would have been worth it had Mila not fled from his chambers. It *was* worth it, he chided himself. To hold her. To kiss her. For her to know who he was. Who he *really* was.

But now he needed to get himself in order and get up to his parents' private rooms. Right after he bathed. They'd forgive him his tardiness.

Thak stripped off his jacket and tunic, custom leather boots and pants—all stiff with sweat and grime from the previous days. Someone had the foresight to have a maid fill his tub with hot water straight from the spring taps, and despite the time it had been sitting, the water was still blissfully hot on his road-weary muscles. The sound that rumbled from him as he sank in up to his chest was half groan and half sigh.

The cedar-scented bar soap lathered easily, and he used it to scrub away not only the oily sheen from his skin, but also a thin layer of self-doubt. He would track Mila down as soon as he'd spoken to the king and queen. He would tell her exactly how he felt. About her. About himself. About all the things he hoped for them together. It might take days, weeks, months for him to mend the fragile thing dancing between them, but mend it he would.

She had come there seeking a reliable alliance, and he would ensure she had exactly what she needed before she left. If she chose to rescind her proposal, he would accept it. It would hurt more than he wanted to think about, but he would do it. More than that, he would still stand beside her and her queendom, the entire Thornscarp military at his back.

The tub wasn't specifically designed for him, but it was large enough to accommodate his physical presence. He submerged his head completely under the soothing waters, knowing full well his horns were likely still protruding above the surface. When he finally emerged, it was with a renewed sense of calm. If he could stare down his foes on the field of battle, he could damn well face his own emotions and his fears for what might come.

He pushed up from the tub, and water sluiced over his body and puddled at his paws. He'd like to trim his beard but simply did not have the time. He grabbed a clean linen shirt and was buttoning his fresh trousers when a knock came at the door.

"Your Highness?" a pinched feminine voice asked.

Fuck. Annissa. What did the manipulative woman want now? He wasn't sure exactly how many times he'd had to tell her she wouldn't be getting more than a passing word from him, much less a proposal, no matter how she tried. He'd never misled her. Never given her any indication he was the least bit interested. Yet she persisted. Every damn day she was popping up in the hall or at his mother's table. She was in the garden sunning herself or at the training grounds strutting by. She was in the kitchen when he wanted a quick bite or in the stables when he wanted a quiet ride out in the hills. He never invited her. Never flirted with her. Had certainly never bedded her. And still she dogged him over and over and over again.

And then her hellion of a cousin thought it wise to attack Mila. Likely under some deluded premise that the princess was in some way usurping her place by his side.

"One moment," he answered, doing the best he could to keep the vitriol from his voice. He pulled his shirt closed and finished fastening the buttons, not needing to give her *anything* to take as a sign of his interest.

When he pulled the door open, Annissa stood glancing back and forth up the corridor. It was furtive. Thak didn't like it. Frowning, he dipped his head out and looked toward Mila's room. The last thing he needed was for the princess to see Annissa lurking about. Who knew what she'd make of it. Thankfully there was no sign of her. Just Dawson, standing sharp and attentive and all too much like he was trying not to see what was happening.

"You need to come quickly, Your Highness." Thak's frown deepened. As far as he knew, no one had given the all clear to address him as such. She should have still been treating him as if he were just another castle guard. He was opening his mouth to tell her as much, when she interrupted him. "It's that odious Gildernosh emissary. He's lost his mind. I saw him cornering the queen, going on about harboring that woman. He looked as if he might do something rash."

"Did you call the guards? Where the hell is Niri?"

She flinched back from his tone. "I . . . no. I don't know where she is. I just thought of you. It was foolish, I know. But I'm always thinking of you." She tilted her head down but looked up at him under her lashes.

He took a deep breath, already heading toward the stairs. As much as he disliked the woman, he understood why she'd come to him instead. Foolish? Maybe. But also understandable given her previous actions. He glanced back at Dawson, and the guard sent him a questioning look. Thak nodded. "Tell the princess not to answer the door for anyone."

Dawson knocked, and when the door cracked open he spoke in a rushed tone before the oak clicked shut again.

Annissa bit at her lower lip. "Maybe he should—"

Thak didn't let her finish. "Where are they?"

"In the wine cellar."

"The wine cellar?"

She nodded.

That made little sense. The cellar was his father's lair. His mother rarely ventured down there, preferring to let the king have something for himself. A space he could go to escape. Even from her.

Annissa must have seen the confusion on his face. "We were in the hall when he appeared and told her he wanted to sample the king's famous gloomberry wine. He was spouting some drivel about taking a bottle home for the Lord Protector. The queen told him he could sample some at the feast this evening, but he insisted. Since the king wasn't available, Her Majesty agreed to escort him. I went along, of course, but when things became heated, she signaled for me to leave. Presumably to fetch assistance. I shouldn't have. Left her, I mean."

"The queen can handle herself, trust me." He wasn't sure why he was trying to reassure her. She *shouldn't* have left. And Niri should have been there as well.

Nothing about this made sense, but he had no time to question it. Dawson joined them on their descent down the steps.

He realized later what an error he'd made. He should have questioned it. He should have called for Ograt or more guards to accompany him. He should have left Dawson at his post. He should have seen Annissa for the viper she was.

He did none of those things. Instead he walked right into the trap she'd so easily laid for him.

23

*A*verage Oak

If Mila hadn't jumped on Thak and made him show her a good time by now, there was no hope for her. Puddi and Glow had given her ample time to get down to business. Puddi understood her hesitation. She was destined to be queen and all, but the poor girl needed to experience some of life's more tasty activities. And that guard was certainly tasty. Her previous husband? Not so much.

If Mila couldn't have Thak for forever, she should at least get to have him for now. The problem, of course, was just how decent and earnest the tall hunky thing was. Puddi knew it was more than possible he'd see it as a betrayal of his duty or a compromise to his morals to take advantage of the visiting princess. And as much as Mila might want to, she wouldn't put him in a position to betray his kingdom or his prince.

While Puddi herself had flirted with the man, she hadn't been serious in her attempts to have him pay attention to her. She was never serious. Life was full of scrumptious men and seductive creatures. She wouldn't be blamed for dipping her toes into the pool of available partners every now and then. But if she ever did settle down, it would only be after Mila had found her one and only. Her partner for life. Her happily ever after. Then, and only then, would Puddi look to do the same. And as much as she was fine with experiencing all the possibilities she could now, she was certain her happy match would come in the form of another gnome.

For now though, the day was growing short, and Puddi was growing hungry. She wanted to freshen up before the celebratory feast. The Corps had returned, and with it all those fine-looking soldiers. It was time to get back to their chambers, check in on Mila, and get them all ready for what could be a very enjoyable evening.

"I hope she doesn't sacrifice her happiness again," she mused.

Only Glow was close enough to hear her, but she knew her surly friend would agree. The surly bit was just an act. The sharp words and salty glares just a way of covering her real feelings.

"Me too." The sprite sighed. Her magenta hair fluttered in the breeze.

How many times had Puddi herself wished for hair the same color as her friend's? Too numerous to count.

Glow wouldn't look at her as she asked, "Do you think Evansband will really invade?" Puddi rarely heard Glow sound worried or unsure. The sprite quickly added, "I mean, it's more important for Mila to go where her heart takes her. I'd never argue against that. But if she backs out of the engagement to Edonier and the clans are able to get their filthy hands on the assets back home. . ." She didn't continue. She didn't need to. Puddi knew exactly what she was thinking.

They'd both had their share of heartache and ugliness before being sent from their respective realms to serve as offerings to

Gildernosh. Puddi often suspected they had been bought rather than graciously volunteered by their own realms, despite being titled political liaisons. Neither could believe their luck when they became ladies to Mila. She was kind and forthright. She'd treated them as long-lost sisters rather than as servants. Puddi would never get over it.

But for Glowildeen, the exchange might have saved her life. She never talked about it in detail, but every now and then, some little truth would spill from her tiny lips and she'd get that feral gleam in her eye. Puddi knew at those moments, Glow was remembering some horrid bit of her history. Puddi was sure to be extra *extra* until the sprite settled and she went back to the grouch they knew and loved.

The fact that Mila had welcomed them with such joy and grace? It had sealed the sprite's allegiance so completely Puddi knew the idea of her birth nation taking any small bit of it away would be seen as an abhorrent possibility.

That wicked gleam was back. Puddi didn't say anything. She opened her arms wide, and the sprite floated in for the briefest of embraces.

"Would you look at this?" a voice boomed behind them. "Wonders never cease, huh? I knew you had the heart of a true warrior under all that bluster."

Glow didn't miss a beat before lifting both hands into the air and throwing Ograt a very vulgar gesture.

The bald soldier laughed from his belly. "It isn't a bad thing, my wee fiendish friend."

Puddi looked to Ograt and was surprised to see him standing with Gregor. So far as she knew, the two weren't particularly close. She never saw them converse, only barely acknowledging each other when they passed, always tense and on occasion close to pained.

"What happened at the border?" she asked. When Ograt

glanced at the prince, she added, "Or are you not allowed to say?"

"We can fill you in as we walk," Gregor said.

Ograt proceeded to enlighten them on the events of the previous week. They in turn updated him on the random bits of happenings from within the castle, carefully avoiding the more salacious details that happened to involve the prince in their company. For his part, Gregor seemed thoughtful when it came to Mila's story about both Annissa and the king. Neither he nor Ograt were exceptionally surprised by either of the encounters.

They'd made it inside and were heading for the stairs when Puddi said, "I still don't understand why Thak was needed with the Corps."

Ograt grimaced, but Gregor remained stone-faced. "That's a bit complicated."

Glow crossed her arms and lowered her chin. "Still don't trust us, do you?"

"No. Not entirely," Gregor answered. The simple statement should have been hurtful, but for some reason, the way he said it, openly and without any sign of deception, made Puddi respect him a bit more.

"But if we ever earn the trust of the realm, you'd tell us?"

"I would indeed."

Glow scoffed.

"Look." Gregor pinched his brow, and Ograt grinned. "I have it on reasonable authority that by the end of the day, some of our secrets will also be yours. Mila will have all the answers she needs, and perhaps we'll form this tentative alliance you so desire. Until that time, let us keep quiet a little longer."

As soon as his words were out, the man in question appeared down the hall. Dawson was at his side, but Puddi frowned when she realized it wasn't Mila who accompanied them. It was that wretched Annissa. Thak didn't see the four of them, focused as he was on getting wherever he was heading. He wore the expression of a man on a mission with little time or thought for anything other than his goal. Dawson caught sight of them, a frown on his face. He gestured for them to follow but didn't wait, determined as he was to keep up with Thak.

Puddi glanced up at Ograt and Gregor. They both had thunderclouds in their eyes. Given their earlier conversation, she wasn't the least bit surprised.

"Well, Your Highness," Ograt's voice was serious and low. "I don't know about you, but I don't like the looks of that."

"Nor do I. My brother loathes being anywhere near the harpy. Can't blame him."

Puddi startled. Brother? He *definitely* just said brother.

She was opening her mouth to ask him what the Maidens he meant by it but snapped it shut at the prince's next words. "And where is the fair Princess Mila?"

Glow cursed at the implication of Mila being in jeopardy.

Ograt dipped his head to the door Thak had disappeared behind. "We best not tarry if we mean to find out."

Gregor thought for a moment, a war of emotions on his face. "I don't suppose I could ask you ladies to accompany Ograt? If need be, you could fetch assistance. I'd like to check on your lady myself."

Puddi wanted to go with him and ensure Mila's safety with her own eyes, but Gregor was swift and she was not.

Glow seemed to be coming to the same conclusion. Her wings beat faster as she flew down the corridor to catch him. "If I hear tales akin to the ones from several days past, prince or no, I'll gut you from balls to gullet."

He nodded but didn't slow his pace. "I don't know what this is about, but something doesn't feel right. Be prepared for anything."

Ograt drew his saber and Glow her dirk, and she turned from the prince. Gregor took off at a sprint for the stairs.

Ograt was moving toward the door. Puddi had to jog to keep

up with his longer strides, but Glow was able to stay ahead of them all, lest they lose sight of the trio.

"Where's this go?" Puddi's voice came in short breathless bursts.

"It's the back passage to the king's wine cellar. Not many use it." He wasn't breathless at all. "Most avoid the cellars completely, but if they don't, they go through the kitchens."

They pushed through the door, and Puddi was immediately struck by the depth of the inky darkness compared to the bright sunshine they'd experienced only moments before.

She could hear muffled voices up ahead, but try as she might, she couldn't make out the words, only a pervasive sense of urgency in the tone.

Lamps dotted the smooth stone walls, and the gnome felt an off-kilter reality as they raced in and out of pools of light.

They were coming around a gentle bend when a door slammed in front of them. Glow pulled up just in time, narrowly avoiding getting crushed by the heavy oak. Thankfully, one of the lamps rested this side of the wood, allowing them to see in the dim light.

Ograt twisted the handle and pushed with all of his considerable force, but the oak didn't move an inch.

"Is it sentient? Can you speak to it and have it open?"

"Average oak, this one," Ograt said. "Plenty thick and just as sturdy."

"Ssshhh." Glow had flown up next to the door and placed one tiny pointed grey ear against the wood. "Did you hear that?"

Puddi didn't know what she meant, but then, through the wood and the gloom, it came to her. A muffled shout. Grunts and tumbles. Flesh hitting flesh. A groan, then a curse, then silence.

Whatever was happening behind that door, it wasn't good. Glow spoke for them all when she spun toward Gregor and said, "We need to get in there. Now."

24

$\mathcal{T}$he Horns and All

This wasn't right. He knew it wasn't right, yet he continued to march toward the wine cellar, Annissa just steps behind. It never occurred to him to keep the woman in view. It never occurred to him she would be any sort of threat. Not to him at least.

Thankfully, Dawson had a brain in his grey-scaled skull. The younger guard never took his eyes from her, walking half a step to the right and behind her.

As they came to the cellar door, Thak turned his gaze over his shoulder. The movement had one horn skimming the wall, a faint hissing emitting as the dense keratin scraped like flint upon the stone. Annissa was trying to see past him into the room filled with barrels. Dawson looked ready for just about anything.

The faint echo of footsteps sounded from up the corridor,

and Thak's senses went on high alert. With any luck, it was Niri coming to Her Majesty's aid.

Annissa looked from Thak to the door and moved, pushing past him and into the cellar.

He had little choice but to follow. Dipping his head, he slipped through the threshold, Dawson right behind him.

More lamps were lit in the open damp space, and Thak knew the moment his eyes roamed the room he'd miscalculated. Badly.

There was no sign of the queen. Of course there wasn't. Unlike him, his mother was not a fool.

The moment Dawson entered, the door slammed shut behind them, and Thak heard a soft thwomp as Dawson grunted, the air leaving his lungs in a rush.

Annissa stood several feet away, clawed hands clasped behind her back and a ridiculous smirk on her face. Next to her stood that fucking Gildernosh bastard, Joaquine. He had the balls to look pleased with himself, as if he'd pulled off the most elaborate plot in the history of Thornscarp. Prince Edonier was all too happy to pull something *off him* instead.

He made it all of one step forward before he felt the strap sail through the air and over his head. It tightened. A leather noose around his neck.

"It's not just mines in Gildernosh, you know," Joaquine said, voice dripping with boredom. "There's the ports all along the coast. *And* we've got the best lands for farming and agriculture too. Ranchers and the like. Apparently taking down a steer is the same as taking down a piece of demon spawn." He waved his hand at his head. "The horns and all."

The leather around Thak's neck tightened, and the world grew dim around the edges. He lifted his hands to the strap, desperately trying to get his fingers between it and his windpipe. He heard sounds of a struggle behind him and knew

Dawson was doing his best to handle whoever else was in the room.

"Enough of that or the prince dies," Joaquine said.

Immediately the sound of metal hitting stone came from behind Thak—Dawson had dropped his sword. The sound of flesh hitting flesh. Another grunt. The smack of a body on the cold stone floor. No further sounds came from Dawson.

It was no surprise Joaquine knew Thak's true identity. He was certain the Gildernosh men had figured it out. It had cost one of them his life. It hadn't taken long for the surviving guard to report his findings. Even if he hadn't, Annissa was clearly a traitor. She must have made a deal of some sort. One she would pay for with her life.

"I told you to bring him alone," Joaquine directed at Annissa.

"I tried. Not like I could tell him not to bring anyone else along. It would have been too suspicious. Besides, you should be thanking me. He's the one who was stationed outside your princess's room. She'll be all yours for the taking now."

Thak's heart plunged at the statement. It made sense. This man wanted Mila. And Thak had just made it infinitely easier for him to get to her.

"Yes, well. That is good news."

The binding on his throat pulled even tighter, and stars danced before his eyes. He clawed at the strap, but it was no use.

"You aren't looking too good, Edonier," Joaquine said. "How does it feel when the tables are turned? I told you I'd see you dead and here we are."

"You can't kill him," Annissa hissed. "You promised."

Joaquine's expression suggested he smelled something foul as he looked at her.

"You get your throne and I get ours, remember?" she said. She genuinely thought after this she had a path to either his bed or his throne? He knew her to be conniving, but he'd never thought her stupid. Clearly he'd been wrong.

The Gildernosh emissary only looked at her with more loathing, perhaps thinking the same thing.

"Your get your throne and I get ours," she repeated. "Or I can make sure everyone knows what you've done. You'll not only die before you step foot outside these walls, but I'll ensure the full force of Thornscarp crushes your precious Gildernosh."

Annissa wasn't helping herself. She had no way to divulge his actions without implicating herself. For this reason, Thak was surprised when Joaquine acquiesced.

"Fine." He nodded to Thak's captor.

Thak fixed his gaze on Annissa, all but ignoring Joaquine. The strap loosened enough for him to rasp out, "If you think for one heartbeat I'd ever take you as a bride, you're grossly delusional."

In a blink, pain bloomed behind his legs and he was forced to his knees.

"Hands," the voice behind him said. He recognized it as the man who'd accompanied him on his campaign against Evansband. The one he *hadn't* killed. Thak didn't respond. "Give me your hands, or I'll tighten this until you pass out and then I'll bind them anyway."

Knowing he needed to keep his wits as much as he could, he did as commanded. Everyone in this room, save Dawson, was going to regret every life choice they'd ever made. He would see to it.

"That's the thing about heirs," Joaquine said. "Once you've got the spare, the eldest no longer is quite so necessary. I keep trying to explain this to Lady Annissa, but she seems to have her heart, or at least her claws, set on you. I don't understand it myself. At least that brother isn't painful to look at. But a deal is a deal."

The man behind Thak pulled his hands back and tied them with a length of rope. Only then did the pressure on his throat truly let up. For one brief moment he thought they were going to remove the strap. The idea died like a candle flame in a thunderstorm as the rope binding his hands was pulled tight and fastened to the leather at the back of his neck. One wrong move, one wrong pull, and he'd strangle himself as easy as snapping a twig.

"How long before someone ventures down this way?" Joaquine asked Annissa.

"Could be hours. Could be days. This is the king's domain, but even he doesn't visit on a consistent schedule."

"I suppose we better get going then."

He walked over and stared down at Thak. "I'll give your regards to Mila. Right before I deliver that whipping I promised."

Rage filled Thak. So much so he could feel it vibrating in the humid air of the cellar. Hear it screeching in his head.

It took him a beat to realize it wasn't his rage that had vibrated and screeched.

It was one very pissed off sprite. Flying straight for Joaquine, with death in her eyes and fishbone-sized blade in hand.

25

Tough Little Warriors

OGRAT WAS A BADASS. GLOWILDEEN KNEW IT FROM THAT VERY first night in the festival hall. It wasn't the earrings or the cat eyes. Not even the bald head or the scars that spoke of battles fought and battles won. It was in the way he smiled and the way he teased. Only folks who were confident in their abilities were able to pull off that attitude and not come across as complete pricks. She worried on occasion that she herself was one of those folks who were just prickish. On occasion. Not always. Her friends knew her and they still loved her and at the end of the story, that was all that would really matter.

But Ograt? He was a badass, and she adored him for it. Not that she would ever tell him of course.

They stood outside the cellar, Ograt grinding his impressive teeth and taking all of a heartbeat to come up with a plan. She was sure he could fix this.

He glanced down at Puddi and spoke with the authority of

the badass soldier he was. "All right now, ladies. This is what we're gonna do. You see that trap?" He pointed to a ground-level opening in the wall adjacent to the door. It was perhaps eighteen inches wide and maybe half again as much in height.

"Yes," Puddi answered hesitantly.

"I'm going to need you tough little warriors to squeeze through to the inside." He drew a dagger from his boot and handed it to Puddi. She took it between two pinched fingers, eyeing it as if it were a writhing painted asp rather than a sturdy utilitarian weapon. "The wall is no more than two feet thick, but the vent there runs a little jog to help with the drainage. It's likely a good five feet through the tight space." He glanced at the gnome. "I'd say to tuck that stinger in your bodice, but well, not sure it'd fit. Maybe in your belt?"

She frowned at him and secured it under one of her shoulder straps. "You want us to go through and do what?" Puddi was clearly not in love with this plan.

"Wiggle on through and see what's what. Distract Annissa somehow. But don't get yerselves damaged, hear." He was already moving back the way they'd come. "I'm going to run round and go through the kitchens. We should have done that first. There's no lock from that side."

Glow smiled her most ferocious smile and winked at Ograt. "Get moving then. We got this side covered."

She didn't wait for the soldier to leave before she shot to the opening. It was dark, but she could see flickering light from the other side.

Puddi frowned at the rectangular hole. "I don't know about this, Glow."

"It'll be no more than a dirty dress for ya." Glow would be able to walk if she ducked her head a bit, but Puddi would need to get down on her hands and knees to crawl the distance. "I'll go first."

She took a tentative step forward and placed one hand on

the wall of the vent, her dirk held out in front of her in the other. The stone was cool to the touch and had a greasy texture she wasn't too fond of. Puddi's dress would certainly be ruined, but hopefully the gnome would take it in stride and simply find it an excuse to get a new frock. She took three steps forward and waited until her friend entered the passage.

"Ugghh." Puddi sounded as if she might retch. "Glow. It's slimy."

"Yep. It is." When she could sense Puddi directly behind her, Glow began to move. The sounds from ahead were muffled and distorted, but she was certain she heard a man's voice. One that didn't belong to Mila's man Thak. "Puddi, quiet your huffing. I think I hear something."

"I'm on my belly in ickiness, Glow. Sorry if it's taking the breath from me."

"Shhh."

She could hear that nasty piece of work Annissa now, and unless the acoustics were very bad indeed, it sounded as if the woman had made a deal for a throne. It didn't take a mage or a seer to know which throne she was after. Glow hadn't missed Gregor's slip earlier about his brother. It all made sense. Edonier had been right in front of them the whole time, and as much as she wanted to hate Thak for his dishonesty, she was secretly relieved. It meant Mila might get her happy ending after all. But first, the dumb lump of a man needed to have his ass saved apparently. At least she'd have something to hold over him for the rest of his life. Her lips curled at the thought.

"Glow, did you hear that? Is she talking about Thak? Is he—"

"Quiet now, Puddi." She loved Puddi something fierce, but sometimes the woman did not know when to hold her blathering.

The man spoke again, and Glow's temper flared. It was Joaquine. "I'll give your regards to Mila. Right before I deliver that whipping I promised."

It was all she needed to hear. The sprite sprinted forward, and the moment she was clear of the stone over her head, she launched into the air, weapon aimed directly for the bastard's left eye.

She didn't know what to expect when she burst forth from the hole near the floor. One quick glance was all she took as she flew straight at the man-shaped pile of excrement who'd dare to threaten Mila. As cocky as he'd sounded while threatening her, he certainly was taken aback as Glow darted straight for him. He flinched at the last moment, and rather than sinking her blade into his orbit as she'd planned, the steel cut a wicked gouge just to the side of his eye.

He reached out to grab her but was too slow. She danced out of his reach and turned for another pass. From this angle she could see Dawson. The guard had been subdued with bindings that wrapped around his torso and pinned his wings in what appeared to be a painful way. The guard had murder in his eyes where he lay behind a bound and equally angry Thak. She'd hoped the big man would be some help as she distracted the bitch and the bastard. That plan was now shot to all the hells. And to add salt to sorrow, the other men from Gildernosh were there, blades drawn and waiting for orders.

"Here I was thinking the princess was where your loyalties should lie," she snarled at them. "But I see you're just another bunch of boot lickers." None of the three showed any sign of having heard her. They stood shoulder to shoulder behind Thak, waiting to do Joaquine's bidding.

How long would it take for Ograt to arrive? She had no idea how far around the kitchen doors were. Could she do any real damage? Not likely. But could she keep them busy? Yes. Yes, she could.

Puddi pulled herself from the vent hole, eyes wide as she took in the scene.

Glow buzzed back to Joaquine. He had a handkerchief

pressed to the side of his face. "We don't have time for this. Pin her down and pluck out her wings if you must."

Two of his men had the decency to look at least mildly disgusted by his statement, but the other seemed quite excited by the idea of a little violence at Glow's expense. He stepped toward her. To his detriment, that step took him within half a foot of the bound big man. With effortless grace, Thak swung his head just as the man moved past him. Kneeling as he was, it put Thak's head even with the unfortunate man's gut. With a wet smack the Prince of Thornscarp drove one of those impressive horns through the man's abdomen and out the back. Glow couldn't be sure, but based on the amount of blood that flowed when Thak pulled back, she guessed he'd hit a kidney. The Gildernosh lackey dropped, screaming. The other two jumped back from Thak, clearly not wanting to experience anything similar.

Glowildeen Rosewink flashed her vicious needle teeth in a wide grin.

Annissa's already pale skin grew even paler.

Joaquine made a retching noise, staggering back a few steps.

Puddi looked momentarily horrified. Then she set her mouth in a firm line and stepped up behind Thak. Glow watched, ever proud of her friend, as Puddi pulled the dagger from her dress and sawed away at the rope binding Thak's hands.

She made no secret of it, yet with all the room's attention on the dying man and the blood dripping from the prince's horn, no one attempted to stop her.

"Time to go." Turning to the men he'd brought along, Joaquine said, "Kill him if you like." Glow was happy to hear the tremor in his voice.

Annissa looked as if she wanted to argue but held her tongue.

The pair of men moved back toward the locked door they'd

come through, obviously not wanting to march through the kitchens in their escape, and Glow cursed Ograt for going the long way around. She understood it, but now the filth was about to slip his capture.

She needed to block the door. Swooping down, she dove for Joaquine's head again. He ducked in time to avoid her stinging blade, Annissa close on his heels.

Several things happened at once. The door from the kitchen burst open, Ograt bellowing a war cry and saber raised. Puddi's dagger made a final slice through the rope binding Thak's hands, and he ripped the leather from his neck as he rose to his feet. Joaquine stepped over Dawson and pulled the back door open. Glow flew over his head and dropped down in front of him, ready to bar his escape.

This time, however, Annissa reacted. With one clawed hand, she swiped at the sprite.

Pain erupted up Glow's back, and with an anguished cry, she fell and landed hard next to Dawson. She tried to stand but found the world dimming. She was vaguely aware of what was happening around her.

Puddi screamed and Thak roared.

Ograt dispatched the two remaining Gildernosh men.

Annissa smiled down on her and turned, disappearing into the gloom, right behind Joaquine.

26

S he Is My Queen

MILA DIDN'T THINK SHE COULD WEAR THE SOFT TURQUOISE GOWN
to the celebration. She'd seen the way Thak's eyes had roved
over her earlier. She'd felt the heat of his stare as he took in her
sun-kissed skin and the way the material brought out the color
of her eyes. As much as she appreciated it, she wasn't sure she
could stand to see the hunger on his face as he pushed her away
a second time. It would be too humiliating. Too pathetic.

She decided to wear one of her original gowns. They weren't
nearly as flattering and they were certainly less comfortable, but
she'd been living in them her whole life. One more night
wouldn't be the end of her.

She undressed quickly and pulled on a thin silk shift. She'd
do her hair and put on the heavy gown at the last possible
moment. The soft cream fabric felt wonderful against her skin.
She was about to climb into bed for a few minutes of rest when
she heard raised voices outside her door. She couldn't make out

230

the words, but she thought she recognized Gregor's voice easily enough. The other though. The other was female and only vaguely familiar. It wasn't Puddi or Glow. Was it Lady Annissa? Why would the vile woman be at her door at this time of the night?

"Please, Gregor. He said to fetch you. It seemed urgent."

Why was Gregor outside her door? Had he come to replace Dawson? The guard had told her he needed to step away for a moment, and she had assumed her door would briefly be left unguarded. Surely the prince had more interesting things to do than stand sentry. Mila could picture him on the other side of the sentient wood. It almost made her laugh.

Mila crept closer to the door in time to hear a loud thunk and then a terrible quiet.

"Gregor?" she called. "Gregor, are you all right?"

No answer.

And then from farther down the hall the sound of a woman's cry. Was that also Annissa? What was going on out there?

All thoughts of assassinations and attacks fled her mind when she heard the thunk and the scream. Despite the level of security put in place on her behalf, she didn't think before opening the door. She was engaged to the most feared man in all the five realms and was a guest in his home on behalf of the queen.

Heir to a throne. Engaged to a warrior prince. And the biggest twit in all the five realms.

"Joaquine." Her stomach clenched.

"Hello, Princess."

Annissa stood across the hall and waggled her claw-tipped fingers at Mila as Joaquine stepped over the body outside her door and over the threshold to her chamber, a disgusting smile stretched across his revolting face.

Normally, she'd have stood her ground against her father's emissary, but something in his eyes and the set of his jaw made cold creep down her spine. Add in Gregor's still form, lying in a growing puddle of blood, and it was evident. This was no political visit or request for her to accompany him home. By attacking a prince of Thornscarp, he'd effectively declared war on the entire realm.

Mila reached for the door and shoved it back against the man. He caught it with his shoulder, grunting with the effort, but pushed his way in and slammed it behind him.

"You need to leave. Now." She took one step back from him then stood her ground, feet planted firmly apart and arms crossed over her chest, all too aware of the thin silk and what it revealed.

"Humorous. I've been telling you the same for days now, and here we remain." Half of his face was awash with blood, a vicious laceration flapping the skin between his eye and his lank hair.

"You could have left at any time. There was no cause for you to stay."

"And leave you to these beasts and your own stupidity?"

"The only beast in this castle is you."

"Maidens above. You actually believe that, don't you?" His face twisted even further into disgust. Blood seeped from his wound, dripping down to his chin. "Please tell me you haven't bedded the monster."

Mila's eyes flew wide with outrage. "Get out of my room."

"No. I don't think I will. And that isn't an answer. Has he put his paws on you, Your Highness? Or is there still some hope you remain untainted?"

Untainted. She would kill this man. She just needed to be smart enough to do it. Joaquine wasn't a skilled fighter, nor was he young or exceptionally fit, but he still outweighed Mila and she hadn't gotten around to those defense lessons with Petra or Thak. Perhaps she could use the element of surprise as she'd done with Gregor.

He took another step toward her, and despite her best intentions of holding her ground, Mila found herself stepping back. She had the good sense to angle her retreat in the direction of the bathing chamber rather than the bed. If she could get inside, she might be able to bar the door from him.

"Your father would be devastated to know how far you've fallen. But no matter. We won't tell him." Joaquine's greasy hair fell over his eyes as his head swung around the room. "If he'd only listened to me from the start, we'd never be here. He should have let me have you. That clod you were wedded to might still be alive, and you'd be ascended by now, my seed already having done its work."

She took another step back, her stomach roiling with every greasy word he spoke.

"Of course it isn't too late, as long as you've not gone and done something vile. He can still have his power, your father. He'll just need to share it with me."

"My father would never trade my ascension for his own power."

"You really are that naïve, aren't you. Of course he would. He already has."

Mila refused to believe him. She took another step back. Closer to the hearth and closer to the bathing chamber.

"It doesn't matter. If I were ascended, neither of you would have any power. When I'm queen I'll see you stripped of any title. You'll be lucky to find a position shoveling pig shit."

"When you are queen, I will be your king unless you'd like me to tell your father all that has transpired here. Chasing after what most would consider little more than bestiality. Then you might have more to worry over than just your crown."

Her anger was rising. How dare he presume to corner her in her own room. How dare he suggest he should have a place in her bed let alone beside her on the throne. How dare he speak about Thak and his wonderful people as if they were creatures not worthy of her notice.

"I never understood what Gidaeon's issue was. You seem fuckable enough to me. But as much as I appreciate the view, you'll need better traveling clothes." Heat sang through her veins. Was nothing in her life private? Her own shames needed to be shared with everyone at court?

He snorted a laugh, and spittle flew from his thick lips.

"You think I didn't know? Believe me. I know so much more than you can imagine. Now get dressed."

Mila had no intention of leaving that room, let alone Thornscarp, with Joaquine. But his instruction to get dressed might play to her advantage. Rather than retreating farther into the bathing chamber, she walked to the wardrobe and pulled out a clean riding dress and leggings, Joaquine's gaze following her every move.

"I can't wait to leave this Maiden-forsaken place. As much as I hate to admit it, I would have liked to gain some inroads with the king though. It'd be well worth our time to get some of these brutes into the mines." He snorted a laugh. "I imagine a little livestock feed and straw pallets and they'd double what the other laborers output."

Mila was going to be sick. Surely her father couldn't agree with this man. Could he?

She didn't know where Puddi and Glow had gotten off to, but if she could delay long enough, they should arrive and sound an alarm of some sort. If that was even necessary. Surely the bleeding form of Gregor wouldn't go unnoticed for long. Thak's room was next door. A conversation with his parents couldn't take much time.

Stepping close to the hearth, she edged toward the bathing chamber, dress in hand.

"What do you think you're doing?" Joaquine's voice grated her every nerve.

"You suggested I dress." She lifted her chin toward the door, disdain dripping with each syllable. She'd be damned if she'd let this worm of a man think he'd unnerved her.

"Keep the door open."

She looked at him with such ill-concealed disgust he chuckled.

Joaquine reached into the sheath on his side and pulled out a dagger. He pointed it at her, but Mila doubted he'd ever really use it. Not when he'd gone to such lengths to retrieve her and drag her home.

"Consider it a favor to your dear little gnomish friend. I'd hate for something to happen to her should you get any other ridiculous ideas."

Puddi. She and Glow still hadn't arrived for the night.

"What have you done?"

"Nothing to *her*. Yet."

To her. Had something happened to Glow then? It was hard to believe. The little sprite could surely hold her own against anything Joaquine had to offer.

"He killed one of my men, you know. Giles. I sent him and Drake with the bastards to the border. I'll admit they're good at keeping secrets here. Never had a clue the big bastard was actually Edonier. But one day on the battlefield across from those whelps from Evansband and it was no secret just who your guard actually was. They tried to take him out. Do what was right for Gildernosh. Prevent this travesty of a marriage from happening, and Giles paid with his life."

Mila hadn't known the Gildernosh men, and she hated any loss of life, but she found she had trouble mustering any sympathy for his death. The bruises on Thak's face. Did those come from the dead man? If so, well...

She had no time to dwell on it. Mila had to think. Could she buy herself enough time to dash for the door instead of the bathing chamber? Was Annissa still out there?

Almost in answer to her thoughts, footsteps sounded beyond the sentient pine. A cacophony of voices calling over one another. She couldn't be certain, but she thought she heard a long string of expletives in Ograt's colorful voice.

Mila took the opportunity of the distraction and dropped her riding clothes from one hand while scooping up the hearth poker with the other. She spun toward the door. Unfortunately the noise had also spurred Joaquine into motion. As she was grabbing the iron, he was grabbing her. His free hand latched onto her shoulder and spun her around so her back was to his chest. He placed the dagger at her throat as a bang came from the door.

"Mila!" Thak's voice roared through the wood.

"Tell them to leave," the emissary hissed. His breath reeked of garlic and stale tea.

Two more bangs on the door. Where was Puddi? She could easily have the door opened in no time, giggling as she felt up the wood.

"If you value your life, Princess, tell them to leave." He pushed the dagger into the soft flesh of her neck.

He wouldn't do it. She had to believe he wouldn't do it. If this man wanted anything, it was the power that came with the throne. He had a slice of that as her father's advisor, but if he wanted more? He'd need her to get it.

"Wait," she said softly. Let him think she was talking to Thak and the fury that waited on the other side of the door. She wasn't talking to Thak. She was talking to herself.

Wait. Just one more second.

His grip tightened. "Louder, Your Highness."

She let her body go soft. Compliant. Easily manipulated. His grip slackened. It was all she needed. She dipped her head forward, enough that the dagger bit into the flesh of her neck a touch. The blade scraped along the skin just above her collarbone, but it gave her the room she needed. She drove her head back into his face at the same time she drove the iron poker down into the top of his boot.

A shriek echoed through the room as the man flailed about, any pretense at being in control swallowed in the sound of his wails. The arm holding her around the waist flew to his face, and the one holding the dagger dropped, slicing into the silk of her shift and drawing a thin line of blood from her hip. She winced but managed to slip from his grip and rush to the door.

Mila flung the door wide and fell into Thak as he raised his hand to pound once again.

Behind him she could see Ograt and Petra. Nox knelt on the ground beside Gregor who was thankfully awake but bleeding profusely from a nasty gash on his head. Niri was leading Annissa away, hands bound behind her back.

Mila thought she'd gotten to see nearly every side of Thak, and even one or two of Prince Edonier the Mighty, during her time in the castle. She had never seen this side of him before. The rage and fury buried under the barest thread of control was unlike anything she could have imagined. A vein bulged in his temple. His normally warm brown eyes were filled with the fire of a thousand devils. His pulse pounded in his neck. In one swift motion, he pulled her into his arms and placed a brief but fierce kiss to the top of her head before pushing her back at arm's length. His eyes roamed from the blood on her neck to the torn cream shift now stained red. His eyes hardened. His lips thinned.

Without a word, he gently placed her to the side. He stepped around her and put his massive body between her and the man trembling in the center of the room.

Blood flowed from both Joaquine's nose and the ragged hole in the top of his boot. He looked at Edonier as if death himself had strolled into the room. And perhaps that was what he saw. Everyone knew the stories after all. Prince Edonier the Brutal. The mighty warrior. Death on the battlefield. Death to his enemies. And Joaquine was now very much his enemy.

Thak padded toward him on silent paws. "You touched her."

Joaquine's thick lips quivered as drops of saliva mixed with the blood and snot streaming from his nose.

"You drew her blood."

Joaquine fell to his knees and began to beg.

"She is your queen and you dared to put a hand on her." Not princess. Not heir to the throne. Queen.

Just as she'd never seen that look on his face, Mila had never heard that tone in his voice. Barely more than whispered words but so full of power the earth nearly trembled with them.

"More than that," he breathed. "She is *my* queen."

He reached down and gathered the other man's shirt in his fist, twisting as he pulled him to his feet.

"Have you not heard the stories? Do you not know my nature? You come here, to my realm, to my home and think to subdue me with ropes? Make a deal with a viper to put her on the throne beside me? Have *the stones* to think you can take that which is under *my* protection? I should kill you now."

Joaquine soiled himself and whimpered.

"Ograt!" Thak barked.

Within a heartbeat the bald warrior was at his side.

"Take him to the cells."

"On it now." Ograt yanked Joaquine's arms behind his back and secured them with a set of heavy iron shackles. "Aye, man, ye reek of piss and cowardice." He nodded at Mila as he marched Joaquine out of the room.

"Petra. Get a healer up here now. Gregor and the princess need tending. Then send word to Ladies Puddi and Glowildeen that Mila is well."

Petra gave a brief nod and turned on her heel.

"Take Nox with you. Dawson may like to see him."

"Then, if you would, update the king and queen. I'm sure

Her Majesty will be more than happy to deal with Annissa. And word will need to be sent to Gildernosh. That man won't be returning home anytime soon."

"No need to fetch a healer for me. I can walk." Gregor tipped a mock salute to his brother. "I'll have one sent up for Mila though. And I can speak to Mother and Da."

It was the first time either of them had called the king and queen something so mundane. So familiar. So loving.

Thak nodded his thanks.

His calm composure evaporated as soon as they were alone. His eyes traveled from her face to her blood-stained and torn shift.

Thak's voice almost broke when he spoke. "How in all of the hells did he get in here?"

It was only as he stepped closer that Mila saw the ring of red angry flesh between his beard and his collar.

She stepped to him and placed a hand on his cheek, turning his face so she could see his injury better. "What happened to you?"

"You first."

Balls and bastards he was stubborn when he wanted to be. She puffed out her cheeks as she exhaled. She'd not win that particular battle. Best to get it out and over with.

"I opened the door and he came in."

He groaned and tilted his head back, staring at the ceiling. "For the love of. . . Why? Dawson told you to keep it shut. I know he did. I thought the mere fact it was there for your protection would be reason enough to use it, Mila."

"I heard screaming. I thought someone was in trouble. I only thought to help, and if that is my crime, I will gladly stand guilty here before you."

"But you almost *weren't* here standing before me. Guilty or otherwise. He could have *taken* you. Or hurt you. And then instead of defending your realm I'd be at war with it."

"Defending it?"

"Yes, Your Highness. Where do you think I've been these past days? At the border. Strongly encouraging Evansband to rethink its position."

"I thought it was just an errand for the king."

"It was. But my particular sort of errand." He reached out and tilted her chin up, exposing the small cut on her neck.

"And is it true? Did my father's men try to kill you?"

He snorted a laugh. "If that was an attempt to kill me, then it's no wonder your queendom is in need of some decent military support. They jumped out from behind a tree while I was . . . taking care of some personal business."

She raised her eyebrows at him.

He grinned. "Let's just say no man enjoys being surprised when he's still got shit on his ass."

Mila nearly choked.

"One of them got a good swing in with a decent-sized hunk of rock." He pointed to his face. "It didn't end well for him. His companion didn't stick around to assist him."

It seemed Giles had chosen his own demise then.

Thak paced in front of the fire. Mila grabbed one of the blankets and sat wrapped in the thick layer as she watched him.

Even in the close space, with Thak's energy running high, Mila marveled at how graceful he was.

"Do you want to tell me what happened?" he finally asked. "What he said?"

"There isn't much to tell." Mila pulled the blanket tighter around her shoulders. "He threatened Puddi. Said some horrid things about your people. His intentions were to get me home to my father and presumably wed me and take my throne for his own. He grabbed me, and I acted foolishly."

"He put his hands on you." Thak stopped his pacing and stared at her but didn't wait for her to answer. "You acted bravely, Mila. Not foolishly."

"My bravery may not be enough in the end. Until I am queen, there is little I can actually do."

Thak sat next to her on the bed. "You will be a great ruler, Mila. Of that I have no doubt," he said quietly.

Mila's hand involuntarily touched her lips. "Some of the things he said." She swiped the tears from her cheeks. "All of it actually. I don't know if I can go back there—"

"Do not continue that thought, Your Highness."

Thak turned to her and pulled a lock of hair into his hand. "I'd have killed him." He twirled the stands between his fingers. "If you hadn't been here. I'd have killed him."

"But you didn't."

He rubbed at his beard and closed his eyes. "You know me as one man, as Thak. But . . . I'm terrified you will eventually be terrified of me. When you see me as Edonier. In the cellar I held on to myself, but then I saw Gregor and knew something was terribly wrong. The gears flipped and I became that man. The brutal prince."

Mila curled in on herself and rested her forehead on her knees.

A soft knock sounded on the door jam. A middle-aged woman with soft grey eyes and a head full of quills stood on the threshold, a worn leather bag grasped in both hands before her.

"You called for me?"

Thak gave the woman a weary smile. "Yes. Thank you, Yandy. The princess has been injured."

"You look like you've been at it again yourself."

"Nothing I can't handle."

"Well then, let's take a look, Your Highness." She turned to Mila who dropped the blanket from her shoulder.

"Where would you like me?"

"Where you are is fine, but if you'd lie back, it'd be helpful."

Mila did as she was bade, wincing slightly as the laceration on her hip pulled with the movement. "I don't think it's as bad as it looks."

"I'll be the judge of that, Your Highness." The older woman set to work first inspecting her neck and then using a small pair of shears to open the tear on her shift to get a better look at the wound on her torso. "Just these two spots then?"

"Yes."

"You're right about the neck wound. It's fairly shallow, but the head and neck tend to bleed like stink. We can get it patched up in no time. Just some salve and it'll be right as rain in a few days. This though"—she nodded where the knife had sliced Mila's hip—"will need a few stitches."

Mila nodded. "Whatever's best."

Yandy set to work mixing up a silky ointment which she smeared on the shallow cut above Mila's clavicle. Then she got busy cleaning the skin over her hip. "This'll sting a bit." It was the only warning Mila got before the pinch of the needle pierced her skin. The healer was swift and competent with her stitches, and the wound was closed in a matter of minutes.

"Keep it clean and apply the salve a couple times per day. You may have a scar, but it shouldn't be too bad."

A scar was the least of Mila's worries. "Thank you."

The woman was packing her kit when she turned to Thak. "Do you want me to have a look or no?"

He shook his head. "Not the worst I've had. I'll be fine."

The angry red welts on his neck made Mila cringe, but she assumed he knew what he could or couldn't handle.

"Well, if your mother sees it, don't blame me for not trying."

"Never." He smiled.

"Oh. And the sprite. I managed to save her wing. She'll be up in the air in no time at all."

Mila's heart leapt to her throat. "The sprite? Did something happen to Glow?"

Thak cringed. "I meant to tell you. Your friends are quite the heroines."

The healer showed herself out as Thak relayed the events of the preceding hours.

Mila's pulse quickened. "Where are they?"

"In the infirmary. I can take you down there now if you'd like. I was hoping to check in on Dawson as well. And I suppose Gregor."

Mila moved to the door. "Mila, wait."

She spun on him, and he raised his hands in a gesture of surrender. "Perhaps you should change first?"

She looked down at the bloodied and battered cream silk shift. "I suppose that isn't a bad idea."

27

A Dozen Plus One

THERE WAS A GAP IN THE DRAPES. A SMALL ONE. TINY REALLY. But the one singular beam that traversed that little gap managed to fall directly on Mila's face, enough to draw her from the deepest dredges of slumber. Her bed was once again comfy and cozy. It had been a long night in the infirmary. The list of their friends who'd been injured on her behalf made Mila nauseous. It also made her angry.

Gregor had blamed himself. The idea that one sniveling coward from Gildernosh and a backstabbing traitor from their own court could wreak such damage to the strongest of them was nothing short of an embarrassment to his position as Master Covert. Thak had reminded his brother that he'd acted rashly by believing Annissa when her story didn't make sense, and Ograt maligned his inability to protect his prince and friend more swiftly. Glow was sullen, blaming her inability to take out Joaquine's eye, and Dawson was miserable that he too had failed his prince.

Only Puddi remained upbeat, proud of her part in the heroics and thrilled with the adventure and romance of the rescue.

"As you should be," Mila told her. "But now that you are all safe and tended to, I want nothing more than a hot bath and some rest.

"I'm staying down here with Glow if that's all right with you."

"Perfectly fine. I won't make the mistake of opening the door to an unknown threat again."

"No, Your Highness, you won't," Thak said. "I'll be guarding it this evening."

Mila looked at him levelly. "Thak, you must be more exhausted than even me. You've not slept in a proper bed in days."

"I'll manage."

She felt like arguing but knew it would be pointless. So, after making their rounds in the infirmary, she waited until they were alone in the hall outside her room. "Perhaps you could guard the door from the inside. Just tonight."

"Perhaps I could."

He followed her inside and dropped into the armchair by the fire while Mila bathed off the day. When she exited the bathing chamber, she found him asleep, head thrown back and long legs ending in paws stretched out before him in the chair. The blood on his horn had dried to a dark brown that looked almost black in the flickering lamps. She hated to wake him, but thought he might like the chance to wash the gore from himself as well.

Walking to the chair, she dropped to a crouch and lifted her hand to his cheek. He moaned and turned his face into her palm, his eyes fluttering open.

A small smile lifted his lips. "Mmm."

"Thought you might want to take a turn in the bath."

"That's very thoughtful of you." He stretched his arms over his head. She marveled at the way he instinctively avoided the tips of his horns. "I can trust you won't get into trouble while I'm in there?"

"Only if the trouble is between the sheets of that bed."

He raised an eyebrow at her, and her cheeks pinked.

"That reminds me," she said as she dropped down and shoved her hand under the mattress. "Oh, that girl." She bit at her lower lip as she fished the first stone out.

"Let me help," he said as he lifted the mattress effortlessly.

Mila's eyes went round, and she laughed.

In the end, a dozen plus one stones were removed from under the mattress. They sat in a small pile near the hearth.

"I'll give it to Quince, she takes her orders seriously." Thak had looked upon the stack with something close to appreciation when the last had been removed.

"My back may never be the same again."

"You're tougher than you look."

"I'll take that a compliment."

"You should."

Thak disappeared into the bathing chamber, and Mila crawled into bed. She was asleep in the time between one breath and the next. She didn't hear Thak as he finished in the bath or when he climbed under the sheets beside her.

When the sunbeam hit her face, she stretched and rolled over. Right into the man asleep beside her. He'd tilted his head away from her, as if even in slumber he didn't want to chance her getting injured by one of his horns.

She studied his face in the stillness. Those incredible lashes. The dotting of freckles. The curl of tousled hair and outline of his jaw.

She wanted to kiss him awake. Wanted to do so much more

than kiss him, but she was worried he might not welcome it. He'd seemed *reluctant* before.

Biting at her lip, she hesitated, and in the moment of indecision, his eyes opened slowly.

"Mila," he breathed her name. "You have a concerned look on your face."

"Do I?"

"You do?"

"I was thinking about something."

"What were you thinking?"

"About the best way to wake you?"

"Hmm." He stilled for a moment. "How about you show me what you were thinking then."

"You might not care for what I had in mind."

"I doubt that very much."

"All right then." She didn't hesitate. Leaning down, she drew her lips briefly across his. Just a touch, but enough to send a shiver through her all the same.

"You thought I wouldn't welcome a kiss?" His brow furrowed.

"I was thinking a bit more than a kiss, if I'm being honest."

"Go on then."

"But you. . ."

"Go on then, Mila. Show me what you thought I wouldn't care for." He stared at her and licked absently at his lower lip.

It was her undoing.

The fabric of her shift pulled tight against her body, and she needed to free herself from it. Rising up, she straddled him and pulled the gown off over her head. Mila was rewarded with the sharp intake of Thak's breath. He lay still beneath her and stared up at her uncovered body.

"And you thought I'd not care for this either?"
She nodded.
He frowned. "It's a shame you would think such a thing."

She didn't speak, just sat looking down on him.

"You are glorious, Mila. So much so, it almost hurts to look at you." His voice was deep and husky. Mila felt the blush warming her cheeks. "Just stay there a moment. I want to capture this in my memory."

He studied her with his eyes first and then with his hands. He traced the line of her collarbones first. Her skin grew tight and pebbled. His fingers danced along until his hands met at the notch of her sternum. Then down her shoulders and around to her back. Feather soft. Those beautiful, strong, scarred and nicked hands felt like silk and heaven and promises kept. Then down over her breasts, weighing them in his palms and gently teasing their peaks.

"These are as far from average as one could get." At first she didn't understand why he'd chosen those particular words. Then he ran his palms down her ribs to the swell of her hips. "And these are certainly not too wide."

She smiled as she remembered the list of things she'd ticked off to him in her inebriated state so many days ago. Her faults. The things deemed not beautiful enough for the people of Gildernosh. Or at least not beautiful enough according to the men who'd been in her life before. She hadn't taken stock of it until then, but Thak had made it a point to praise each of those things. Her dimples and sun-kissed skin, her height and her waves of hair.

Finally he cupped the back of her thighs where they met her rounded backside. "And this ass? I've been fantasizing about this ass for weeks now."

He ran his fingers in a massaging motion that had her coming apart at the seams.

When she could take it no longer, she bent forward and kissed him again. Thak ran his hands down her legs where they rested on the mattress, returning to once again cup her backside.

She moaned into his mouth. It seemed to undo his restraint. In one fluid motion, he rolled her beneath him and stood and removed his clothing.

Now it was Mila's turn to gasp in surprise. He was superb. Each muscle was defined as if he'd been sculpted from marble. She drank in his perfection. Her eyes roamed from the bottoms of his paws up the length of his lower legs to just below his knees. The soft brown fur transitioned into the same smooth skin that covered the rest of him, all the way over his glorious torso to the tips of his magnificent horns and back down again. His shoulders and chest were sprinkled with the same faint freckles that dotted his nose. Like his beautiful hands, the rest of him showed signs of a dozen small wounds. She wanted to touch each spot. Trace each scar. Faint silvery imperfections over his shoulders and arms, on his knees and one over his hip. Touching her own newly stitched skin, she wondered if the scars would eventually match.

She loved his chimera attributes as much as his human ones. She loved the myriad of small imperfections on his long strong fingers. She loved the smattering of freckles over his otherwise smooth skin. She loved the red-tinged facial hair that covered his jaw and chin. She loved his warm brown eyes, his soft chestnut curls, and his crooked smile. She loved his horns and his claws and everything in between. The chimera and the human. Her gaze finally rested on a very human and very excited body part.

When he noticed where she was focused he chuckled softly but then grew quiet and serious. "Ograt was right. There will never be need of a maid in this chamber with us, Princess."

When she'd had her fill, she grabbed his hands and pulled him back into the bed with her, already smiling at the thought of not having to lie to the queen about her lack of sleep.

She stayed on her knees, and he matched her stance and put his hands on her face and pulled her to him.

When he kissed her, she melted. When she kissed him back, he groaned. When he trailed those warm soft kisses down her neck and over her shoulder before finally focusing on her breasts, she arched back in the deliciousness of it all.

Barely able to focus as he tugged and licked, she breathed words that had him stopping. "Will you marry me, Thak? Will you marry me and love me like I love you? Will you stand beside me in Gildernosh and let me stand beside you in Thornscarp?"

"Yes, Mila. Yes, I will."

And then his tongue was working again and she let thoughts of the future drift from her mind and simply enjoyed the present. He pushed her back, and his mouth continued to explore every inch of her. When she thought it couldn't possibly get any better, he covered her body with his massive weight and gently pushed into her, joining them in the most perfect of ways.

The heir to the throne of Gildernosh was not a girl. She was not a maiden. She had lain with a man before. She had not been made love to though. She'd not been worshipped and caressed and taken in the way that Thak worshipped and caressed and took her. When he played her body with his, causing her to tighten and spiral and fracture, she cried out in equal parts ecstasy and astonishment. Prince Edonier Thakeri Thorn the Mighty followed her into bliss.

They lay tangled together, sweat soaked and breathless.

Mila ran her hands over his back and up the tight muscles of his neck, stroking them through his hair and around the bases of his horns.

"The first time I saw you, I avoided looking at these."

"Mmm."

"I can't believe I was such a fool."

"Not a fool, Mila. You had every right to be wary."

She snorted. "Wary. Good word."

"Mmm-hmm."

"Puddi wasn't scared of you for a minute."

A chuckled rumbled in his chest, and the vibration sent a whole new wave of longing surging through her body. "Of course she wasn't. She was too busy feeling up the door and planning her next conquest. Will she ever forgive me, you think?"

"She already has."

"They are a credit to you. Lady Puddi and Lady Glowildeen both."

"They are a credit to themselves. I'm just lucky to have them as my friends. My sisters. Just as you are lucky to have Ograt and Petra, Nox and Ram."

He played with her hair as she rested her head at the joint of his chest and shoulder. "When we make the journey to Gildernosh, I'd like you to have your own detail. Of guards I mean."

"Do you think that's really necessary?"

He looked at her as if she'd lost her mind. "Do I think it's necessary? Mila, more than one someone doesn't want you to be queen. That much is evident." She grimaced. "And Dawson has already asked for the job."

She smiled and sat up, long raven locks falling around her naked chest. "Dawson?" Her smile fell. "But what about Nox? I hate that they could be separated like that."

"Did you think I'd not be taking some of my own soldiers, Mila?" He smirked as he brushed the locks back behind her shoulders. "Or perhaps you still think me a lowly castle guard with little say in who I might choose to travel with?" He sat up and kissed the tip of her nose. "If I remember correctly, you indicated previously your father might be less than pleased with this union. I'll not take chances. I'm bringing my most trusted with us."

Mila grew pensive, not looking at him when she spoke. "What I asked you earlier, Thak. About marrying me. . ." She studied her hands.

He tilted her chin up, forcing her to look him in the eye.

"I know it may seemed rushed. But"—she took a deep breath—"I don't want to wait. Gregor scoffed at the notion before. And it may seem desperate. And even if I wasn't desperate, I know what I want, and I want you. Even if you weren't the prince and even if my people didn't need it. But they do and I am and. . . Can we wed now, before I go home?"

"Now?" His face grew serious. "My men have seen me in this state, but Lady Puddi might get more of an eyeful than I like."

She stared at him until his face broke into the lopsided smile she so enjoyed. "I'm jesting, Mila. Yes. We can wed as soon as you would like. Today, tomorrow, next week. You say the words and I will oblige."

She sagged in relief until he spoke again. "We should probably tell the king and queen."

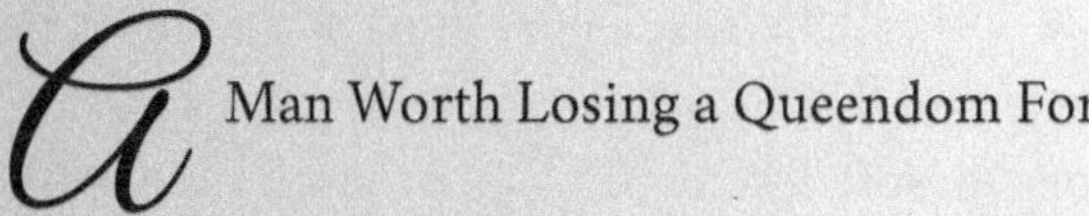Man Worth Losing a Queendom For

THE WEDDING WAS A SMALL AFFAIR. MILA WAS DRESSED IN A gown of shimmering silver that moved about her legs in falls and swirls. The bodice was twisted and tight, hugging her breasts and leaving her back open to the cool evening breeze. Puddi had done her hair in long flowing waves dotted and twined with small periwinkle buds and threaded through with silver chains.

The gnome had dressed herself in turquoise, and Glow was a dainty dream in diaphanous lilac. Her wing had been mended, but rather than fly at Mila's side, she rested upon the shoulder of Ograt as he stood next to Gregor at Edonier's back. The prince and the soldier seemed to have gotten over the tension between them and shared the ease of brothers. The wicked grin on the sprite's face was outdone only by Ograt's, all canines and mischief. The warrior's siblings, Niri, Dawson, and his twin Wren made up the remainder of the small party.

King Edon of Thornscarp presided over the union, Queen Augustina at his side. Her Majesty seemed at peace with the turn of events, and when she wiped a small line of silver from her eyes, Mila was surprised to realize the tear was one of joy for her son rather than sorrow.

Joaquine wasn't invited. When he left his cell, he would be escorted back to Gildernosh under heavy guard. Mila would eventually return to her people. Thak didn't like it, but Mila had insisted. She still believed her father would see reason when the time came. Thak did not seem as convinced.

Eloise and Annissa would soon stand trial. Thak refused to comment on what he thought the outcome would be, but Gregor had been more forthcoming. He was sure the queen would choose exile for their misdeeds. For someone like Annissa it was a fate worse than death.

As Edon wrapped a soft length of leather around Thak's wrist, the prince laced his fingers with hers. The king continued the figure eight and tied Mila to Thak. Her cheeks warmed when he raised their bound hands to his lips and kissed each of her knuckles in turn.

"You have a symbol of your people as well, do you not?" the king asked her.

Without pulling her bound hand from Thak she reached out to her side. "I do. Puddi?"

The gnome reached into her bodice and produced a set of thick gold hoops. They were simple in design but heavy and thick. Each latched with a hinge on one side. The larger set held a deep sapphire gem in its center. The smaller, a delicate opal with veining of the same deep azure hue.

Puddi gave her the small set first. Mila handed it to Thak but kept her wrist extended.

Single-handedly, he clasped it to her outstretched wrist and clicked it shut. Mila took the larger one and fastened it on Thak's empty wrist.

In the hours before the ceremony, Mila had explained. "This was my mother's father's band. She left it to me. It never touched Gidaeon's flesh. He didn't seem worthy. I had this one designed to match it but likewise have not worn it yet. I'd ask you to have a smith weld mine closed. It's our custom, and I have no intention of removing it. But you may leave yours hinged. It may be an encumbrance during battle."

He had frowned a little but not replied.

Standing before those gathered, Thak pulled her hand to his heart and dropped his forehead to hers. "The smith can weld them both. It'll come off only when I leave this world. In battle or otherwise." He tilted his face and captured her mouth with his. The kiss was lingering and sweet.

Puddi clasped her hand to her bosom and sighed in the most dramatic fashion.

Glow sent up a cheer, and the warriors of Thornscarp—including the king and queen—joined in.

Mila had never been happier in her life. When she'd set out on the journey, she'd hoped it was the right thing for her people. Soon she'd see if she was right. But in that moment, it didn't matter if she'd failed miserably. She'd come in search of an alliance with a demon prince. She was leaving with a man worth losing a queendom for.

She'd worry about the rest later.

Thank you for taking the time to share in Mila and Thak's story. I'd love to know what you think. The Best way to support authors is to leave a review on Amazon, Goodreads, your social media channels, Bookbub, or anywhere else you review books!

As always, this book would not have been possible without the support of so many—my family, friends, and those who continue to pick up my books to escape from real life for a page or two. You know who you are and you know how much I appreciate you.

I enjoy pulling these tales from my head, but I am the first to admit, punctuation and attention to grammatical detail are not my strong suits. I was lucky to have found a fantastic editor several books ago and without her meticulous eye, these stories would be a bit of a mess. Karen Robinson, you are the best!

To all of the amazing readers out there, thank you from the bottom of my heart. Whether I've known you since I was a child or we see each other at work, whether we have connected on social media or at live events, whether I know you name or you anonymously read my books for free, knowing you take the time to share in these little stories gives me a special joy I cannot put into words.

Thank you, thank you, thank you!

ABOUT THE AUTHOR

Kami King Larsen is a native of the desert southwest and studied biology before attending medical school. Although she is a practicing pediatrician by training, she is a lover of great stories and all things whimsical by birth. Kami lives in Nevada with her husband, daughters, and two dogs.

MORE FROM KAMI KING LARSEN

A Simple Tale of Water and Weeping
A Simple Tale of Ink and Bindings
Blood and Wonder (Medicus Corpus Book 1)
Breath and Starshine (Medicus Corpus Book 2)

Writing As Aster Rye
Bittersweet Breadcrumbs
Vespertine Dreams

Let's Connect

If you are interested in the opportunity to receive free Advanced Reader Copies for future releases and keep up with other exciting news, join my mailing list via my website or follow me on social media. www.kamikinglarsenbooks.com
Instagram @authorkamikinglarsen
@lilyfernbooks
Or find me on Facebook Kami King Larsen Books and Bits